Ca

Steal You

for a

Second?

Can I Steal You for a Second?

JODI McALISTER

**SIMON &
SCHUSTER**

London · New York · Sydney · Toronto · New Delhi

CAN I STEAL YOU FOR A SECOND?
First published in Australia in 2023 by
Simon & Schuster (Australia) Pty Limited
Suite 19A, Level 1, Building C, 450 Miller Street, Cammeray, NSW 2062

10 9 8 7 6 5 4 3 2 1

Sydney New York London Toronto New Delhi
Visit our website at www.simonandschuster.com.au

A catalogue record for this
book is available from the
NATIONAL
LIBRARY National Library of Australia
OF AUSTRALIA

ISBN: 9781761104992

Cover design: Alissa Dinallo
Cover illustrations: Marcela Herrera
Typeset by Midland Typesetters, Australia
Printed and bound in Australia by Griffin Press

The paper this book is printed on is certified against the
Forest Stewardship Council® Standards. Griffin Press hol
chain of custody certification SCS-COC-001185. FSC®
promotes environmentally responsible, socially beneficial
and economically viable management of the world's fore

For Kate and Adele,
who refused to tell me this was a bad idea.

1

'All right, Amanda,' Murray said. 'This is going to be pretty standard stuff, okay? Nothing that wasn't on your application, nothing groundbreaking, no gotchas. All good?'

'Yes,' I replied, crossing my legs. I really wasn't used to wearing dresses, and the thought that I might accidentally flash the camera had given me nightmares on no less than three of the nights we spent in hotel lockdown.

'Look at me, not at the camera,' Murray said. 'Remember to answer in full sentences. The audience isn't going to hear my question, only your answer.'

'Full sentences. Yes. Got it.'

Someone re-angled a light and it shone right in my eyes. For a second, it felt like someone had sent a laser beam right through my brain.

'Sorry, sorry,' the tech guy said, moving the light again. 'There was a weird shadow on your face.'

'It's okay,' I said, dabbing at my watering eyes. 'Don't worry about it.'

'Make-up, can we get a touch-up, please?' Murray said.

A make-up woman scurried over to me.

'Unless you want to keep the tears, Amanda?' Murray said. 'You just broke up with your ex, right? If you're going to cry anyway—'

'No,' I said firmly. 'I'm not going to cry. No more tears.'

'All right, then.'

The make-up woman dabbed at my face with a small brush, touching up the contouring around my eyes. She was wearing a bright purple mask with little white polka dots. It was much cuter than the ones I had. I made a mental note to ask her where she got it, sometime later, when I wasn't devoting all my energy to looking like a proper holding-it-together adult.

'Okay, Amanda,' Murray said, when she was finished. 'Are you ready?'

'Yes,' I said. 'I'm ready.'

'Why did you come on *Marry Me, Juliet*, Amanda?'

'I came on *Marry Me, Juliet* because I believe in love,' I said, willing myself with all my being not to cry. 'I'm here because I've had my heart broken, but I don't want it to be broken forever. I'm here to try and put it back together.'

It was about two pm on a Tuesday afternoon when I decided to apply for *Marry Me, Juliet*. It was two months, three weeks, five days, and twenty-ish hours after Jac broke up with me. I was at work, writing up some maintenance instructions for a client. He leaned over the desk, looked at what I was writing, and said, 'Nice handwriting.'

'Thanks,' I said, genuinely a bit flattered. 'I don't think anyone's ever complimented my handwriting before.'

'Most mechanics write like doctors,' he said. 'Totally unreadable.'

'I do my best,' I said, finishing the instructions, folding them neatly in half and handing them to him. 'You look after that beautiful car now, all right? I don't want her back here in car hospital again.'

'I don't know,' he said, winking at me. 'If she has to come back, then I get to see you again. If I weren't already married...'

I made myself keep smiling as I rang up the cost of his repairs on the till.

'You single?'

'Yes!' Dave, one of the other mechanics, called over his shoulder. 'She got dumped!'

I shot him an *Oh, come on* look. He gave me a *What? You did!* look back.

'Trust me,' the customer said, leaning a little too far over the counter, 'the guy's an idiot.'

I gave Dave a pre-emptive look before he could shout, *She got dumped by a chick, mate!* I was already being propositioned by a married man. I knew from far too much experience that the grossness factor would go up at least ten times if said married man knew I was into women.

But the customer just looked thoughtful. 'You should go on that dating show,' he said, handing over his credit card. 'That Romeo and Juliet one. You're hot enough.'

If he hadn't said that thing about the dating show, I would have forgotten the interaction immediately (well, immediately after I'd given Dave the 793840329840th version of my 'Can you please not tell customers I'm single? You know it makes them hit on me' lecture). Being a petite blonde lady mechanic meant that men said far grosser things to me on a daily basis. I mostly just filed them away in the 'ugh, just another day in the office' box in my brain.

But he *had* said that thing about the dating show.

I knew exactly which dating show he meant. I watched *Marry Me, Juliet* (where a bunch of women compete for one man), *Wherefore Art Thou Romeo?* (where a bunch of men compete for one woman), and *Juliet on the Beach* (where a bunch of rejected contestants get drunk and hook up on a beach) religiously. I followed a lot of past contestants on Instagram, too. I was a pretty dedicated fan.

The thought of actually being on the show had never occurred to me, though.

Huh.

Interesting.

I wish I could say it was more complicated than that. That I weighed up all my options carefully. That I really thought about it seriously.

But nope. I decided to apply for *Marry Me, Juliet* just after lunch on a Tuesday because a customer suggested it while indulging in a spot of light sexual harassment.

'Mandie, no!' Mum said, when I told her my plans over dinner that night. 'That's a terrible idea.'

'Don't you want me out of my old bedroom?' I asked,

spooning more potato bake onto my plate. 'Just think, Mum –
if I got on the show, you'd have your house to yourself again.'

'You know I love having you here,' she said. 'You can stay
as long as you want. But that doesn't change the fact that this
is an awful idea.'

'No, it's not,' I said, shifting my attention to the salad.
Mum had put croutons in it, the fancy kind that she made
herself from sourdough. 'It's a great idea. It'll be fun. It'll be
an adventure. Think of all the ballgowns I'd get to wear. All
that free champagne. Those fancy dates they go on, with
all the boats and planes and things.'

Mum put her fork down. It clinked loudly against her
plate. 'Amanda,' she said. She never called me by my full
name unless I was in trouble, but I kept talking anyway.

'It's exciting,' I said, picking up a crouton with my fingers
and biting it in half. 'I've never been single during application season before. There was always Chloe or Mark or Jac or
whoever. I might never get another chance to have an experience like this. Great croutons, Mum.'

'Amanda! Stop!'

I stopped.

'Firstly, don't think you can distract me by compliment-
ing my cooking,' Mum said. 'Secondly, *think* about this
before you do something stupid.'

'I have thought about it,' I said, leaving out the *for about
six seconds* part. 'And I want to do it.'

'Why?'

'I told you. It'll be an adventure.'

'Don't lie to me, Mandie.'

'I'm not!'

'Then don't lie to yourself,' Mum said. 'You want to make Jac jealous.'

'That's not it,' I said. 'I swear.'

'That never crossed your mind?' she said. 'The thought of her watching a handsome man fall in love with you and realising she made a horrible mistake?'

'Of course it crossed my mind,' I said. I'd never been a good liar, and there was no point even trying with someone who knew me as well as Mum did. 'It's not *why*, though.'

'Because she didn't make a horrible mistake,' Mum said. 'Her breaking up with you was the nicest thing she ever did for you.'

'This isn't about Jac,' I insisted. 'It's about me. Moving on.'

'With some fantasy man? Mandie, come on.'

I stabbed at the half-crouton on my plate with my fork and said nothing.

'That show is a fantasy of a love that hardly ever comes true,' Mum said. 'Jac realising she made a mistake and coming back to you is a fantasy too.'

Tears sprang to my eyes. I blinked them back.

But I couldn't fool Mum. 'Swapping one fantasy for another isn't going to help anything, sweetheart,' she said, reaching across the table and taking my hand. 'You need to make some real steps forward, towards a new life of your own. A real life. Without Jac.'

I heard what Mum was saying. I really did.

But when I headed upstairs after dinner, to the bedroom that had been mine as a kid and had suddenly become mine again two months, three weeks, six days, and three hours ago, I opened up my laptop and went to the application website.

Mum wasn't wrong. In fact, I could write a list of all the things she was right about, like:

1) *Marry Me, Juliet* absolutely was a fantasy.
2) The chances of me finding a soulmate on the show were minuscule, even if I was ready to put myself back out there.
3) No matter how hard I tried, Jac wasn't going to get jealous and she absolutely wasn't coming back.

I was right too, though. My application wasn't about Jac. Or at least, it wasn't *just* about Jac. It was about me.

Jac hated *Marry Me, Juliet*. 'What can you possibly get out of this?' she'd asked me once in frustration. 'It's heteronormative, it's misogynistic, and on top of that, it's garbage.'

'I like seeing them fall in love,' I replied.

'You know they don't actually fall in love, right?'

'Some of them do! Luna and Roger have been together for more than two years now. And Basil and Megan—'

'Mandie,' Jac said, 'I'm not interested. Come to me when you have something worthwhile to talk about.'

I'd tried so hard to be the girlfriend Jac deserved, someone smart and clever and deep. I'd bent and broken parts of myself trying to become that girl. But I'd never stopped watching *Marry Me, Juliet*.

7

I didn't know how to put it into words in a way that would make Mum understand. I couldn't even really explain it to myself.

But *Marry Me, Juliet* didn't have Jac's fingerprints all over it. *Marry Me, Juliet* was just *mine*.

The first page of the application was full of pretty standard form questions that I filled out quickly: name, age, occupation, clothing sizes, whether or not I had any serious medical issues, that sort of thing. The last question was: *What is your sexual orientation?*

Whenever this question turned up on forms, I usually just clicked *bisexual* and got on with it. I'd been out since I was fifteen. It had been tough for a while until I found my place and my little queer community, but I'd done that work a long time ago. I was comfortable with who I was now. It wasn't a big deal.

But this wasn't a drop-down list, it was just a blank space. I paused, finger hovering over the *b* key.

There hadn't been a lot of out bi contestants on *Marry Me, Juliet*, but there'd been a few. Every single one of them had been treated horribly, either in the Villa, by the audience, or both. It was a sort of escalated version of what usually happened to me at work: as soon as people found out you were into women as well as men, they found a way to be gross about it.

No matter what my reasons were for wanting to go on the show, that was . . . not the experience I wanted.

I date men, I typed in the box.

Jac would be furious with me. She talked a lot about the

importance of media representation. She'd want me to come out immediately, loud and proud.

But Jac had given up any right to a say in what I did two months, three weeks, six days and counting-the-hours-was-a-pointless-waste-of-time ago. I saved my answers and clicked through to the next page.

The next page of the application was all short-answer questions – quite a lot of them, I discovered, as I scrolled to the bottom. *What are you passionate about? When did you last cry?* (God, the answer to that one was going to be embarrassing.) *What are your favourite outdoor activities? Your five best features? Your five worst features?*

There must have been forty or fifty questions altogether. Ooof. This was going to take a while.

I cracked my knuckles. If I'd been wearing long sleeves, I would have rolled them up. I didn't mind hard work. That could go under 'best features'.

I scrolled back up, planning to start at the top, but one of the questions caught my eye and made me stop. *What scares you?*

I leaned back in my chair and looked around my old room. It was exactly the same as it had been when I moved out to start my apprenticeship when I was eighteen, nearly ten years ago.

Every day, I woke up in my single bed, stared up at the decade-old posters of cars and pop stars, and thought about Jac. I went to work, put on my coveralls, started tuning up whatever car needed tuning up that day, and thought about Jac. I had lunch, thought about Jac. Knocked off, thought about Jac. Came home, had dinner, argued with my poor mum about how I was thinking about Jac too much and needed to stop.

Then I thought about Jac.

I lived in a small town. There wasn't a thing I could do or a place I could go that wouldn't make me think about Jac.

I'm scared I'll never get over my ex, I typed. *I'm scared of repeating the same patterns, over and over again. I'm scared of never growing, never changing, never moving forward. I'm scared of feeling like this forever.*

I deleted the last sentence in the end. It needed context, and if I started trying to explain what 'feeling like this' actually meant, I'd still be sitting here in another ten years.

But it was true. And it was the reason that I hadn't been able to articulate, the reason I needed to do this.

If I stayed here, in this place where everything had Jac written all over it, I might actually feel like this forever. I needed to be somewhere *else*.

I finished my application two nights later. I teared up when I hit the send button, and for once, I let the tears fall instead of blinking them back or wiping them away. It might be a small step, it might be a stupid step, it might be a step that never came to anything, but it was a step I'd taken on my own. It felt like a win.

It felt like another win when a producer named Carrie called me a few weeks later to tell me they wanted to see me for an audition. 'We loved your application,' she told me.

'Really?!' I asked.

'Really,' she said. 'You're exactly the kind of contestant we look for on *Marry Me, Juliet*, Amanda.'

I knew that probably just meant 'you're blonde and pretty', but I let myself count it as another win. *Be kind to yourself* was a very common theme in all the 'How To Get Over Your Ex' articles I was reading, and I was trying my very best.

The audition was in the city, about two hours away by train. I told Mum I was going to visit my friend Bec and that I was going to stay the night. I hadn't talked to her about my application since that night at dinner.

I felt guilty as hell when Mum dropped me off at the train station. 'Are you sure about going?' she asked. 'There's that virus everyone's talking about. I don't want you catching it in the city.'

'The virus isn't even in this country, Mum,' I said, desperate to get out of the car before I chickened out. 'I'll be fine.'

She pressed a brown paper bag into my hand. 'Some lunch,' she told me.

'Mum!' I protested. 'I'm twenty-seven, not five. I can get my own lunch.'

'I know,' she said. 'But you still need looking after sometimes, Mandie. Don't go getting hungry. Say hi to Bec for me.'

I can tell you one thing: if you're already feeling guilty about lying to your mum, her giving you lunch in a brown paper bag intensifies the feeling about fifty times over. My lunch was my tell-tale heart, muttering *what are you doing what are you doing what are you doing*, over and over again.

'Are you all right, Amanda?' the psych asked me in my mandatory evaluation. 'You seem a bit down, and a bit distracted.'

'I'm fine,' I lied, and then immediately felt even more guilty for lying. 'Sorry, what was the question?'

'What are you looking for in a romantic partner?'

A million images of Jac immediately flashed before my eyes. Her smiling. Her laughing. Her face when I'd first told her I loved her, the long, deliberate pause before she'd looked me in the eyes and said it back.

'Someone who . . .' I bit my lip.

'It's all right,' the psych said. 'Take your time.'

'Someone who knows what they want,' I said at last. 'I don't care what that is, as long as it includes me.'

After the psych evaluation and the medical and the group exercises they gave us lunch, some sad platters of soggy sandwiches and trays of fruit that were ninety-five per cent honeydew melon. I took my brown bag outside into the sun instead and sat on the steps of the building, hoping that if I ate the lunch, it'd stop tell-tale-hearting me.

The first thing I pulled out of the bag was a note. *Have a great day, darling. I love you. Mum xoxo*

And right there, sitting on those very public steps, on a very public street, in the middle of a very public city, I burst into extremely public, extremely embarrassing tears.

'Hey,' a woman's voice said. 'Are you all right?'

'I'm fine,' I sobbed.

'No, you're not.'

She sat down beside me. 'Come on, the audition wasn't

that bad, was it? I know the group exercises were like fingernails on a blackboard, but this reaction feels slightly disproportionate.'

A few of my sobs turned into laughs, before regressing back into sobs.

'Anything I can do? Anything I can say? I could give you a hug, or I could go away. Whatever you want.'

I shook my head, too choked up to say any actual words.

'I'm going to put my hand on your back, okay? You can cry for as long as you want.'

Her hand was a warm weight, rubbing gently at the base of my neck, as I pressed my eyes into my palms and tried desperately to get myself under control.

I couldn't tell you exactly how long I cried. It was probably only a few minutes, but in that way where time slows down at the worst possible moment, it felt like hours.

It had only taken a few seconds for Jac to say 'I don't want to be with you anymore.' But I could tell you everything about those seconds, every tiny little detail. What she'd been wearing. Where she'd been standing. Which eye a stray piece of her hair kept falling into. How it had felt when I'd said, '. . . What?', and she'd blown that piece of hair out of her eye and said, 'This isn't easy for me either, but it's what's best. I don't love you anymore,' and I'd started crying, and she'd said, 'Not now, Mandie, please, we need to be adults about this.'

'That's the way,' the woman said, still rubbing my back as my sobs eventually began to peter out. 'Deep breaths, all right?'

'I'm so sorry,' I managed to say.

I looked at her for the first time, and blinked. The person who'd just witnessed my extremely public breakdown was one of the most beautiful women I'd ever seen.

She wasn't my type. When I date women, I tend to go for Kristen Stewart types – short hair, kind of masc aesthetic, soft butch. Jac, with her undercut and her librarian glasses and her love of tweed blazers, had been the epitome of my type.

This woman was not that. She was Pasifika, with long dark hair partially restrained by a bright orange headband. Her dress was bright orange as well, belted at the waist, with a full skirt that looked like it would flare to about mid-calf when she stood.

And her eyebrows. My goodness, her eyebrows. I had never seen anyone with eyebrows as sharp and perfect and knife-edged as hers.

She might not have been my type, but I would murder anyone who said a word against those eyebrows.

'How are you feeling?' she asked, still rubbing my back.

'Embarrassed,' I replied. 'Really, really embarrassed.'

'This probably doesn't help,' she said, 'but if you get on the show, they're going to embarrass you way worse than this.'

She wasn't wrong. I might have sidestepped the fact that I was bi, but there had to be plenty of other ways they could make my life a nightmare. I certainly had enough weaknesses to exploit.

Why hadn't I listened to Mum? Why didn't I *think* before I did anything?

'You'll definitely get on the show, don't worry,' the woman said, misreading my expression. 'I'm amazed they even made you audition. They've probably already written your name on a bunch of the date cards. Pretty pint-sized blonde like you, you're catnip to these people.'

I managed a weak smile.

'You want to talk about whatever's got you out here crying?'

Wordlessly, I passed her the note.

'You're crying because your mum loves you?' she asked, arching one perfect eyebrow as she read it. 'I don't want to be insensitive, but you need to get bigger problems.'

'No,' I said. 'Well, kind of. She doesn't think this is a good idea. I lied about where I was going.'

'I just didn't tell mine,' she replied. 'I figure I'll cross that bridge and deal with the "This is what you want to do with your life? *This?*" lecture if I come to it.'

'Smart,' I said. 'I should have done that.'

She nudged me with her elbow. 'That the real reason you're crying, though?'

I sighed. 'I'm crying because my mum loves me,' I said, 'but my ex doesn't.'

'Ah,' she said. 'Now that's a problem worth crying about.'

I realised about a second too late that I probably shouldn't provide gossip fodder to someone who might be on the show with me. This was classic potential humiliation material.

But she just nudged me with her elbow again. 'I'm sorry that happened to you,' she said. 'I've been there. Done that. Got the T-shirt. It hurts like hell.'

'Yeah.' My voice was croaky from crying. 'It does.'

'Any kids?'

'No. We'd been talking about it, but . . . no.'

'Then comfort yourself with this: it's not as bad as it could have been. I got the T-shirt *and* the kid *and* the custody battle *and* the having-to-look-the-new-wife-in-the-eye, and I can tell you that it's not all it's cracked up to be.'

'That sounds horrible. I'm sorry.'

She shrugged. 'Not your fault. Not my fault either. It's his fault, the lying bastard. Did yours cheat?'

'No.'

I kind of wished she had, though. Something about 'Jac fell in love with someone else' felt preferable to 'Jac just doesn't love you specifically anymore, Amanda, and would rather be alone than spend another second in your company'.

'Girls, you need to come back in now,' a producer – Suzette, I thought her name was – said, sticking her head out the door. 'We're starting the one-on-ones.'

'Don't call us—' my new friend started, but Suzette was already gone. '. . . girls,' she finished, sighing. 'I hate it when people call adult women "girls".'

'The one I hate is "miss",' I said. 'I've got this customer who calls me "Miss Amanda" every single time he comes into my shop. I can't stand it.'

'Ugh,' she replied. 'So, it's Amanda? Your name?'

'Yep.'

'Dylan,' she said. 'Nice to meet you.'

2

'Hey,' I said to Dylan at the end of auditions. 'Can I buy you a drink? To thank you for today?'

'Babe, no thanks needed,' she said. 'But I'd love to grab a drink. There's a cute little wine bar around the corner.'

It really was just around the corner, only a couple of minutes' walk (although it would have been more like five minutes if I'd been on my own – Dylan was taller than me, and I had to walk fast to match her stride). Most people hadn't knocked off work yet, so the bar was relatively empty. 'What do you want?' I asked her, pulling my wallet out of my bag.

'Let's get champagne,' Dylan said. 'It's basically the official beverage of *Marry Me, Juliet*, after all. We'd better get used to drinking it if we're going to be on the show.'

'Oh no, what an enormous problem for us,' I said. 'You're right. We'd better start training.'

She laughed. She had a great laugh, full-throated, border-ing on a cackle, the kind that made you want to join in immediately.

We took our champagne and sat at a little high-top table near the window. It had hooks on the underside for our handbags, and they gently knocked together: mine a pale pink one that I'd taken out of my rotation because Jac hated it, and hers a brighter pink which should not have gone with her orange dress at all, but somehow did.

'Cheers,' Dylan said, holding up her glass. 'To our future reality TV glory.'

'Cheers,' I said, clinking my glass against hers.

We drank. 'You feeling better?' Dylan asked.

'Well, I am now,' I said, gesturing to my champagne.

She chuckled.

'But yes, I am feeling better,' I said. 'You caught me in a . . . how should I put this?'

'Rocky moment?'

'Exactly,' I said. 'But I'm okay now. Or I will be. Or some-thing. I'm not actively crying, which is the important thing.'

'I remember what it's like,' she said. 'When my marriage felt apart . . . Rocky moment is the wrong phrase, really. It's more like a quicksand moment. Like you're trying to stand and you're trying to get your balance but the ground just wants to suck you up.'

'Yes!' I said. I meant to tap my fingers in emphasis against the table, but I was a bit too enthusiastic, and we both had to steady our glasses. 'That's exactly it. And the tiniest little thing can knock you over. Like – and this is just an example, it definitely never happened – your mum putting a nice note in your lunch.'

Dylan grinned. 'I know everyone says this, but it really does get better with time. The ground turns solid again. I promise.'

I let out a breath. 'I hope so.'

She held up her glass again. 'To finding solid ground.'

'Absolutely.'

I took another sip and then set my glass down. 'So that's why I'm here,' I said. 'Why are you trying to get on *Marry Me, Juliet*?'

'In a way, it's the same sort of thing,' she said. 'I'm at a – I was going to say crossroads, but that's not right. I'm at a dead end. This is, like, an attempt to go off-road until I find the highway.'

I must have looked confused, because Dylan laughed and started explaining. She was a nurse, but she'd been slowly coming to the realisation that it wasn't for her. 'I like looking after people, but the reward isn't worth the cost,' she said. 'The work is long and hard. The pay is garbage. The respect is non-existent. I don't get to spend anywhere near enough time with my kid. I've been thinking about leaving for a while anyway, but now there's this virus on the horizon, and it's kicked me into gear. I want to help – and I will help, don't get me wrong, as much as I possibly can – but I know how nurses get treated. I already know we're going to get thrown under the bus.'

She picked up her almost-empty champagne flute, drank the dregs, and started twirling it in her fingers. 'Going on

19

Marry Me, Juliet is a bit of a Hail Mary,' she said. 'I'm not desperate to find a man or anything, but you've seen how much money some of the old contestants make, right?'

I nodded. I followed a lot of ex-contestants on Instagram, and some of them were clearly making big bucks in sponcon.

'It's not like that's what I want to do with my life either,' Dylan said. 'I don't know what I want to do, really. Just not what I'm doing right now.'

'Me too!' I said. 'I don't have a goal for the show. If I find someone there, great, but if I don't, that's fine. I just need to do something completely different for a while. Reset.'

We ordered another round and began talking about the show. It turned out we'd both watched every season, and we shared a lot of the same opinions. 'Yes!' Dylan said, slapping her hand against the table. 'Thank you! Brett absolutely should have picked Mary-Ellen! Some of my friends were like "noooooo, he has so much more in common with CJ, they have an intellectual connection," but—'

'But there was no spark, right?' I said, gesturing wildly and nearly knocking over my champagne glass again.

'Yes!' Dylan said. 'When they kissed, it looked like someone mashing a Barbie and Ken together. And didn't you get the sense that CJ didn't even really like him?'

'What do you mean?'

'She was always making these little comments,' she said. 'Like, he'd tell her something personal about himself, and she'd smile and pat him on the shoulder, and then they'd cut to an interview with her and she'd be like, "We can work on that once we're together." Like he was some house she was renovating instead of a person she might end up in a relationship with— 'hey, are you okay?'

'You know how in the application form you had to write down your five worst features?' I said, brushing my tears away with my wrist and blinking furiously. 'Number one on my list is that I cry too much. Sorry.'

'Don't apologise,' she said, reaching over the table and taking my hand. 'You cry as much as you want.'

'I don't want to cry, though,' I said. 'It's the quicksand thing again. The smallest thing makes me think of my ex, and . . . waterworks. Every time. I hate that I'm like this.'

'So your ex was a bit of a CJ?'

I dabbed at my eyes with a serviette while I figured out how to phrase my response.

'My ex is brilliant,' I said at last. 'Jac had – has – really high standards, and after a while . . .'

'Go on,' Dylan said comfortingly.

I took a deep breath. 'Let's just say,' I said, 'that I turned out to be one of those houses that gets abandoned because the renovation is too hard.'

Dylan eyed me shrewdly. 'Have you considered that maybe your ex absolutely fucking sucked?'

I made a strangled half-laugh.

She squeezed my hand. 'I know I've only known you for, like, six hours,' she said, her eyes warm as they looked into mine, 'but I can tell you this with absolute certainty: you deserve someone who actually likes you.'

Now my laugh was a little more full, a little less strangled. 'Maybe I'll find them on *Marry Me, Juliet*.'

'Maybe,' she said. 'You and Mr Cardboard Cut-out Handsome Man could be the next Basil and Megan.'

'Luna and Roger is probably more my speed.'

Dylan took another sip of champagne. 'I'm interested. Explain.'

'Basil and Megan are great together, but I always found him a bit intimidating,' I said. 'Roger's so gentle. He has kind eyes. I like that in a man.'

We chatted for another half an hour or so before Dylan got a text from someone. 'Shit, I have to go, sorry about this, Amanda,' she said. 'Sorry.'

'That's okay,' I said. 'I have to go and meet my friend anyway.'

Dylan and I hugged and exchanged numbers, but as I walked – slightly unsteadily, after two glasses of champagne, but on more solid ground than I had been for a long time – towards the bus stop, I wondered if I would ever see her again. They auditioned thousands of people around the country for *Marry Me, Juliet*. The chances of one of us getting on the show were slim, let alone both of us.

Maybe, I thought, sitting on the bus to Bec's, it was like the one-night stand version of a friendship. I'd never had an actual one-night stand (I was very much a serial monogamist), so perhaps this was the closest I would ever come: one very nice, very pleasurable afternoon with a cool woman who could put into words some of the things I'd been struggling to express.

At 11.30 that night, though, my phone buzzed. I was three-quarters of the way asleep on Bec's couch, and I rubbed my eyes sleepily as I looked at it.

Hey! Dylan had written. *I had such a good time with you today & I want you to know I meant what I said – you deserve someone who actually likes you.*

The three dots were blinking underneath. She was writing another message.

I remembered what you said about the worst features list on the application. Idea: go back and look at your best features list! You deserve someone who will see those things in you.

I sat up on the couch and shoved my hair out of my face.

Do it now, she wrote. *I can see you saw this message. Don't leave me on read.* 😉

OK, OK, I sent back. *I'm doing it now.*

I found my application receipt buried deep in my email. Under *What are your five best features?* I'd written:

1) I'm not afraid of hard work.
2) I'm organised and methodical.
3) I'm not insecure about my looks.
4) I'm good at my job.
5) I have nice handwriting.

Oh no, I sent to Dylan.

???? she sent back.

One of my things was 'I have nice handwriting'. Babe!!!!!!!!

I know.

Project for you, she said. *Come up with a new one.*

I drew my legs up and rested my chin on my knees, thinking about it.

Another message popped up. *This isn't me trying to do some weird house renovation on you btw. Just trying to help you see what's already there.* 😊

I get it, don't worry, I sent back. *How about 5) I'm not going to let the quicksand drag me down?*

She sent back an emoji of two champagne glasses clinking against each other.

OMG! I texted Dylan a few weeks later. It was a subject change – the last thing we'd been talking about was the fashion at the Met Gala and how bad everyone was at following the theme. *You'll never guess who I just got off the phone with?!!!!*

I bet I can guess, she sent back almost immediately. *Gruff? Scruffy? Mid-thirties-ish? Somewhere between daddy and dad vibes?*

I shifted position on my bed and leaned up against the wall, my head resting against the bottom of an old Halsey poster teenage Mandie had ripped out of a magazine. *You think producer Murray has daddy vibes?*

Like, *I* wouldn't call him daddy personally, but I can picture a universe in which *someone* calls him daddy, she replied. *But he called you? You're on the show?*

I literally just got off the phone with him, I sent. *Which you guessed very easily, so – he called you too?!*

You bet, she replied. *Officially on my way to the Juliet Villa, bayyyyybeeeeeeee.*

You said yes straight away?

Of course I did. Didn't you?

I told him I had to think about it.

Babe!!!!!! Dylan sent. *What is there to think about?*

It was a totally valid question. I'd been just as surprised as she was now when 'Can I think about it, Murray?' had come out of my mouth.

??? she sent.

But there were reasons. *1) My mum hates the idea. 2) I'm not over my ex. 3) I don't understand why they picked me.*

She sent back a list of her own. *1) Your mum will get over it. 2) This is an absolutely iconic way to move on. 3) They picked you because, a) you rule, b) you're interesting, and c) you're hot.*

Another text arrived before I had a chance to reply. *Also d) you're blonde. You know how horny the show is for blondes.*

I sent back a row of laughing emojis.

Plus, we can't forget e) the whole audience is going to fall in love with you, she added.

Like clockwork, the break-up started playing in my mind again. Jac blowing her hair out of her eyes. Telling me she didn't love me anymore. Me crying. Her telling me to grow up.

And bonus: I'll be there!! Dylan sent. *Who wouldn't want to hang out with me?!*

I definitely want to hang out with you! I replied, forcing the memory away. *But there's work too. They'll be pissed.*

Trust me, so will mine, she sent back. *But I'm still going.*

How is work? I asked. *Everything I hear on the news is so terrible. I worry about you all the time.*

25

She sent back a selfie. She was in full PPE, the mask digging into her face, leaving deep hollows under her eyes, dark and bruised. *It absolutely fucking sucks,* she sent back.

Oh God. I'm so sorry.

It's brutal, honestly, she said. *The virus numbers are climbing every day, and we're just getting slammed harder and harder & the PPE they're making us work in is bullshit. I've worn that mask for four days straight. I'll be lucky if I don't catch the damn thing before the show starts.*

Don't say that!!

I feel so guilty about leaving when we're already so under-staffed, but I can't go on like this, she sent. *I had to send Noah to his dad's. I can't put him at risk. It's killing me.*

God. I wish there was some way I could help. Make things easier for you.

The three dots appeared, disappeared and reappeared a few times before her next reply came through.

Some things can't be fixed, she wrote. *Sometimes you just have to sit with it, no matter how badly it sucks.*

Tears pricked my eyelids. I blinked them rapidly away. I wasn't going to do this. I wasn't going to take someone else's very real, very serious, potentially life-or-death problems and make them about me and my stupid quick-sand feelings.

Well, if you need someone to sit with, I wrote back, *you know where I am.*

Don't tempt me, Frodo, she replied. *Or I'll run out of this hospital, jump on a train out your way, and land right in your lap.*

My fingers hovered above my phone screen as I tried to figure out what to say next.

I tried to imagine Dylan here with me, in my childhood bedroom. Her seeing me not just sitting with my heartbreak, but wallowing in it.

Waiting.

. . . and there it was. The real reason I'd blurted out 'Can I think about it, Murray?' when he'd offered me a place on the show.

I was still waiting for Jac to come back. She didn't love me anymore – and even if she did, she'd be way too proud to admit she'd made a mistake – but here I was, still. waiting. anyway.

Was that the kind of person I wanted to be? Was that the kind of person that a grown-ass woman like Dylan would ever want to talk about her actual serious adult problems with? Was that the kind of person anyone would ever want to come back for?

No.

Fuck that.

I was going to call Murray, and tell him yes.

Mum would be disappointed in me. Work would be annoyed with me. And I was going to have to deal with whatever came after – all the attention, positive and negative, even if I didn't come out on TV.

I genuinely didn't know if I was tough enough. Most days, I was one strong gust of wind away from being blown right into the quicksand and never resurfacing.

Future Mandie was going to have to deal with that,

though. Because Present Mandie wasn't going to hang around dreaming of having Past Mandie's life back anymore.

Soon, I wrote back to Dylan. *You, me, Juliet Villa. I'll sit with you as much as you want.*

Much as she asserted over and over again that she was one hundred per cent absolutely definitely going on *Marry Me, Juliet,* I was worried Dylan wouldn't be there when I arrived at the lockdown hotel for two weeks of quarantine before shooting. Our text convo was now *very* long, so I knew how guilty she felt about leaving her job. I also knew how badly she was missing her son. I wouldn't have been at all surprised if she'd ditched at the last minute and chosen to spend the next eight weeks with him instead of on TV. It would have been a very sensible, completely reasonable thing to do, even though the thought that she might do it made me feel a bit sick.

Which was very selfish of me. Surely even I wasn't so pathetic that I'd put my desire to go through this experience with a friend over her getting to spend time with her child.

I stopped myself. That was a quicksand thought pattern.

Dylan had sent me a few more 'How To Get Over Your Ex' articles. (*Let me know when you're done with these,* she'd texted. *Plenty more where they came from.*) One of them had specifically been about being dumped, and described strategies for building your confidence back up. One strategy it suggested was that when you slipped into being negative about yourself or calling yourself names, you countered that by identifying one thing you liked about yourself.

6) I am good at making friends, I added to my best features list in my mind. It had only taken me an afternoon to become friends with Dylan. If she didn't turn up, I could make other friends. It would be okay. *I* would be okay.

But I didn't need to worry, because Dylan was there. 'Mandie!' she said when I walked into the conference room for our pre-lockdown briefing. She was wearing a bright pink mask, so I couldn't technically see it, but I knew she was smiling. 'You made it!'

'Of course I made it!' I replied, smiling back at her and giving her one of those awkward six-feet-away pandemic air hugs. 'What, you thought I was going to bail?'

'I thought your mum's intense opposition to you coming on the show might have got to you at the last minute.'

'She's still not thrilled about it,' I replied. 'She thinks I'm throwing myself into a fantasy world instead of dealing with the real one. But I'm on such reduced hours at the shop right now that I'm not really making any money. She might not be a fan of me being on the show, but she is a fan of me having an income, and a hundred bucks a day is better than nothing.'

'Aren't mechanics considered essential workers?'

'Technically yes, but only in emergencies. With everyone in lockdown, hardly anyone's driving, so . . .'

'I still can't believe you're a mechanic,' Dylan said, shaking her head as we took our seats. The ones we were allowed to sit in were marked with stickers, carefully spaced for social distancing. 'That blew my mind. Whenever you talked about the shop where you worked I was picturing, like, a cupcake shop or something.'

'I'm more complicated than I seem,' I said. 'Slightly, anyway.'

'Why cars?'

I shrugged. 'I've always been good with my hands.'

'God, men must love you,' Dylan said. 'You're like a whole category of porn in one person.'

You should see how they react when they find out I like women, I thought, but didn't say.

It wasn't that I thought she would react badly. I'd developed a good radar over the years, and I couldn't imagine Dylan having any kind of problem with me coming out to her.

But I'd learned from years of watching *Marry Me, Juliet* that if you shared a secret with even one person, it would eventually get out. Even if that person was trustworthy – which I fully believed Dylan was – it'd get out. How could it not? They were filming you constantly. That was how a contestant had been outed as pan a few seasons back. She'd told her best friend on the show, and somehow – producers, probably? – it got back to the Romeo, and he'd immediately started angling for a threesome.

So no. No thank you. None of that for me, please. 'Oh hey, I'm bi, BTW' was a conversation that could wait until after filming.

'Ladies!' producer Murray called, standing on the little stage at the front of the room. 'If I can have your attention, please?'

'You see what I mean about the dad meets daddy vibes, right?' Dylan whispered to me, leaning across the space between our seats. 'He's, like, perfectly in the middle.'

I stifled a laugh behind my mask.

Murray launched into a long lecture about how the show was going to work –about how we'd be locked down for two weeks in the hotel and tested regularly for the virus before filming started, about the virus-free closed-set bubble that the show was going to shoot in, about our contracts, and about how Tom Zelig is the host, not a second Romeo, besides, he's married so please please please stop being horny for Z, *he is not for you.*

I listened intently. I always made sure I was clear on the instructions for things so I didn't make silly mistakes. I took notes on my phone so I wouldn't forget anything.

. . . which was why I saw the text from Jac the instant it popped up.

You're going on reality TV? What the actual fuck, Mandie.

'. . . shoot for six weeks – about two episodes a week, twelve altogether – then there'll be a gap of a couple of months before the premiere,' I dimly heard Murray say.

The second text came through a moment later. *Don't you have any self-respect?*

I'd been punched in the stomach twice in my life: once in high school in a drama class incident gone wrong, and once when I was doing my apprenticeship, by a dude desperate to prove that chicks just couldn't hack it in the industry.

Jac, it turned out, could deliver that same kind of blow – the one that doubles you over, that makes it impossible to breathe, that takes you down to the ground – in a single text.

'Are you all right?' Dylan whispered.

I couldn't speak. I just showed her the phone.

'Your ex?' she asked.

I nodded. Murray was talking about money now and how much (little) we were all going to get paid, and I knew I should be listening, but . . .

Don't you have any self-respect? How did Jac always know exactly which combination of words would hurt the most?

'Delete it,' Dylan said.

I looked at her, wide-eyed.

'Delete it,' she said. 'You don't need this kind of bullshit. First step to getting rid of an ex: delete everything. Lose their number. Block them.'

I bit my lip, hard.

'You can't let an ex's voice stay in your head,' she said. 'They'll suck you right back down into the quicksand.'

Slowly, I hovered my finger over the little text bubbles.

Don't you dare, Jac whispered in my mind.

'Do it,' Dylan said. 'I dare you.'

I swallowed. *Don't you have any self-respect?*

No. Not much. Hardly any.

But enough.

I gritted my teeth. I deleted the texts.

And I blocked Jac's number.

3

They tried to take our phones away during hotel lockdown, but Dylan pitched an absolute fit. 'I have a seven-year-old son,' she told Murray fiercely. 'You're telling me you're going to lock me up for two weeks and not let me talk to him?'

He did indeed try to tell her that – 'You're not going to be able to have your phone on the show, and this is a logical extension of that policy. We can't have any details leak.' – but Dylan was a force of nature, and he caved. 'And you're going to let me have daily conversations with my kid during filming!' she said to his retreating back. 'Or I'm not doing the show, do you hear me?'

'Yeah, yeah, whatever,' Murray said, waving his hand dismissively as he walked away.

'I want that in writing!' she called after him.

He made another vague hand gesture without turning back.

'Would you really have quit the show?' I asked her, as we stood in the lift with a production assistant who was showing us to the rooms we would be locked in for the next fortnight.

'No, but he doesn't need to know that,' she replied. 'Please don't tell him,' she added, to the production assistant.

'No worries,' the PA replied.

'If there's one thing I've learned from being a parent, it's that the first rule of getting control is acting like you already have it,' Dylan said.

'Would you say that's more dad energy or daddy energy?' I asked her, waggling my eyebrows.

Her cackle of a laugh lasted all the way up to our floor.

Our rooms were next to each other, and we leaned against the wall outside them as the PA gave us a lecture. 'Once these doors close behind you, you won't be coming out for two weeks,' she warned us. 'When meals are delivered, they'll knock, but you should wait a full minute before you open the door. The only person you should open these doors to straight away is the nurse when they come to do testing. Is that clear?'

It was only slight, but I felt Dylan flinch when the PA mentioned nurses. I curled my fingers around hers and squeezed. She squeezed back gratefully.

'You going to be okay?' I asked her, when the lecture was over.

'Yeah, yeah, I'll be fine,' she said. 'Just another attack of the guilts. What about you?'

'What about me?'

'You've got your phone,' she said, gesturing. 'I know you

just deleted your ex's number, but you must still be connected on like fifty different kinds of social media. Are you going to be all right?'

I thought about it. 'I don't know,' I said. 'Good question.'

'Come on, ladies,' the PA said. 'It's time to go inside.'

We separated, and I opened the door to my room. 'Tell you what,' Dylan said, opening her door. 'If you feel yourself getting weak, you call me, okay?'

'You wouldn't say that if you knew how often I'll take you up on that.'

'Mandie,' she said, 'there's a special place in hell for women who don't help other women get over their shithead exes.'

Our quarantine hotel rooms were tiny, the kind where the bed took up ninety-five per cent of the floorspace. 'Can you believe it?' I said to Dylan when we FaceTimed that night, after I made her order me not to look at Jac's Instagram. 'I had all these plans to get into yoga while we were locked away, but there's barely enough space to stand, let alone do a downward dog.'

'It could be worse,' she said. 'It will be worse, in the Villa. I very much doubt we'll be getting our own rooms there.'

'Good point,' I said. 'No TV in the Villa, either. We should make use of all the fancy channels they have here while we can. I'm going to become an expert on the Kardashians.'

'We should pick a show to watch together. Keep ourselves sane.'

That was why, two weeks, several virus tests, and a whirl-wind day of hair, make-up, dress fittings, and interviews later, the first thing I said to Dylan when we were face to face again was, 'I can't believe they never made a second season of *Real Housewives of Auckland*.'

'I know, right?' Dylan said. 'How do all the other *Real Housewives* franchises get a million seasons and the literal pinnacle of the franchise only gets one?'

'It's a tragedy.'

'Agreed,' she said. 'Also, hi babe! It's so nice to see you properly again!'

'You too!' I said, as we hugged.

She pulled back and held me at arms' length. 'Mandie, I knew you were hot, but damn.'

She gestured up and down my First Night Party dress, the ensemble I'd be wearing to meet the Romeo on the red carpet. It was a short-ish pale pink dress with a frothy, layered skirt, shot through with something sparkly, giving off a very 'ballerina from the inside of a jewellery box' vibe.

'Thank you,' I said. 'But why are we talking about me when we could be talking about you? You look incredible.'

She grinned. 'I do, don't I?'

'Dylan Gilchrist and Amanda Mitchell?' a PA said, coming up to us. 'You're both in Limo 1 with Murray. This way, please.'

The train of Dylan's First Night Party dress swept along the ground as we followed the PA. It was electric green and sequinned, and it made her look like a sea witch – like she might sit on a rock and sing, and sailors would fall over themselves for the honour of drowning in her presence.

Incredible was too weak a word for how she looked. She might not have been my type, but in that dress, Dylan was stunning. The Romeo was going to fall to his knees and beg her to step on him.

There was a prickle of something in my stomach. I looked pretty enough in my ballerina gown, but in the blandest, most basic, pedestrian way.

I stamped firmly on the thought before I got stuck in the quicksand again. *7) I am supportive of my friends,* I added to my list of positive features.

Part of the sea witch dress spilled over my lap as we packed into the limo. I was the smallest, so I was in the middle, squashed between Dylan on one side and a pretty brunette in black tulle on the other. 'Sorry, sorry, sorry,' I told the brunette. 'I really don't mean to invade your personal space like this. I'm so sorry.'

'It's all right.'

'Tell me if I elbow you or anything,' I said. 'I don't want to accidentally hurt you.'

'I will.'

'I'm Amanda,' I said. 'Nice to meet you.'

'Cece,' she replied. 'Nice to meet you too.'

I could feel her leg jiggling ever so slightly against mine. She was nervous.

So was I, I realised suddenly.

Fourteen days in lockdown should have been plenty of time to process the fact that I was about to go on reality TV and try to fall in love. But between watching *Real Housewives* and chatting with Dylan and doing my best not to stalk Jac's social media and trying to erase the words *Don't you have any self-respect?* from my brain, I hadn't actually given it much thought.

Typical Mandie, Jac used to say, ruffling her fingers through my hair. *Never thinking ahead.*

'Can you tell us who the Romeo is?' I asked Murray.

He'd been absorbed in an argument with the East Asian woman sitting next to him (her huge yellow skirt was spread over his lap, and Murray was making it clear that he would very much like her skirt *not* to be spread over his lap), and he looked slightly surprised to realise that there were other people in the limo. 'You'll find out soon enough.'

'I heard it was Chris Gregory,' the blonde woman on Big Yellow Dress's other side said. I remembered her from the pre-lockdown briefing, because Dylan had pointed her out and said, 'Look, Mandie, your clone.'

'The TV gardener?' Big Yellow Dress said, making a disgusted face. 'Eww.'

'What do you mean, "eww"?' the Mandie Clone demanded. 'He's a babe. Haven't you seen his abs?'

'He's always so sweaty. I bet he reeks. Probably worse than you, Murray.'

Murray's face took on a stormcloud expression.

'I wouldn't mind if it were Chris Gregory,' I said. 'He has kind eyes.'

It wasn't a lie. Mum loved lifestyle shows, and I'd seen a lot of Chris Gregory's landscaping program since I'd moved back in with her. He spent a lot of time gently patting fertiliser down around plants and gently helping children design vegetable gardens and gently stroking trees before he pruned branches off.

He'd be a great Romeo. Jac had been a lot of things, but gentle hadn't been one of them. I could use some gentle in my life. I'd be gently attracted to him, and he could be my extremely gentle rebound. 'I'm sorry, Amanda, but your heart isn't the other half of mine,' he'd tell me gently when he broke up with me, and I'd paper over my agonising heartbreak with a gentler one, and then I could just get on with my life.

'It's not Chris Gregory,' Murray said.

Oh. Well. There went that fantasy.

'Here's what's going to happen,' Murray said. 'Listen up. That means you, Lily.'

Big Yellow Dress rested her chin on his shoulder and smiled sweetly up at him. 'What is it that makes you think I'm not listening? I'm starting to think you don't like me.'

Yikes. Chris Gregory had clearly made a lucky escape. This woman would have eaten him for breakfast.

'In about five minutes, we're going to pull up in the driveway,' Murray said, apparently deciding to pretend Yellow Dress Lily wasn't there. 'You'll stay in the limo until I say you can get out. Say what you need to say to the Romeo, but make it quick. We have to film this whole thing – all the entrances, the First Night Party, and the Necklace Ceremony – while it's still dark, so we don't have time for you to take forever.'

'Isn't the First Night Party usually filmed over a couple of nights?' Dylan asked.

'Usually, yes,' Murray replied. 'But we can't take you back out of the Juliet Villa once we put you in because of the bubble, so this year we have to get it all in one. Get in, get out, be memorable. The Romeo's meeting fifteen girls tonight, so if he can't remember your name, he's probably going to cut you.'

Something about that sentence made my stomach clench.

I was good with people. I knew that. *6) on my list – I am good at making friends.*

But just because I was good with people didn't mean I was good at making them *remember* me.

I didn't stand out. I was vanilla ice cream. Everyone likes vanilla ice cream, but no one ever goes 'mmmm, wow, delicious, what a memorable vanilla ice cream I just had, I'm going to tell all my friends about it'.

What's the worst that can happen? I asked myself. *Even if you get eliminated on the first night, you still tried something new. You still took a big step forward. You still stopped waiting.*

But Jac would *know* I got cut straight away.

Pathetic, she'd say. *You can't even do that right.*

Dylan squeezed my fingers. 'Hey,' she whispered to me. 'I'm nervous too.'

'Thanks,' I whispered, squeezing back. 'I'm just worried he won't remember me.'

She leaned in close, her lips almost touching my ear. 'Trust me, Mandie,' she said. 'The way you look? He's going to remember you.'

Some of her hair brushed my shoulder. It tickled. I shivered.

'How many is he cutting tonight?' the Mandie Clone asked.

'Z will tell you that before the Necklace Ceremony,'

Murray said. 'Remember: when Z comes back into the First Night Party, the party ends. Because we have to film everything tonight, the party is going to be much shorter than it would normally be, so take your chances. If you haven't taken the Romeo aside by the time the party ends, chances are you'll get cut because he won't remember you.'

'Do you really think someone could forget me, Murray?' Lily said, batting her eyelashes at him again.

'Yes,' Murray said. 'Some of the Romeos we've had have been pretty dense.'

Was this Romeo going to be dense? I could work with that. My taste in men ran in a pretty distinct himbo direction.

It would drive Dylan absolutely up the wall, though. What were the chances that the Romeo was going to be some kind of magical unicorn who we were both interested in? Who was interested in two women as different as we were?

I had no doubt that my friendship with Dylan would survive the show. I wasn't sure *I'd* survive the show without Dylan, though.

'You've been working on this show for a few seasons, right, Murray?' I asked. 'Do you have any tips? Apart from making him remember us?'

He looked contemplative for a second. 'Just don't get too drunk,' he said at last. 'And try not to fall in the pool with your mic pack on. They're expensive.'

Well, that was something. Even I could probably manage that.

'Right, we're approaching the property,' he said. 'One of our guys is going to open the door. Dylan G, you're out first.'

41

'Right,' Dylan said.

The fact that they were giving her an initial meant there must be another Dylan on the show. Interesting. It wasn't the most common women's name ever, so it was a bit surprising that there were two of them.

'Shit, really?'

It took me a second to realise Murray was talking to someone in his earpiece. 'Really what?' Cece asked.

'Brief Z,' Murray said, ignoring her. 'Give me half an hour to get my girls through intros, and I'll come and troubleshoot.'

'Brief Z about what?' Cece asked. Her leg started to jiggle even more violently.

'We're here,' Murray said, still ignoring her as the limo slowed and then stopped. 'Get ready, Dylan.'

'I'm ready,' she said. 'And it's "women".'

That snapped him out of whatever was happening in his earpiece, because he looked right at her. 'What?'

'You called us "girls". It's women. We're all adult women.'

'You're right,' Murray said. 'Sorry about that. Bad habit.'

That's what I'm talking about, Mandie, Jac would say, gesturing wildly. *If you'd just stand up to people once in a while, things might change.*

My mouth went dry. *Don't you have any self-respect?*

'You good to go?' Murray asked.

Dylan glanced at me, smiled, and squeezed my hand again quickly. 'Yes,' she said.

'Open the door,' Murray said into his radio.

Like magic, it opened. 'See you in there, Mandie,' Dylan whispered.

42

Her sea witch dress got caught as she got out of the car. I unhooked it before it could rip (God, it would be a crime to rip a dress like that), and then she was gone.

'You should have let it tear.'

It took me longer than it should have to realise Lily was talking to me. 'What?'

'Her dress,' Lily said. 'This is supposed to be a competition. We're not here to make friends.'

A tougher person might have argued. Dylan certainly would have.

But I just said, 'Whatever you say,' and turned back to the window.

I was hoping I could watch Dylan meet the Romeo, but the door-opening person was standing in the way. It made sense. There must be rules about laying eyes on the magical man himself before it was your turn.

My throat was still dry. There were some tiny bottles of water wedged in the car door. I took one, cracked it open, poured nearly half of it down my throat, and tried to breathe slow and deep.

'All of you need to be quiet now,' Murray said. 'I have to listen. We can't have any background noise pick up in the intros, or we'll have to refilm them.'

'Get out of the way,' Lily ordered Murray.

She'd had the same idea as me, clearly, because she basically climbed into his lap in her effort to see out the window. 'I want to get a look at the Romeo.'

'Lily, sit down!' Murray said, jerking his body. 'And for the love of God, shut up.'

43

The look Lily gave him was full of venom. 'Don't you dare tell me to shut up,' she told him icily. 'Don't you dare.'

Murray tugged at his already scruffy hair, making it even scruffier. 'I'm sorry. But – just – please, I need you to be quiet. All of you. I have to think.'

I sipped at my water. The door guy's arse was still blocking my view of Dylan and the Romeo.

He was going to like her. Of course he was going to like her. How could he not?

'Go. Now. Out,' Murray said.

He was looking at me. My throat instantly went dry again.

I drained the dregs of my water and wedged the empty bottle back in the car door. 'All right,' I said. 'Good luck, everyone.'

'Do I look like I need it?' Lily said, waving a hand dismissively.

Yikes again.

I stepped out of the car and into a fairy-tale.

I knew, on some level, what it was going to look like. I knew there were going to be fairy lights and lanterns and outdoor chandeliers and sparkles as far as the eye could see.

But there was a difference between watching it on TV and being there in real life. It looked *amazing*.

'Wow,' I breathed.

It really hit me in that moment, what I'd done. I'd taken that little spark of an idea that had formed that Tuesday afternoon in the shop, and I'd followed it all the way through. I'd taken a step. It might be a step into a fantasy world, but it was still a step. A step that *I'd* taken. One foot out of the quicksand.

Jac was going to hate that I was here. She was going to absolutely fucking *hate it.*

I smiled, and started walking up the driveway, camera crew in my wake.

Mandie doesn't have an ounce of self-respect, Jac'd be saying to herself, but she'd be the one sitting there watching a show she swore she had zero interest in and that was actively bad for society.

'Hi!' the Romeo called to me.

Hell yes, he was perfect. The Romeo was a gorgeous South Asian man: tall and broad-shouldered, with perfectly coiffed dark hair, filling out his grey suit like nobody's business. He was exactly the kind of clean-cut handsome that Jac hated.

'Hi!' I replied. 'I'm Amanda. Lovely to meet you!'

'Lovely to meet you too,' he replied, taking my hands and kissing me on both cheeks. 'I'm Dylan.'

I blinked. 'Dylan? Like—'

'– like the last contestant, yes,' he said. 'Let's hope it doesn't get too confusing. But tell me about you, Amanda. What do you do?'

'I'm a mechanic.'

He smiled, one of those wide-eyed, genuinely excited smiles some people have. I liked him instantly. 'No way! Really?'

'Really,' I replied. 'You don't want to look too hard at my manicure. There's definitely still grease under my nails.'

'I'll make you a deal,' he said. 'I won't look at your nails if you don't look at my calluses.'

I immediately turned his hands over in mine. 'Oh my God, those are some beauties!' I said, tracing one with a fingertip. 'How did you get those?'

'I'm a sailor.'

'What, like in the navy?'

'No, not like that,' he replied. 'As a sport. I went to the Olympics.'

'Sorry. That was probably a stupid question. I don't know much about sailing.'

'I don't expect you to, don't worry,' he said, smiling again. 'But I do expect you to keep up your end of the bargain, and I can't help but notice you broke our deal *immediately*. So show me those nails, girl.'

I laughed and held out my hands for him. He made a production of studying them. 'No,' he said. 'No grease here.'

'I don't think you're looking hard enough.'

'Look, you might be right,' he said. 'I can't see shit without my glasses.'

I pictured him with glasses and went a little weak at the knees. Oh, I could *definitely* work with this handsome man in glasses.

'Dylan!' the director called. 'No swearing!'

'Fuck,' Romeo-Dylan said. 'Sorry, Amanda.'

'I'm a mechanic,' I replied. 'I work around men all day. I promise you that I've heard it before.'

'Take it back,' the director said. 'Say the thing about your glasses and then wrap it up. We've got thirteen more girls to get through, and we're on a schedule.'

'You good?' he asked me.

I nodded.

'I can't see anything without my glasses,' he replied. 'But I promise I'll see you inside the Villa, all right, Amanda?'

'It's a deal,' I replied. 'I hope you're better at holding up your end of bargains than I am.'

His chuckle followed me as I floated away from him towards the door to the Villa, light as air.

This might work. This might actually *work*. Romeo-Dylan was gorgeous and non-threatening and easy to talk to, and Jac would hate his enthusiastic loveliness *so much* and it would be *so good*, and—

'He's a hottie, right?' Dylan said, her sea witch dress trailing behind her as she swept over to me, a glass of champagne in each hand.

– and why would he pick me when he could pick her?

You went on reality TV and got eliminated on the first night, Jac would say. *You can't even do that right.*

'Yeah,' I replied, making myself smile and taking the glass she held out to me. 'He is.'

4

On the very first day of my mechanic apprenticeship, aged eighteen, I walked into a garage full of men. Every single one of them possessed at least six different calendars featuring blondes in bikinis draped over cars.

Obviously, I did not wear a bikini to work, but it didn't take a genius to notice basically every one of my co-workers look at me, look at their calendars, look back at me, look at one of the many cars in the garage, and mentally drape me over the hood.

I tried so many things to get them to stop. So many. For example:

- Ignoring all the comments and looks (You know how they tell you in school that if you ignore bullies they go away? Not true, at least in my experience.);
- Calling them out when I heard the comments or saw the

looks, even though I am extremely bad at standing up for myself ('Can't you take a joke?');

- Complaining to my boss ('Just ignore them; anyway, can't you take a joke?');
- Being so much better at my job than they were that they *had* to respect me (turns out men hate it when you're better at things than them);
- Getting my boyfriend at the time to pick me up and drop me off from work (mildly effective for a while, but . . .);
- After we broke up, getting my new girlfriend to pick me up and drop me off (extreme opposite effect); and
- Joining in with their gross sexist banter (made me feel like I was selling my soul to the devil).

It took years before I hit on the only tactic that seemed to work, at least a reasonable percentage of the time: make them see me as their mum.

It was not easy. I've never wanted to be one of those women who complains about being pretty and blonde and how it makes their life sooooo haaaaaard, but it is not easy to put yourself in the mum zone when you look like I do, even if the only thing you ever wear is boxy coveralls. Plus, the line between 'mum zone' and 'wife zone' is distressingly thin, as I found out when I went a bit too hard in the 'mum who bakes for you' direction.

It was also not fun. Turns out being a mum involves a lot of work. I had to listen to a lot of men tell me about very trivial problems, and give very sensible, very obvious advice. Then there was my long lecture series about Cleaning Up Around

Here, which didn't achieve much other than changing the conversation from 'I'd do her' to 'what a nagging bitch'.

But at least it meant that they stopped seeing me as a sex object and started seeing me as a person (at least seventy per cent of the time, anyway). When other men came into the garage and made gross comments about me, they got 'How dare you talk like that about Our Mandie!' rather than 'I know, right?'

It might not have been progress. Jac had been very clear that it was not progress. But it made things survivable, so now whenever I was in a situation where I felt uncomfortable, out of place or threatened, my instinct was to go Full Mum.

My First Night Party victim was my limo neighbour Cece, who'd stumbled into the mansion looking like she'd seen a ghost, turned around to run, and seen yet more ghosts. The leg-jiggling in the limo had clearly only been the start of it. She hadn't stopped shaking the whole time we were here, and now she seemed to be trying to disappear into the corner of one of the couches.

'Hey you,' I said, sitting down on the other end of the couch. 'How's things? You looked all lonely over here.'

The look she gave me was somewhere between 'please don't talk to me' and 'please don't leave me'. 'I'm okay,' she managed, her knuckles white around her champagne flute. 'I'm just . . . this is so weird.'

'So weird,' I said, putting on my best comforting voice. 'It's such a surreal situation, you know?'

As I was wondering if I should try and extricate the champagne flute from her hand before she crushed it and blood got everywhere, one of the crew appeared. 'Amanda, I want you to say that again, but sit closer,' she said. 'We can't get you both in frame.'

'Sorry,' I said, moving so I was sitting right next to Cece. 'I'm just so used to social distancing. It's instinct now.'

'Yes! Great! Say that!' the AD said. 'That'll make a great grab for the ads. Rolling. In three—'

'Wait!' Cece exclaimed. 'I don't know what to say. What were we talking about?'

'I've got it,' I said, reaching out and patting her hand gently, one of my favourite Mum Manoeuvres™. 'Just follow my lead, okay?'

She nodded, looking like she wanted to throw up.

I felt like I was on much steadier ground after I mothered Cece through a little conversation about social distancing, so when they summoned all fifteen of us over to a different collection of couches and sat me beside Dylan, I was able to be all, 'Oh, I was just talking to people' when she asked me where I disappeared to.

. . . rather than telling her the truth: that I was having an attack of 'Why would he like me when he could have her?'. Dylan might already know plenty about my regular crises of self-confidence, but some things were too embarrassingly teenager-y to say out loud, even to your new best friend. *You were* intimidated *by me?* she'd say, raising a perfect eyebrow. *Oh, babe, you're deeper in the quicksand than I thought.*

'How dare you wear my colour?' Lily snapped at another woman, who'd had the audacity to also wear a yellow dress. 'Yellow is mine. Don't ever do it again.'

Dylan rolled her eyes. 'Lily, stop being ridiculous. You can't claim a colour.'

'Please address me by my full name. Lily Fireball.'

'I am not fucking calling you Lily Fireball. What kind of influencer bullshit is that?'

Dylan had probably never been intimidated by another person in her life.

I wondered if that was a skill that could be taught. If Dylan could write me some kind of instruction manual. *How to Stand Tall, Stand Your Ground, and Stand Up For Yourself (For Dummies).*

'– cheer,' the director was saying. 'We need to keep the energy high.'

'Wait, what?' I whispered to Dylan. 'I zoned out. What are we cheering about?'

'Hello, Juliets!'

'That,' Dylan whispered back, as Tom Zelig walked in and everyone went absolutely nuts.

I'm not going to lie: I also went absolutely nuts, even though it was about two seconds after everyone else. You don't watch as much *Marry Me, Juliet* as I have and *not* have a special little place in your heart for Z.

Dylan laughed beside me. 'You're adorable,' she said in my ear.

'Welcome to *Marry Me, Juliet*,' Z said. 'I'm your host Tom Zelig, and it's my absolute honour to be here right now with all of you on your journey to find true love.'

I think that's what he said, anyway. I was a bit busy rolling the word *adorable* around in my mind.

'Obviously, we're all living in tough times right now,' Z said. 'The pandemic has changed everything, and it's made it a lot harder to look for love. But we hope that here, on *Marry Me, Juliet*, we can help two people find their forever love story, one that will bring hope to the nation at a time when we need hope more than anything.'

Oh, thank you! I'd said once to Jac, when she gave me a vase she'd blown herself in her glassblowing class. *This is so nice. You're adorable.*

Don't call me adorable, she said. *Adorable is a word for puppies and small children. I'm a grown woman.*

I spent the rest of the night apologising, the vase forgotten on our coffee table.

'So, here he is!' Z announced. 'Olympic gold medallist in sailing, founder and spokesperson for Ties Out For The Boys day, your Romeo, Dylan Jayasinghe Mellor!'

There was more cheering and applauding as Romeo-Dylan walked in. I applauded too, but even though he was definitely still extremely hot, my heart wasn't all the way in it.

Adorable.

What was it that Dylan had said to Murray in the limo? *Don't call us girls – we're grown women.*

Would you call a grown woman *adorable*?

'Hi everyone,' Romeo-Dylan said.

'Dylan, you've got to call them Juliets,' the director said. 'Let's go again.'

'Hi, Juliets,' he said obediently. 'It's so lovely to meet you all.'

Yet more applause, yet more cheering. Romeo-Dylan smiled sheepishly and ran his hand through his hair.

I glanced sideways at Dylan. *You're adorable.*

What did that *mean*?

'Welcome, Dylan!' Z said to Romeo-Dylan. 'What does it feel like to be the Romeo?'

'It's absolutely surreal,' he replied. 'I feel incredibly blessed and privileged to be here with all these wonderful women who've given up their time just for a chance at love.'

Dylan glanced back at me, smiling.

And I immediately felt like a massive idiot. Obviously, by 'you're adorable' she just meant 'you're adorable' not 'I secretly think you are extremely childish'. When had she ever given me any evidence that she was trying to neg me?

I forced my attention back to Romeo-Dylan. He really was so handsome.

'Tell us why you decided to come on this journey,' Z was saying. 'What are you looking for?'

'Isn't everyone looking for the same thing?' Romeo-Dylan said. 'Love?'

I imagined being on the press tour with him after the show. *I'm so glad I met Mandie,* he'd say, *she's adorable,* and I'd look up at him and say, *You're pretty adorable yourself,* and he'd flash those white teeth and smile and say, *I adore you,* and I'd say, *I adore you too,* and Jac would be watching despite herself and she'd be grinding her teeth so hard that she'd have to get a new mouthguard because there would be *nothing she could do about it.*

'What do you like, though?' Lily said. 'Blondes? Brunettes? Redheads? Fireballs?'

'I think what Lily Fireball is very subtly trying to ask,' Z said, 'is: what's your type, Dylan? What do you look for in a potential Juliet?'

'Physically, I wouldn't say I have a type,' Romeo-Dylan replied.

Jac would watch every single TV appearance and listen to every single radio spot. She wouldn't be able to help herself. I'd be happy, and she'd be miserable, and—

'But I like strong women. Tough women. Women who like a challenge and who don't back down.'

. . . well, shit.

Seriously. He might as well have taken a can of spray paint and graffitied ANYONE BUT AMANDA across the front of the Villa.

'God, she's quick,' Dylan muttered beside me.

It took me a second to realise that she was talking about Lily Fireball, who was towing Romeo-Dylan away by the hand. 'Yeah,' I agreed half-heartedly.

'How long do you think I should give them before I interrupt?'

I blinked. 'You're going to interrupt?'

'Of course I am!' she said. 'You think I'm going to sit back and let her monopolise tall, dark and handsome over there? Not a chance.'

I forced myself to smile, even though 'Why would he like me when he could have her?' had started churning around in my stomach again.

This was ridiculous. Was I really going to do this? Was I actually going to be that person I always laughed at when I watched the show, who was all like, 'OMG! I have such deep feelings!' on the very first night?

I might be a bit of a head-in-the-clouds romantic sometimes, but even I didn't think it was possible to fall in love that fast.

And I hadn't! Of course not. But Romeo-Dylan seemed so *nice*, and he had kind eyes, and . . . God, there was something very compelling about the thought that I could rub him in Jac's face.

'I'm going to do it,' Dylan said, grinning. 'It's been, what, three minutes? Plenty of time.'

'Good luck,' I managed.

'Thanks, babe,' she said, patting me on the hand in a pitch-perfect rendition of my Mum Manoeuvre before disappearing in a trail of sea-witch sequins.

I headed to the bar. Suddenly I very, very badly needed a drink.

Thank goodness for Cece, honestly. She was obviously having a terrible time, but going Full Mum was familiar ground for me, and trying to make her feel more comfortable was making me feel a whole lot more comfortable.

We got drinks at the bar and then I towed Cece out towards the pool, glimmering bright turquoise against the dark of the night sky. It took some effort – she really was struggling, poor thing – but I small-talked at her for long enough that she finally managed to get some words in of her own. 'I, um, probably wouldn't be here if it wasn't for the pandemic,' she said. 'I lost my job, and . . .'

'Oh, that's so tough,' I said. 'I lost hours, but not my whole job. That must be brutal.'

'Like you wouldn't believe,' she replied. 'I haven't been this stressed about money since I was eighteen.'

'I'm so sorry.'

'I'm still here for the right reasons, though,' she said hurriedly. 'Not just money. I promise.'

'I wouldn't think otherwise,' I said reassuringly. 'You can be here for the right reasons and also appreciate that there's some money that goes along with it.'

The relief in Cece's eyes was palpable. 'So, um, why did you decide to come on the show?'

'It was a bit of an impulse decision,' I replied. 'I've loved the show for a long time. I've watched every season. But this is the first time in quite a few years I've been single. I went through a break-up a few months ago.'

In the early days, right after the break-up, I'd started crying whenever I had to tell someone Jac and I had split.

Not this time, though. I got through that sentence as smoothly as if I'd been telling Cece about the weather.

Maybe it was the champagne, but I decided to splash out and award myself another item on my positive features list. *8) I'm getting better at keeping it together.*

'Ouch,' Cece said, wrinkling her nose. 'I've been there. I'm sorry.'

'It's all right,' I said, patting her arm. 'That's in the past.'

'So is it—' She paused. 'Are you here for . . . revenge? On your ex?'

Over her shoulder, I caught sight of Dylan: both of them. Dylan had clearly been successful in ousting Lily Fireball, because she was sitting next to Romeo-Dylan, sea-witch dress glittering against the white of the couch cushions. He was laughing at something she said, head thrown back, and she was smiling too – one of those smiles that went all the way to her eyes – hand resting gently on his knee.

They looked like a stock photo. *Beautiful happy couple*, it would say. It would be an expensive stock photo too, because they both looked *so* beautiful, *so* happy, *so* perfect together.

'I meant it as revenge at the time,' I said faintly, 'but corny as it is, I really am here for love.'

They were going to be dynamite on the press tour. Everyone was going to go *wild* for Double Dylan.

Cece wasn't saying anything. The silence was stretching out, longer and longer.

'I know the chances of winning aren't very high,' I said, forcing my attention back to her, 'and even then a lot of Romeos don't stay with their Juliet, but . . . what if it was me, you know? Why not me?'

I was lucky that Cece a) was so nervous that she was having problems thinking, and b) didn't know me that well. 'Exactly,' she said, instead of *well, there's the fact that you're none of the things that the Romeo is looking for, and also the fact that you're such a vanilla ice cream person Jac would rather be with no one than be with you, so the chances of you beating fourteen other women isn't high – I mean,*

*could you really see a world where someone picks you instead
of her?*

Cece's eyes were beginning to look desperate again, so
I pushed the thought away. I *wasn't* going to fall apart. I *was*
going to keep it together. 'Plus, even if you don't win, there's
always *Juliet on the Beach*,' I said, pulling Full Mum around
me like a suit of armour. 'There's a few contestants from
past seasons I wouldn't mind seeing there, if you know what
I mean.'

It wasn't a lie. There were definitely several whose
Instagrams I followed closely, men and women.

Maybe that would be a better environment for me,
actually. *Juliet on the Beach* featured contestants from
previous seasons who'd been dumped by their Romeo or
Juliet, so everyone there would know the sting of rejection.
The playing field might be a bit more even.

'I wonder if they'll even do *Juliet on the Beach* this year,'
Dylan said, appearing next to me as if by magic. 'How do you
create a virus bubble on a beach?'

. . . except if Dylan was also on *Juliet on the Beach*, the
playing field would be just as uneven as it was here. Who'd
look my way if they could look hers?

'There's still time, isn't there?' I said, because Cece clearly
wasn't going to be the one to carry the conversation, and
I wasn't going to do this, I wasn't going to be this person. I
had enough bad features without adding 'jealous monster' to
the list. 'They've still got to film a season of *Wherefore Art
Thou Romeo?* after us, so maybe by the time they're ready to
do *Juliet on the Beach*, all of this will be over.'

'I really, sincerely doubt it,' Dylan said. 'I'm a nurse. I've seen how this bastard of a virus operates. We'll be living with it for a while.'

'You're a nurse?' Cece said.

I was strangely proud of her for managing to contribute to the conversation. I had to resist offering my congratulations.

'I am,' Dylan replied. 'For seven years now.'

'I – should I be thanking you for your service?' Cece said. 'I don't quite know what to say.'

Dylan snorted. 'You can thank me by not making me think about it,' she said. 'I am fully committed to living in fantasyland in here, thank you very much.'

Back past her shoulder, I caught sight of Romeo-Dylan again. He was chatting to the Mandie Clone now, listening just as attentively to her as he had been to Dylan.

'Speaking of fantasyland,' Dylan said, waggling her perfect eyebrows, 'can we talk about the Romeo? Because that man is fine.'

Now there was something I could wholeheartedly agree with. 'Oh my God, so fine,' I said.

'Really fine,' Cece agreed.

'I was just with him,' Dylan said. 'He's a nice guy. Really down to earth. Easy to talk to. I liked him.'

'I liked him too, when I met him on the driveway,' I said. 'He has really kind eyes.'

Dylan gave me an inquisitive look. 'That's a thing for you, isn't it?' she said, poking me gently in the shoulder with her index finger. Her nail polish was sparkly green too. 'Kind eyes.'

'You can tell a lot about a person by their eyes,' I answered.

It was true. When you worked around as many men as I did, you learned to gauge pretty quickly how they were thinking about you by the way they were looking at you.

Dylan grinned. 'What about my eyes?' she said. 'What do they tell you?'

'Hmmm,' I said. 'Come closer. I can't quite see. You're too tall.'

She bent down, still grinning.

The world went away.

Her face was close to mine. I could feel her breath on my skin. Maybe I was living in fantasyland too, because I was nose to nose with a sea witch, and I was going to live to tell the tale.

Probably, anyway. It was a big call to think that I would survive this.

'Your eyes tell me that you're strong,' I said, somehow. *8)* must be true. I really must be getting better at keeping it together. 'You're no nonsense. You're firm.'

'I think the word you're looking for is "ball-buster",' she said.

'Be quiet,' I said, because I could feel her words against my lips, and I was genuinely worried I might die if she said anything else. 'I haven't finished.'

She grinned even wider. It was incredible. I wanted to trace the curve of her eyebrows gently with the very tip of a finger, featherlight, like a butterfly.

'But you're also gentle,' I said. 'Tender. Protective, when you care about someone, but—'

'How dare you!?'

It was like someone had thrown a bucket of cold water over my head. I sprang away from Dylan, and only just managed not to fall over.

'How dare you?' Lily Fireball exclaimed again, sweeping towards us with a gaggle of cameramen.

She poked Dylan hard in the shoulder. 'That was my time with the Romeo!' she yelled. 'How dare you interrupt?'

Dylan didn't move. 'We all want time with him. That's what we're all here for. You don't get to keep him all for yourself, Lily.'

'It's Lily *Fireball*!'

It was like dominoes. Lily pushed Dylan, and Dylan stumbled backwards, but I was close behind her, and I was already unsteady, so I fell back too, into Cece, and then – splash!

'Oh my God, Cece!' I exclaimed as she surfaced, spluttering, in the pool. 'Are you all right? I'm so sorry.'

'I'm – I'm okay,' she said. 'It's okay. It's all okay.'

I offered her my hand and helped her clamber out of the pool. 'I'm so sorry,' I said again. 'Your beautiful dress – your hair—'

'It wasn't your fault, Mandie,' Dylan said, folding her arms and glaring at Lily.

'That's right,' Lily said back sweetly. 'It's *your* fault.'

'Excuse me?'

'You stole the Romeo from me,' Lily said. 'If you hadn't, then what's-her-face wouldn't have ended up in the pool.'

'Cece,' I said. 'Her name is Cece.'

'Honey, do I look like I care?'

'Mandie, you take Cece to get dried off,' Dylan said, her death stare unwavering from Lily. 'I'll deal with this.'

'Oh, will you now?' Lily said, raising an eyebrow.

Cece shivered, and I put my arm around her. 'Come on, let's get you into some new clothes,' I said, in my mumsiest voice, wondering all the while how Lily could survive going toe to toe with an angry sea witch.

Cece was whisked away by Murray before we could get more than two steps inside the Juliet Villa. 'Shit, fuck, shit,' he muttered to himself. 'Suzette? I need you to monitor the fight between Dylan G and Lily.'

'They're your girls, Murray,' one of the other producers said.

'I'm well aware of that, but I'm not a fucking octopus,' he said. 'Just do it, okay? I've got to deal with this.'

Cece looked like she was being hauled to the principal's office, but before I could open my mouth to say 'Do you want me to come with you?' Murray was herding her away. 'Wardrobe!' he said into his headset. 'Get me some new outfits for Cece, stat. Maximum bedraggled.'

That left me standing there, in the middle of the living room, alone for the first time in what seemed like forever.

. . . unless you counted the two weeks I'd just spent in isolation, I guess. But I'd spent most of that time chatting with Dylan, so it probably didn't *really* count.

Dylan.

What the hell had just happened?

'Amanda?'

I turned, startled. 'Oh! Hello!'

'What are you doing in here by yourself?' Romeo-Dylan asked.

'I could ask you the same question,' I replied. 'How have you escaped the clutches of everyone stealing you for a second?'

'Even Romeos occasionally need to take a minute,' he said. 'I haven't been so worried I was going to piss my pants since I was three years old.'

I laughed. 'Wow. Charming.'

'Sorry,' he said. 'I probably shouldn't say shit like that to you. I'm supposed to make you like me.'

'Dylan!' someone said from behind me. 'Swearing!'

He threw his head back. 'Shiiiiiiiiiiiiiiit. Sorry.'

'I promise you, I can handle it,' I said, patting him gently on the arm.

'Network can't,' the crew person behind me said. 'Go again.'

'What did I say?' Romeo-Dylan asked me.

'Um . . . you said you shouldn't talk about pissing your pants in front of me, because you were supposed to make me like you.'

'Ah. Yes. I was being charming.'

I laughed again.

'Ready?' he asked.

I nodded.

'Sorry,' he said. 'I shouldn't say stuff like that in front of you. I'm trying to make you like me.'

'Well, you're doing a great job,' I said, patting him on the arm again. 'I like you fine.'

'You like me fine? Wow. That's some high praise right there. I might never recover.'

'Hey,' I said. 'It's a start.'

'It is, isn't it?'

He looked outside, where there was still a gaggle of people standing around the pool. 'Since everyone else seems to be otherwise occupied, can I turn the tables and steal *you* for a second?'

'Are you sure?' I said. 'There's big drama going on outside. You don't want to go sort that out?'

'Hmmm, let me think,' Romeo-Dylan said. 'I could go outside and wade into what sounds like a screaming match and probably make it worse, or—' he gestured to the couch, 'I could sit here on this couch and talk to a pretty girl. What a tough decision.'

'Really?'

'Really,' he said. 'Sit down, Amanda. I want to hear more about this mechanic thing. What made you want to go into that field?'

By the time the Necklace Ceremony rolled around, I was sure of three things:

1) Romeo-Dylan was a very nice man and I liked him a lot.
2) I had a good shot at getting a necklace.
3) Being Cece's show mum was going to be a full-time job.

The poor woman was shaking in her boots – well, heels – beside me. When she'd re-emerged (dry) into the cocktail party, she'd tried to confront Lily about pushing her into the pool. I'd tried to have her back, but she'd looked like a house-cat trying to confront a lion. Then, to add insult to injury, Z had come in and announced that the First Night Party was over. Poor Cece hadn't had a chance to say a single word to Romeo-Dylan.

I felt a bit bad about that, to be honest. If Romeo-Dylan had gone to sort out the Lily/Dylan screaming match instead of talking to me, surely he'd have managed a moment with the innocent victim of their feud.

I glanced at Dylan, standing a few people away from me, between a tall Persian woman in red and the Mandie Clone. She'd apologised profusely to Cece, but I knew she still felt awful. 'If she gets eliminated because of this, I'm going to pitch a fit,' she'd growled to me as they herded us into the ceremony room.

'If she does get eliminated, it won't be your fault,' I'd whispered back.

She'd arched one of her knife-edge eyebrows at me, and my breath had caught in my throat.

'But she won't,' I said, summoning Full Mum. 'He's a nice guy, right? Cece'll get a pity necklace, if nothing else.'

Dylan had looked off into the distance. 'I hope so,' she'd murmured.

I'd wanted to pat her arm, but I was too scared to touch her, because there was a fourth thing I was much too far on the way to becoming sure of.

'Good evening, Juliets,' Z announced. 'Welcome to your first Necklace Ceremony.'

I forced myself to look away from Dylan and back to the front of the room. *Focus, Mandie,* I ordered myself. *Get your head in the game.*

'This is an important part of the *Marry Me, Juliet* process,' Z said. 'If our Romeo feels like you have a connection and he could see a future with you, he'll give you one of these broken heart necklaces, in recognition of the fact that your heart might be the other half of his. If he doesn't, you'll leave the Villa tonight.'

Romeo-Dylan walked into the room. Next to me, Cece let out a long, shaky breath.

'Hi, everyone,' he said.

'You've got to call them Juliets,' the director said, a note of exasperation in his voice. 'Go again.'

'Hi Juliets.'

We'd had to stop at three different points in our conversation because Romeo-Dylan had accidentally tripped over another of the many things you weren't supposed to say. 'Shit, sorry,' he'd said every time, and then had to apologise again for swearing. I was proud of him for managing not to do it this time.

I tried to focus on that feeling. Nice man. Handsome man. Man who I liked a lot.

Don't think about her eyes.

'I just wanted to tell you what an honour it was to meet you all,' Romeo-Dylan said. 'It's really hard for me to believe that so many beautiful women came out here just to meet me, when the world is in this state. So thank you. So much. From the bottom of my heart.'

Definitely don't think about her eyebrows.

'Unfortunately, there are fifteen of you,' Z said. 'Dylan only has twelve necklaces to give out, which means, I'm sorry, but three of you are going to have to leave the Juliet Villa tonight.'

Cece let out another shaking breath. 'Good luck,' I whispered to her.

'You too,' she replied. We'd all had make-up touch-ups before the Necklace Ceremony, but even so, I could tell that her lips were white.

She really was shaking quite badly. Was she going to faint? We were standing on bleachers like we were in a choir, and we were both on the top row. If she went down, would I be able to catch her before she hit the ground?

'Amanda.'

It took me a second to realise what was happening.

Then, just for a moment, my mind went blank, and I was absolutely, perfectly, radiantly happy.

'You rely too much on validation from other people,' Jac had told me once. 'You need to take pride in things for your own sake.'

She probably wasn't wrong. But as I walked up to get my necklace from Romeo-Dylan, it felt like walking out of the shade into the sun.

Not just any necklace, either. The *first* necklace, the one that meant you'd made the best impression.

'Thank you so much,' I said, beaming up at him. 'I can't believe this.'

'It's my pleasure,' Romeo-Dylan replied, smiling back, a smile that went all the way to his kind eyes. 'Amanda, I want to know if your heart is the other half of mine. Will you take this necklace and commit to finding out with me?'

'I will,' I said, and meant it. 'Of course.'

He was perfect, this lovely man. He was everything I could have hoped for. He was exactly what I needed – and God, watching him give me this necklace was going to make Jac *green*.

I held my hair out of the way so he could put the necklace around my neck. His fingers were warm against my skin as he tried to fasten the catch. 'This will take forever if I'm this bad at putting these on,' he said. 'Sorry, Amanda.'

'You're fine,' I said. 'Take your time.'

Ultimately, someone from wardrobe had to fix the clasp for me, but I didn't care. I floated back up to my spot next to Cece. 'Congratulations,' she whispered.

'Thanks,' I replied, only half-listening.

This might work. This might actually work. Romeo-Dylan was lovely and sweet and handsome, and he had those kind eyes, and he would never say shit like *you rely too much on validation from other people* to me, and Jac would hate it *so much* if we ended up together, and—

'Dylan,' he said.

And *shit*.

Romeo-Dylan had kind eyes. But they weren't the eyes that had made the whole world go away.

'The other Dylan, I mean,' Romeo-Dylan said. 'Dylan G. I'm not quite vain enough to try and declare my love to myself.'

There was a titter of laughter as Dylan swept towards him in her trail of green sequins, but I didn't join in.

I'd had a lovely time talking with Romeo-Dylan on the couch. Truth be told, we might actually be able to make it work, if it weren't for the fourth thing that the First Night Party had made me sure of.

I'd looked into her eyes, and everything had changed.

She was my friend. We were dating the same man. She was straight; or at least, she'd given me no indication otherwise.

But I'd looked into her eyes, and it had been tectonic.

'Dylan,' Romeo-Dylan said, 'I want to know if your heart is the other half of mine. Will you take this necklace and commit to finding out with me?'

'Of course,' she said to him, and it hurt like hell.

There was only one thing I could do: ignore it.

I focused intently on Romeo-Dylan handing out necklaces to other women. I studied every line of his handsome face. I poured my attention into Cece, standing beside me, her shaking becoming increasingly violent as more names were called and none of them were hers.

I might as well have tried to ignore an earthquake.

Even when I wasn't looking at Dylan, I could feel her, feel the energy of her presence, radiating out from her like sunshine.

No. Not like sunshine. That was too gentle. It was like lightning, crackling around her, and – God, I had to get it together. I absolutely could not be feeling like this.

It's been a long, stressful night, and you've drunk a lot of champagne and eaten, like, one mini-quiche, I told myself. *You just need to go to bed and sleep it off.*

Hopefully that would be sooner rather than later. Romeo-Dylan was down to his last necklace.

'I thought long and hard about who to give this last necklace to,' he said. 'I told you at the beginning of tonight that I like strong women. Ballsy women. Women who aren't afraid to go for what they want.'

Cece. I was only going to think about Cece. I wrapped my fingers around hers and held on tight, because if I was busy worrying about Cece, then surely I wouldn't have room in my brain to think about how Romeo-Dylan was straight-up describing my Dylan, and how perfect they were going to be together.

'Sometimes, though,' Romeo-Dylan said, 'it's possible to take things too far.'

They'd have such beautiful children.

'I like a woman who stands up for herself. Someone who stands up for what she believes in. Someone with a strong sense of justice. Someone who fights for what she wants.'

Maybe I'd be godmother to one of them. I'd stand beside the Dylans in some church somewhere and promise to guard their baby with my life, and Dylan would stand beside Romeo-Dylan and smile at me and say, 'Thanks, babe,' and I'd just smile back and say, 'Any time,' even though all I wanted to do was run my finger over those smile lines at the corners of her eyes.

'And I believe in second chances,' Romeo-Dylan finished. 'Which is why I'd like to give this last necklace to . . . Lily Fireball.'

Dylan caught my eye and made a face as Lily flounced up to claim her necklace. *Kill me now,* she mouthed.

I could only manage the weakest of weak smiles back.

But still, I managed it. I was hanging on by my finger-nails, but I was keeping it together.

And I was going to keep keeping it together. I was going to get this – whatever *this* was – under control.

It was only feeling out of control because of this whole bananas intense situation, anyway. And because of Jac! Couldn't forget Jac! Of course I'd glomp onto the first pretty person who was nice to me! It was late and I was tipsy and confused and all of this was going to be better after I had some sleep. Definitely.

'Samantha, Rani, Cecilia, I'm so sorry,' Z said, 'but this is the end of your journey.'

Cece was shaking so badly I was worried she was going to fall. 'I'm so sorry,' I said, hugging her tight. 'I'll miss you, Cece, really.'

It was the truth. I was going to have to find a new project to work on to distract myself.

'Ordinarily, this is where you'd leave the Juliet Villa,' Z was saying, 'but as we all know, this isn't an ordinary year, and this isn't an ordinary season of *Marry Me, Juliet.*'

Cece's shaking was getting worse. Her eyes were so wide I could see the whites all the way around, and her breath was coming in huge, heaving gasps.

'We've been informed that, as we filmed tonight's First Night Party, Stage Four restrictions were implemented by the government in order to control the spread of the pandemic,' Z said. 'Those restrictions mean that wherever you spent the night last night is where you need to stay for the next six weeks.'

Cece was literally swaying on her feet. Shit, was she going to faint?

I wrapped my arm tight around her waist. 'You're okay,' I whispered to her. 'You're okay, Cece. I've got you.'

'What does that mean?' one of the other eliminated women was saying. 'Are we back on the show?'

'No,' Z replied. 'You'll be staying in another house on the property. You won't have any contact with our Romeo, but as more Juliets get eliminated, they'll relocate to that house with you for the duration of filming.'

'Will we be paid?' Cece choked out.

'I'm not sure now is the most appropriate—'

'Answer me!' she shrieked. 'If you don't know – Murray? What's the deal? Are we getting paid? Because I've got rent, and if I'm here and I'm locked down and I'm not getting paid, then I can't afford it. What if my flatmates lose their jobs too? I need to look for work! Are we getting paid? Tell me! Are we getting paid?'

'I think she's having a panic attack,' I said, as Cece's knees gave out and she collapsed against me.

She was taller than me, and I sagged under her body weight. 'A little help, please!' I called.

Jodi McAlister

'I'm a nurse. Get out of the way,' Dylan said, shoving past the women between us. 'We need to give her space. Cece? Cece? Can you hear me?'

'Nnnnnghghnnngh,' Cece moaned.

'We need to get her on her back,' Dylan said.

'I've got it,' Romeo-Dylan said, appearing next to me. 'Let me give you a hand there, Amanda.'

He put one arm behind Cece's knees and then wedged the other between her body and mine so he could support her shoulders, accidentally brushing my breasts. 'Sorry, Amanda,' he said, hefting Cece effortlessly into his arms. 'Didn't mean to grope you there.'

'It's all—' I started, but he was already moving away from me, Dylan in his wake.

Romeo-Dylan laid Cece down on the floor. She moaned again. 'Hey, hey there – what's her name?'

'Cecilia,' Dylan said.

'Cecilia, I've got you, okay? You're all right. I've got you.'

Dylan was checking her pulse. 'Her heart's racing,' she said. 'It might not be a panic attack. It might be hypoglycaemia.'

'Low blood sugar?' Romeo-Dylan said. 'Murray? Suzette? Someone? Can we get her some apple juice or something?'

'We need to get her down to the other house,' Murray said.

'Like hell you do,' Dylan said. 'I'm a medical professional, and—'

'So is Georgie,' Murray said, as a young man with flaming red hair pushed past the crowd to kneel beside Cece. 'This isn't your job here, Dylan.'

74

'It's always my job,' she protested.

Cece moaned incoherently again. 'We need to get her somewhere quieter,' Georgie the medic said.

Romeo-Dylan folded his arms around Cece and picked her up again, like a princess. 'Lead the way,' he said to Murray.

'I'm coming with you,' Dylan said.

'No, you're not,' Murray said firmly. 'Georgie's got this. This way.'

And just like that, they were gone, cameramen scrambling after them as they swept out of the room.

Dylan raised both her hands to her head as she looked after them, fingers clutching at her hair. 'Fuck,' she said. '*Fuck.*'

'Hey,' I said, putting my hand on her shoulder. 'You did good, Dylan. You looked after her. She'll be all right.'

She turned around and looked at me, wild-eyed. 'What the fuck am I doing here, Mandie?' she said, a desperate note in her voice. 'What the fuck have I signed up for?'

5

I wanted nothing more than to take Dylan aside, sit her down and rub her back like she'd done for me at the auditions, but there was no time. 'Okay, that's a wrap up here!' someone called. 'Girls! Hand your necklaces back to the PA!'

'We don't get to keep them?' one of the other women asked.

'You think they have that kind of budget?' Lily said. 'Cute.'

'Don't patronise me!'

'Don't say stupid shit and I won't have to.'

'Girls!' producer Carrie snapped. 'Necklaces! To the PA! Now!'

Don't call us girls, Dylan didn't say.

Lily, shut up, she didn't say either.

Instead, she just stood there, clutching at her elbows, nostrils flared, breathing shallow, looking like she'd seen a ghost.

76

I reached out and unfastened my necklace. 'Hey,' I said quietly, touching her arm. 'Dylan. Your necklace.'

'Oh. Um.'

She fumbled with the clasp, but she couldn't get it undone. 'Here,' I said. 'Let me.'

Her skin was warm under my fingers, and I could feel her shaking. I had the strongest urge to press my lips to the curve where her neck met her shoulder. *Hey*, I'd whisper in her ear. *It's all right. You're all right.*

WHAT THE FUCK ARE YOU DOING MANDIE GET YOURSELF UNDER CONTROL.

I took her necklace off and handed both of them to the PA. 'Here's mine and Dylan's,' I said.

'Already so possessive?'

I blinked. 'What?'

'Mine *and* Dylan's,' Lily said, in a high-pitched, sickly sweet voice. 'Getting the first necklace doesn't mean shit, sweetheart.'

'Oh,' I said, realisation dawning. 'Not that Dylan. I meant—'

'Shut up, Lily,' Dylan said hoarsely.

One corner of Lily's mouth curved upwards in a smirk. 'Getting the second necklace doesn't mean shit either.'

'Getting the last necklace does,' I blurted out.

Lily's eyes turned on me, and I instantly regretted my words. There was something incredibly terrifying about the smile that spread over her face.

But, 'You're lucky the cameras didn't catch you saying that,' was all she said.

77

'Can someone please tell us what the hell is going on?' asked Parisa, the tall Persian woman who'd been standing next to Dylan at the Necklace Ceremony. 'Stage Four restrictions? What does that mean?'

There was a murmur that rose to a roar as everyone started asking questions, before producer Suzette stuck her fingers in her mouth and whistled. 'Girls! Listen up!'

I glanced at Dylan. *We're adult women,* she didn't say. Her jaw was clenched.

'I know you've got a lot of questions about the Stage Four restrictions and what they mean,' Suzette said. 'We're going to do a proper briefing for you tomorrow or the next day, but for now all you need to know is that it's not going to change life in the Villa that much for you. All it means is that once you're eliminated, you can't leave the set.'

'What does *that* mean, though?' asked a Japanese woman I was fairly sure was named Kumiko.

'We're going to repurpose the Romeo Residence as a space for the eliminated Juliets,' Suzette said.

'Wait, what?' another woman asked. 'The Romeo is going to stay with the eliminated girls?'

'No, of course not!' Suzette said, a note of exasperation in her voice. 'We'll put him somewhere else. Look, we're still figuring out the details, but you don't need to worry about any of this. Things will proceed as normal in the Villa. The only difference is that when you get eliminated, instead of going straight home, you'll go to the Convent until the end of the filming period.'

'The Convent?' Lily said. 'You're calling the house for rejected women the Convent?'

'Blame Murray,' Suzette said shortly.

Lily started laughing. Like, she started *laughing*. Tears beaded at the corners of her eyes, leaving black smudges of mascara as they fell. She clutched at the wall with one hand, holding her side with the other like she had a stitch.

Everyone was looking at her strangely, but she either didn't notice or didn't care. 'Tell him it's perfect,' she gasped out. 'Tell him he's a genius.'

Well, nearly everyone was looking at her strangely. Beside me, Dylan still had her arms wrapped around herself, fingers digging into her elbows so tight her knuckles were pale. She was staring at the floor.

'For now, just get to bed,' Suzette said. 'You've got a big day tomor— well, today, actually. Get some sleep while you can.'

'All right, room assignments!' Carrie said, reading off a clipboard. 'Bedroom 1: Kanda, Heather, Belinda, Kumiko, Parisa and Jess D! Bedroom 2: Marija, Amanda, Naya, Jess K, Dylan G and Lily Fireball! Any problems with that?'

I looked at Dylan again. Her eyes were still fixed on the floor.

Even now, even like this, so stricken, so upset, she was magnetic.

'Good, because we're not changing it!' Carrie said. 'Bedroom 1 girls, you're with me. Bedroom 2 girls, you're with Suzette. Let's go.'

The layout of the Juliet Villa reminded me of the house in *The Sound of Music*. When we'd first entered the Villa, we'd come down a flight of stairs into the main part of the house, but there were also two staircases leading up from the entryway, one going to the left, one to the right. Carrie led the Bedroom 1 women up the left staircase. Suzette led the rest of us up the right one.

I half-expected Dylan to stay rooted to the ground, frozen in place. She didn't, but she moved slowly, dragging her feet, like she was walking through water.

I didn't dare touch her again, not when I still had the feeling of the nape of her neck on my fingers, but I leaned in close. 'Are you okay?' I asked in an undertone.

'What am I doing here, Mandie?' she said. 'What was I *thinking*?'

'It's all right,' I said. 'You're all right. I promise.'

Her arm shot out and she grabbed my hand, her fingers squeezing mine so tight it was almost painful.

I wanted to pull away. Should have pulled away.

Would have pulled away, if it weren't for the fact that I actually didn't want to, not even a little bit.

I could practically hear Mum's voice in my head. *This is a fantasy, Mandie,* she was saying. *It isn't real.*

But I laced Dylan's fingers through mine and squeezed back. 'You're all right,' I repeated. 'You're here. With me.'

The bedroom Suzette led us to was nowhere near big enough for all the furniture it held. It was crammed full with three sets of bunk beds, so close together that if you were lying in one, you could reach out and touch the bunk next to you. Each bed had an identical dark green bedspread and beige pillow. Our luggage was lined up against the far wall, under the window. None of us had brought much – we were only allowed two bags each, and had been given very strict guidelines about what to pack – but considering the room was already stuffed to the gills, it meant that to move anywhere you had to walk sideways, like a crab.

'Right,' Suzette said. 'Listen up, ladies!'

Dylan hadn't let go of my hand. I could feel a racing heart in our clasped palms, and I genuinely couldn't tell if it was hers or mine.

'I'm not going to keep you long,' Suzette said. 'This isn't boarding school, and I'm not your mum. That said, there are still some ground rules we expect you to follow.'

It was probably my heart that was racing. *What are you doing, Mandie?!* the one sensible part of my brain screamed at me. *Stop! Think!*

But that part of my brain had never been very big. There was a reason that *I am way too impulsive* appeared so high on my Worst Features list.

'One, get enough sleep!' Suzette said. 'Our filming days are long, and our make-up artists are good, but if you wind up with giant dark circles under your eyes from not sleeping, there's only so much they can do.'

The make-up artists were going to hate me. I was exhausted, but there was no way I was getting to sleep anytime soon. Holding Dylan's hand felt like holding onto a jumper cable.

'Two, leave the crew alone!' Suzette went on, ticking them off on her fingers. 'We're working with a skeleton crew this season. A skeleton with half its bones missing, if we're being honest. We're all very busy all of the time and we don't have time to be your friends. Be your own friends.'

I had just enough restraint not to look at Dylan. Any look I gave her right now would probably be a bit too, ahem, *friendly*.

I glanced over at Lily Fireball instead. There might not have been much space in our bedroom, but she'd still somehow managed to carve out a place for herself. She was leaning artistically against the bathroom doorway, the train of her enormous yellow dress looped up over her arm. I might be good with people, but the thought of trying to be friends with her terrified me.

Or it would have terrified me, if I had room for any thoughts in my brain other than *oh my God oh my God oh my God you can't feel like this Mandie oh my God she's holding my hand oh my God oh my God*.

'Three, no wandering the grounds at night,' Suzette said. 'There's a lake on the property, and I don't want to have to fish anyone out of it. Let's hope Cece's dunk in the pool is the only drowning we have this season.'

'Is she all right?' Dylan asked. Her voice was raspy.

'She'll be fine,' Suzette said. 'Four!'

'Not "she'll be fine",' Dylan said. 'I want specific information. Is she all right?'

'The medic's with her.'

'That's not an answer!'

82

Suzette sighed and touched her earpiece. 'Murray, status check on Cece,' she said. 'How's she doing?'

There was a moment of silence, then, 'All right, thanks,' she said.

'Well?' Dylan asked.

'She's fine,' Suzette said. 'The medic checked her out, and there's no harm done. Just low blood sugar and stress. Dylan JM looked after her.'

'The fainter's getting more time with the Romeo than the rest of us put together,' someone muttered under their breath.

'All right?' Suzette asked Dylan. 'Satisfied?'

Dylan nodded. She squeezed my fingers even tighter.

Get it together, Mandie, I ordered myself. *She is your friend. She is holding your hand because she is upset and she needs support. Stop fantasising.*

I couldn't stop myself from squeezing back.

'Finally, four!' Suzette said. 'Don't complain about the bathroom space. I know there's not enough, but there's nothing I can do, so don't come crying to me about it. Any questions?'

'Yes,' one of the other women – Jess K, I thought – said. 'You said the rejects are taking over the Romeo Residence, right? So where does the Romeo sleep? Is he moving into the Villa too?'

'Absolutely not,' Suzette said. 'And even if I did know where we were going to put him, I wouldn't tell you. I know Juliets have snuck into the Romeo Residence for alone time in some previous seasons, but our Romeo this year has been very clear that he doesn't want that to happen. Any other questions?'

'Where do you sleep?'

The question came from Lily. 'Why do you want to know?' Suzette asked, a sensible amount of wariness in her eyes.

'Just curious,' Lily said airily. 'If things are so dire that you had to turf the Romeo out of his Romeo Residence, where the hell are production sleeping?'

'I'll be sleeping down the hall from you,' Suzette said. 'Carrie will be sleeping near the girls in the other bedroom. That's all you need to know.'

The corner of Lily's mouth twitched.

'If that's it, then you can start getting ready for bed,' Suzette said. 'Wake-up time is ten am.'

'Are you serious?' Jess K said. 'That's in, what, like four hours? Look, the sun's coming up.'

'We're on a schedule,' Suzette said.

'You just told us we have to get enough sleep!'

'Then I suggest you get to bed now,' Suzette said. 'This is reality TV, ladies, not a holiday.'

Dylan didn't say a word to me as we all got ready for bed.

To be fair, I didn't say a word to her either. I didn't have a chance to. The bathroom the six of us were sharing was tiny. There was only mirror space for two at a time, and I ended up elbow to elbow with a fellow blonde named Marija as we took our make-up off, while Dylan was . . .

Well, I didn't know what she was doing.

It was probably best I didn't think about what she was doing. The best way to pour cold water on this little crush I'd drunkenly developed was just to starve it of oxygen, right?

That's a mixed metaphor, Jac's voice said in my mind.

Ugh. I shook my head.

Marija caught my eye in the mirror and offered me a brief smile. 'It's a bit like that, isn't it?' she said.

'Yeah,' I agreed. I had no idea what she was talking about.

All I knew was that even though we were no longer holding hands, I could feel Dylan's fingers wrapped around mine.

She was still in her sea witch dress when I emerged from the bathroom, sitting on the edge of the bottom bunk against the furthest wall. She was staring at her hands resting loosely in her lap, her face morose.

Some people suit morose. There's a reason that 'broody' is low-key code for 'mega-hot'.

Dylan wasn't one of those people, though, and seeing her look this way cracked something inside me.

I was suddenly overcome by a rush of guilt. She'd been holding my hand because she was *sad*. What kind of selfish, shallow person was I to get all caught up in my attraction to her when *my friend was sad*?

'Hey,' I said, walking over and sitting down beside her. I didn't take her hand again – I didn't think I could handle it – but I gave her a little nudge with my shoulder. 'What can I do?'

She shook her head. 'Nothing,' she said, her voice still a little hoarse. 'I've just got to . . . sit with it.'

'What?' I asked. 'What are you sitting with?'

'I shouldn't be here,' she said. 'I should be out there. Helping.'

That made me feel even worse. *This* was what she'd been struggling with while I'd been fantasising about tracing my fingers across the curve of her perfect eyebrows?

'You did help tonight,' I said. 'When Cece fainted.'

'No, I didn't,' Dylan said. 'Not really. They wouldn't let me. They just took her away from me, and . . . fuck, Mandie, what have I done?'

'The right thing for you,' I said, digging deep and finding Mummy Mandie, the most supportive, sexless tool in my arsenal. 'We've talked about this. Nursing isn't what you want to do with your life.'

'Fuck what I want!' she said, looking at me, her beautiful eyes wild. 'I'm needed. *They* need me, out there. Stage Four restrictions means that things are really, really bad. I could help – and what, I'm just not going to? Because I don't *want* to?'

'Dylan,' I said. 'You're a strong woman. But you don't have to be strong enough to carry all of that on your own.'

'I did one of those talking head interviews with Murray during the First Night Party,' she said. 'Before Z came in, while you were talking with Cece. He asked me how it felt to be a hero.'

'You are a hero,' I said. 'You've been on the frontlines for weeks.'

'But I'm not there now.'

'You can always go back,' I said. 'If you feel like you need to – like it's something you have to do – you can go back.'

'No, I can't!' she said. 'Because I'm here! And I – we – can't leave!'

She buried her head in her hands, her fingers clutching at her temples. 'This is the worst idea I've ever had, Mandie,' she said, her voice muffled. 'I'm used to being – I *need* to be – in control. When they took Cece away from me, it just drove home that I'm not in control in here. I can't help, even if I want to. I've got no say over anything. Not who I see, what I do, if I stay, if I go, when I talk to Noah—'

Her voice cracked.

'I can go down the hall and get Suzette, if you like,' I offered. 'She's got a phone. I know it won't fix everything, but you could call Noah, see how he's doing.'

'No. It's too early. He'll still be asleep.'

Dylan took a deep breath, and then took her hands away from her face. 'I just need to accept that I've signed my life away.'

'You've signed your six weeks away,' I said. 'Not your life.'

I took a risk and put my hand on her knee. The sequins of her dress were scratchy beneath my palm.

'We've been up all night,' I told her. 'We're tired. We drank a lot of champagne. A lot happened. But I promise it's going to be okay.'

She took another deep breath, closing her eyes for a moment.

'We just need to go to bed,' I said. 'Get some rest. I bet you anything things'll be clearer afterwards.'

She looked sideways at me and smiled. It was a weak smile, one that didn't go all the way to her eyes, but it was still a smile. 'You're a good egg, Mandie,' she said.

'So are you,' I said, giving her a very Mummy Mandie pat on the knee before forcing myself to take my hand away.

'Want to bunk with me?' she asked. 'The top one's free.'

'Sure.'

'Now get up and get out.'

I blinked.

'So I can get out and take my make-up off,' Dylan clarified. 'You couldn't swing a cat in here.'

'Oh.'

Obediently, I stood and edged out of the narrow gap between our bed and the bunks next to us so Dylan could do the same. Naya and Jess K emerged from the bathroom, and Dylan walked in, closing the door behind her.

I took a few of my own deep breaths. My whole body was still vibrating. It was frankly amazing that I hadn't blurted out something like, *Here's something that'll distract you from your guilt! You're so beautiful it hurts to look at you and I want to bury my face in your neck and never come up for air.*

I needed to take my own advice. Sleep. Somehow. Things would be clearer once my brain had a chance to reset.

I climbed up into my bunk and tested it out. The sheets were a little scratchy, but the mattress was firm, and there was a fuzzy blanket the same colour as the bedspread across the foot of the bed. Jac and I used to have exactly the same blanket in magenta, and I'd inherited it in the break-up.

I knew for a fact it cost $23, because I'd bought it. Who knew *Marry Me, Juliet* was so cheap?

'Hey,' Marija said suddenly, 'where'd Lily go?'

We all looked around. Despite the fact that Lily had been wearing the most conspicuous dress in the entire world, she'd somehow managed to vanish into thin air.

6

I knew, coming onto *Marry Me, Juliet*, that there would be a lot of conflict. The word they always used for it on the show was 'drama'. Lily getting into it with Dylan last night, and Cece getting dunked in the pool, was classic drama. Drama wasn't always big – sometimes two people would have a mild disagreement and all the ads would be about how there would be OMG! so! much! drama! – but it always happened. 'I'm just hoping for a nice, chill week with no drama,' some contestant would say at the beginning of nearly every episode, a wish that would never, ever come true.

Let's make a vow, Dylan had texted me during hotel quarantine. *Neither of us are allowed to be the 'I hope there's no drama this week!' person. We're both too smart for that.*

So yes, I'd been expecting conflict. But I hadn't been expecting the drama to begin pretty much the second we woke up, when we weren't even being filmed.

The skeleton-missing-half-its-bones crew meant that there weren't enough hair and make-up people to go around, so we were being sent to them in dribs and drabs to get made up for filming that day. 'Come on, up!' Suzette had said, hammering on our bedroom door at exactly ten that morning and then walking straight in without waiting for an answer. 'Dylan G, Marija, you're in hair and make-up in half an hour. If you want a shower beforehand, you've got to move now.'

Dylan being first on the roster meant I hadn't had a chance to speak to her yet. I didn't know if that was a good thing or a bad thing. On the one hand, I wanted to know if she was feeling any better this morning, if sleeping on it had helped.

On the other, I was very frightened about what would happen if I looked at her in the cold light of day and the earth shifted under my feet again.

While the rest of us waited around, Carrie had given us a simple task: to make our shopping list for the week. 'This has got all the information you need on it,' she said, putting a piece of paper down on the kitchen island. 'Your weekly budget is here –' she tapped a figure, '– and a list of all the items available to you is here.'

'We have to get avocados,' said one of the other blondes (not the Mandie Clone, whose name was Heather, but a tall woman with long straw-blonde hair whose name was either Melinda or Belinda).

'They're pretty expensive,' Kumiko said, flicking through the list. '$2 a pop, wow. We'll blow through our budget in about two days if we do that.'

'We don't need avocados every day,' Jess D said. 'Maybe avo toast brunch could be a once-a-week treat.'

'We'll need good bread for that,' said another woman whose name I couldn't remember – K-something?

'We should always have good bread,' Melinda/Belinda said. 'Do you know how much sugar is in most bread?'

'What are our bread options, though?' Naya asked, leaning over Kumiko's shoulder to see the list. 'That's a staple. We'll need a lot of that.'

'Not if you're doing keto!' Jess K said. Several people groaned.

Lily snatched the list out of Kumiko's hands. 'Here's what we need to do,' she said. 'Look for what we can buy in bulk, and go from there.'

'I can't believe I'm saying this, but that's good advice,' Dylan said from behind me.

I turned. She was propped in the kitchen doorway, wearing a lime green dress that was swishing around her calves. Her hair was piled up on top of her head. She looked stunning.

I mean, her make-up looked stunning. It was all hair and make-up. It was fine. I was fine. Definitely.

'Oh really?' Lily said. 'It's good advice? You think so? Goodness, I'm so honoured.'

'Don't start,' Dylan said shortly, coming into the kitchen and slotting herself beside me at the island. 'Kanda and Naya, they want you in hair and make-up.'

'What will happen if I do start?' Lily said, batting her eyelashes at Dylan.

I put my hand on Dylan's elbow. I didn't spontaneously

combust, and the earth didn't tilt wildly beneath my feet, which I took as a positive sign. 'We need to make a list of everyone's dietary requirements,' I said.

But no one was listening. 'I'm not a buy-in-bulk kind of girl,' Heather said. 'You think I'm going to eat rice all day?'

'No one's saying you have to eat rice all day,' Parisa said. 'But there are a lot of things we can make with rice, so—'

'What is this, *Desert Island Castaway*?' Heather demanded, at the same time as Jess K exclaimed, 'Keto!'

'We need to make a list of everyone's dietary requirements,' I said again.

'You could do a lot worse than taking *Desert Island Castaway* as a starting point,' Lily said, jabbing her finger into the list so hard it nearly tore. 'They survive, don't they?'

'Have you seen what they look like by the end?' Melinda/Belinda said. 'I am not getting to the end of this looking like some kind of fairy-tale hag.'

'What makes you think you're getting to the end of this?' Jess D said.

'I can't believe you just said that,' Melinda/Belinda said.

'We're getting off-topic,' I said. 'We need—'

'It's a legitimate question,' Jess D said.

'So, like, you're going to win, then?' Melinda/Belinda said. 'On your diet of rice and beans? Are you going to go fishing in the lake for protein?'

'Hey!'

Everyone shut up and looked at Dylan.

'This is getting us nowhere,' she said. 'Shut up, all of you, and listen to Mandie.'

. . . how did she do that?

Maybe I really had just been confused the night before. Maybe instead of desperately wanting to be with her, I just wanted to *be* her.

'What were you saying?' Dylan asked.

She looked at me. Our eyes met.

The earth wobbled, just a little.

'We should start by making a list of everyone's dietary requirements,' I said hurriedly, looking around at the other women. 'And food allergies. That'll give us a place to start.'

'I am not eating keto for the next six weeks,' Heather said.

'No one's asking you to,' Kumiko said. 'That's a good idea, Amanda. Let's start there. Is there a pen and paper in here somewhere?'

We found a notebook and a bundle of pens held together with a rubber band in one of the kitchen drawers, and I started taking notes. 'All right, so we have three vegetarians, a pescatarian, two vegans, a dairy allergy, a shellfish allergy, a nut allergy, one person on low FODMAP, and two people doing low-carb,' I said.

'Keto isn't just low-carb,' Jess K said. 'It's about changing the way your body creates energy so—'

'Shut up!' four or five people said at the same time.

'You know keto is hell on your kidneys, right?' Dylan said. 'Not to mention your bowels.'

'Can we not talk about bowels while we're ordering food, please?' Marija said.

'Can we all agree to three vegan days a week, where we all eat together?' I asked.

'No!' Melinda/Belinda said. 'I'm paleo! I need meat!'

'Don't get me started on paleo,' Dylan muttered.

'Look at the price of meat,' Parisa said, flipping over to the third page of the list. 'Three days vegan sounds like the bare minimum, if you crunch the numbers.'

I ripped a page out of the notebook. 'All right, three vegan days a week,' I said, drawing up a grid and writing the days of the week down the side in one column. 'Does anyone know what days Last Chance Parties are? There are canapes at those, so we don't need to do a dinner. If we plan our vegan days to line up with those, then those of you who really need meat can get some there.'

'Oh yes, like a tiny meatball is going to help,' Melinda/Belinda said.

'You know who's not helping?' Jess D said, eyeballing her fiercely.

'I have dietary needs!'

'And we're doing our best to accommodate them,' I said, reaching over the island and giving her a Mummy Mandie hand pat. 'All right. On the other days, what if we do a vegan option and a non-vegan option?'

One hour and two rotations of women to hair and make-up later, we finally finished our shopping list. Several pieces of notebook paper covered in my handwriting were stuck to the fridge. One had our meal plan for the week, complete with vegan and non-vegan options. One was a cooking roster. One was blank, except for the heading THINGS WE FORGOT at the top. 'So we can do a better job next week,' I said to Dylan, using Blu Tack to stick a pen to the fridge above the blank piece of paper.

'You did a plenty good job this week, Mandie,' she said, studying my handiwork as some of the other women started to filter out of the kitchen. 'You're an organisational machine.'

'I've just had a lot of practice,' I said. 'When you're the one woman working with a bunch of men, they start assuming that you'll do all the organising. You should see the morning tea rosters I've created.'

'However you got the skills, they're impressive as hell,' Dylan said, slinging an arm around my shoulder and squeezing me briefly.

I felt my cheeks turn red. 'I like lists,' I said.

'I like you,' she said, kissing the top of my head.

Not like that not like that she doesn't mean it like that, I chanted in my head.

'Dylan and Parisa!' producer Carrie called. 'Phone call time!'

Dylan dropped her arm from my shoulders. 'I've got to go and talk to Noah,' she said. 'If you've miraculously managed to put together a cleaning roster by the time I'm done, could you do your best not to give me vacuuming? I hate vacuuming.'

'You got it,' I managed to croak.

She left. I turned around and leaned against the kitchen island, taking a deep breath and tapping my fingers on the surface.

I'd been at least partially right the night before. Sleeping on it had changed things. Things were different in the cold, sensible light of morning. The drunken crush that had suddenly exploded like a firework last night had . . . not fizzled, exactly, but receded, like a wave.

Dylan was attractive. I was attracted to her. That was a fact.

But there were lots of people who were attractive and/or I was attracted to, and I could put them in the friend zone just fine. That was a fact too.

This wasn't going to be a thing. I wasn't going to let it be a thing.

Dylan was my friend, and that was plenty. It had been a long time since I'd had someone as ride-or-die as her. In my fragile post-break-up state – a state in which I was definitely very vulnerable and confused! – her friendship was exactly what I needed.

It was all right to enjoy it when people liked me, no matter what Jac used to say about me relying too much on external validation. But it wasn't all right to get so drunk on being liked that I fell headlong into unrequited, self-sabotaging love with a straight woman and ruined a wonderful friendship. That way was quicksand.

So I wasn't going to do it. I was actively choosing not to.

Maybe that should go on my list. *9) I do my best to make good choices.*

Kumiko and I were called for hair and make-up a few minutes later, the last two contestants in the rotation. 'Did I hear you talking about a cleaning roster?' Kumiko said as a PA walked us over. 'Because that's a really good idea.'

'We can totally make one,' I said. 'Or maybe a chore wheel? To make things fair?'

'Oooh, good idea.'

The PA got us some paper, and we worked on it together while having our hair done. 'What chores should be on it?' I asked Kumiko. 'Vacuuming, obviously. Mopping. Bathrooms. Kitchen. Do you think we need to clean the windows?'

'Put it on there anyway,' she said. 'We can always take it off.'

I jotted it down. Kumiko looked over. 'You have really nice handwriting.'

I chuckled.

'What?' she asked.

'Nothing,' I said. 'Don't worry about it. How about dusting?'

By the time we were done with hair and make-up and the twelve of us were finally called for filming, I was feeling a lot more settled. There was something so satisfying about getting things organised. It was one of my favourite things about my job, seeing something that was a big ol' mess and figuring out not just how to make it work, but how to make it work well.

There were three long couches in the Villa's main living area, set out in a U-shape. Carrie and some of the PAs arranged us on them. 'We can't have all the blondes together, you look like Stepford Wives,' Carrie said. 'Amanda, you move over there. Belinda, you move over there.'

I moved onto the centre couch. Dylan sat down next to

me, looking brighter than she had the whole time we'd been here. 'Hey,' I said. 'You look like you're feeling better.'

'I am,' she said. 'Thanks for last night, babe. Really.'

'What are friends for?' I said, because I was making good choices, and I was in control of my own actions, and I was going to fake it until I made it. 'Did talking to Noah this morning help?'

'God, so much,' she said. 'Hearing his voice . . . it reminded me why I'm here. I had to make a change if I was going to be the kind of mum I want to be. If I was going to be there for him at all.'

She looked into the distance wistfully for a moment. I wondered whether she was also faking it until she made it.

But then her eyes refocused on me, and she relaxed. 'You'll have to meet him when we get out of here, Mandie. He's such a great kid.'

'I'd love that,' I said. 'I'm a very good aunt. I've got a reputation for spoiling my friends' kids rotten.'

'That doesn't surprise me at all.'

Some of the crew adjusted the lighting. I couldn't tell you what they did to it precisely, but I can tell you that it made Dylan look luminous. God, she was pretty.

. . . which was a fact I was simply noticing about my friend. Because it was true. I was attaching no further meaning of any kind to it.

I could stare at her for hours, though. Just drink her in. Bathe in how beautiful she was.

Or at least, I could if she wasn't still looking at me. 'What?' I asked.

'Oh, nothing,' she said. 'You've just got this little smile on your face, that's all. Like you just had a really good meal, or a really nice glass of wine. Or really good sex.'

If I'd been drinking something, it would have gone up my nose. 'God, I wish,' I managed to choke out.

'Tell me about it,' she said.

She leaned a little closer. 'You must really like lists, though, if they're putting that kind of smile on your face.'

'Dylan! Amanda!' producer Carrie called. 'Pay attention!'

'Sorry,' we both said at the same time, and then exchanged glances. Hers was amused. I desperately hoped mine hadn't crossed over into aroused.

Carrie gave us a quick lecture about what was going to happen. 'Z is going to come in with your first group date card,' she said. 'You need to keep the energy upbeat, all right? Remember: you want to be on this date card. Time with the Romeo is your most precious resource in this experience.'

'We know,' the woman on my other side said.

'I know you know, Kanda, but there's a difference between knowing and remembering,' Carrie said. 'This is reality TV, not real life. That means we might have to shoot your reactions several times, from several angles. You need to bring the same energy every single time, all right?'

No one said anything.

'All right?' Carrie demanded.

There was a chorus of agreement.

'Good,' she said, and touched a finger to her earpiece. 'Bring in Z.'

We had to shoot Z's entrance five times, but eventually

he/we/everyone finally got it right. 'Good morning, Juliets!' Z exclaimed. 'How was your first night in the Villa?'

We all murmured various garbled versions of 'yeah, good'. Next to me, I swear I heard Kanda literally say the words 'mumble mumble'.

'We're diving right into the experience!' Z announced. 'Today is your first group date with our Romeo Dylan!'

We all did more excited semi-verbal murmurs.

'So I'm going to leave you with this—' Z grabbed at the back of his pants.

'Cut!' the director called. 'Let's go again.'

Someone rushed over to fiddle with the back of Z's pants. He turned slightly, and I couldn't help but smile. Whenever I watched *Marry Me, Juliet*, I'd always wondered how Z produced the date cards seemingly out of nowhere. The answer, it seemed, was that they were literally stuck to the arse of his pants.

Dylan elbowed me. *Oh my God*, she mouthed.

I know, right? I mouthed back. Z's apparent ability to pull date cards straight out of other dimensions had been one of the very first things we'd ever texted about.

Which was a very normal friend thing to text about.

Deep breaths. Fake it 'til you make it, Mandie. Make good choices.

'Go again,' the director said.

'So I'm going to leave you with this—' This time, Z succeeded in pulling the date card off his arse. It made a ripping sound, but none of the production team reacted at all. They could probably edit it out later. '– so you can find out which lucky Juliets will be spending time with the Romeo today. Remember: nothing's more important than time in this game, so if you get time with Dylan JM, make sure you don't waste it!'

We had to sit around for about twenty more minutes while they filmed other angles and some other stuff with Z before they actually let us do anything with the date card. 'Parisa,' Carrie called, 'you read it.'

Parisa jumped up from the end of the couch on the left. 'All right,' she said, pulling the card out of the envelope. 'It says—'

'Cut,' the director said. 'Go again. This time, take the card out slowly. This is a big moment.'

Parisa had to take the card out of the envelope seven more times before they were satisfied. 'Roses are red, seagulls are birds,' she was eventually allowed to read. 'A picture's worth a thousand words.'

'It's a photo shoot!' Kanda exclaimed.

'Of course it's a photo shoot,' Lily said. 'The first group date's always a photo shoot. Haven't you watched this show before?'

Dylan rolled her eyes. Lily caught her doing it, and the terrifying expression that crossed her face made me want to shrink back into the couch.

'Do you want to know who's on the date?' Parisa said, thankfully interrupting whatever it was Lily was about to do.

Everyone murmured their agreement.

'Okay,' she said. 'First of all: Kumiko!'

Everyone cheered as Kumiko beamed.

'Kanda!'

Everyone cheered again.

'Naya!'

And again.

'Marija!'

Carrie stopped us so we could shoot that cheer again. 'You've got to keep the energy high, ladies!' she said. 'No one watching will believe you actually want to spend time with the Romeo if that's all you can muster. Go again, Parisa.'

'Marija!'

This time we went too big and it looked like we were more excited for Marija to go on the date than anyone else.

Just like Goldilocks, though, the third time was the charm, and Parisa was allowed to move on. 'Amanda!'

'Oh!' I exclaimed, surprised. 'That's me!'

Everyone laughed. I joined in after a second, when I realised Dylan was laughing too and they weren't laughing at me.

'Lily Fireball!'

'Oh!' Lily said, in a mock high-pitched voice, clutching a hand to her heart. 'That's me!'

All the air left me like a deflated balloon.

That was how she saw me. How everyone here saw me.

Insubstantial. Childish. Ridiculous.

When you told me you were a mechanic, I thought you'd be this hardass, carving out a space for herself in a male-dominated industry, Jac said to me once, not long before she ended things. *I didn't realise you were mechanic Barbie. Isn't there anything underneath the surface, Mandie? Don't you have any hidden depths?*

Hot tears pricked my eyes. Thin-skinned could go on that list too. *I'm not saying this to be cruel,* Jac said. *I'm saying it to be constructive.*

'Lily, shut up,' Dylan said.

'Don't tell me to shut up.'

'Stop being a bitch to someone who's done nothing to you and I won't have to tell you to shut up.'

'Me!' Parisa said. 'I'm going on the date!'

More half-hearted cheers, which we had to film twice to get the energy right. I blinked the tears back and tried to run through the list in my mind. I was getting better at keeping it together. I wasn't going to let the quicksand drag me down. I was doing my best to make good choices, and bursting into tears right here and now would be a terrible one. I didn't want to let myself down.

'There's only one name left on the card,' Parisa said. 'And it's – drum roll, please –'

There was silence. Dylan and Lily were still trying to murder each other with their eyes.

Carrie sighed. 'Come on, ladies, look alive. Give her a drum roll. Say that again, Parisa.'

'There's only one name left on the card. And it's – can I have a drum roll?'

We all drummed our hands against our knees. Dylan, I noticed, had looked away first. She was shaking her head. Lily was smiling like . . . well, like she'd just had a really good meal, or a really nice glass of wine.

'Dylan G!'

Carrie made us film the reaction four times – not because

we weren't cheering right, but because Dylan didn't look excited enough. 'Come on, Dylan,' Carrie said to her. 'This date will be a real chance to get to know the Romeo. Don't you want to spend time with him?'

'Of course I do,' she said. 'Sorry. Let's do it again.'

'Are you feeling all right?' I asked Dylan, as we walked down the hill towards the site for the group date.

'What?'

'You just seemed a bit off at the end there,' I said. 'A little down.'

'I'm okay,' she said. 'You don't need to worry about me. It's kind of the same thing as last night, really. I'm just . . .'

Her voice trailed off. She reached up and pushed her headband a bit further up her forehead.

'I guess I'm finding it a little bit trickier to adjust to this whole thing than I expected,' she said at last. 'That's all.'

'It's big and weird and strange,' I agreed. 'But you've got me. For what that's worth.'

She smiled, a much more natural smile than the ones she'd been forcing out during filming. The sunlight caught in her hair and – nope, wasn't dwelling on that, wasn't letting myself dwell on that. 'It's worth a lot, Mandie,' she said. 'Thank you.'

'Thank *you*,' I replied. 'For having my back with Lily Fireball.'

'There is no universe in which I'm letting that high-school mean-girl shit stand,' Dylan said. 'I got a lecture afterwards about how I need to rein myself in or the audience is going to see me as this angry monster—'

'Oh,' I said. 'I'm sorry.'

'Babe, no need,' she said. 'I know this is all for TV and they want us all to play these perfect simple characters, but I want – no, I *need* – to stay me, or I'm going to lose my mind.'

The drawn, worried look was coming back onto her face, so I nudged her with my elbow. 'Thank you for this morning, too,' I said. 'For making everyone listen to me with the shopping list thing.'

Dylan smiled again, and the clouds cleared. 'No problem,' she said. 'You ever need something shouted, you come to me. My mum voice can be heard across the other side of a soccer field.'

'I wish I could get people's attention like that,' I said wistfully.

'Well, I wish I had your organisational skills,' she said. 'Putting together that meal plan was like solving a fucking Rubik's cube.'

'It wasn't that hard.'

'Yes, it was,' she said. 'If you ever get sick of mechanic-ing, you should go into, like, project management. You'd be great at it.'

'Maybe,' I said. 'If I could ever get people to listen to me.'

'We could be a project management duo, then,' she said. 'I'll shout at 'em, you organise 'em. You be the carrot, I'll be the stick. Perfect team.'

'Sounds like a plan,' I said. 'Now we just have to think of

a name for our new project management company, and we're in business.'

'We could Brangelina our names together,' she said. 'Dylanda. Dylandie. Dylda. Dyldie – nope, we should probably stay away from anything that sounds like dildo.'

'We might get some interesting clientele.'

She laughed. 'Oh God, totally,' she said. 'What about . . . Amandylan? Mandylan?'

'That last one might be the winner,' I said. 'One, it's got both our names. Two, it'll remind everyone how we met.'

'Hmmm?'

'Man Dylan,' I said. 'We met dating Man Dylan.'

She laughed again. 'That's absolutely it, then. Mandylan Project Management Pty Ltd, at your service.'

'What do you think of him?'

'Hmmm?'

'We never really got a chance to talk about it, with everything that happened,' I said. 'Not properly. What do you think of Man Dylan?'

'Oh,' she said. 'Hot. Super hot. Absolute flames. Hottest Romeo they've had in years.'

'Do you think they'll make him take his shirt off today? Get his abs out?'

'For photo shoot day? Definitely,' she said. 'He's a professional sportsman. He has to be ripped. Plus, he probably already used up like fifty per cent of his allowable Shirt Wearing Screen Quota for the season last night.'

'I just hope we get the chance to talk to him some more,' I said. 'I had such a lovely conversation with him last night. He's so sweet. So nice. I want to get to know him better.'

I meant it, too. I wasn't sure entirely *when* I'd decided it – sometime between Dylan standing next to me in the kitchen in that swishy lime green dress and making everyone listen to me, and my eight thousandth lecture to myself about how I was making only good choices from now on – but I had.

Encouraging my attraction to Dylan was a bad, self-sabotaging, friendship-destroying idea. But she wasn't the only Dylan on *Marry Me, Juliet* I could nurture an attraction to.

In fact, if you ignored the whole thing where I looked into Dylan's eyes and various tectonic events occurred, the First Night Party had gone as well as it possibly could have. I liked Romeo-Dylan, genuinely liked him. And it seemed that he liked me back, or he wouldn't have given me the first necklace. I could do a whole lot worse than that lovely, kind-eyed man as a rebound.

'Oh, sure,' Dylan said airily. 'But, like, pace yourself.'

'What do you mean?'

'I get the feeling it's easy to get swept up in things in here,' she said. 'I know he's great, but . . . I just don't want you to get hurt, Mandie.'

'It's Day Two,' I said, a little confused. 'I've known him for twelve hours. I'm not about to get down on my knees and propose. I just want to talk to him some more.'

'I know, I know,' she said, laughing. 'Sorry. That wasn't, like, a "hands off my man" warning or anything. It was more a "you just went through a big break-up, ease yourself back into things" kind of deal.'

'Thank you for worrying,' I said. 'But I promise you: this

is an emotionally healthy decision zone. No rushing into things. No falling head over heels. Good choices only.'

She laughed again and then changed the subject, and for the rest of the way down the hill, we planned ways to overcome the strong resistance some of the other women had put up against the chore wheel Kumiko and I had developed.

Part of me, though, was still stuck on what she'd said.

Three years ago, *Marry Me, Juliet* did this gimmick-y season where they cast contestants in pairs. There were sets of sisters and cousins and friends (and one mother-daughter pair, which was . . . interesting), all competing for the one Romeo.

Everyone was super happy at first. 'It's so nice to have someone to lean on during this experience!' they'd say in their talking head interviews. 'This is such a tough process, so it's nice not to have to go through it alone!'

But it wasn't like *both* members of the pair could end up with the Romeo. (I wasn't dating Jac when the season aired, but I could imagine the exact lecture about mono-normativity that would have prompted from her.) At some point, the pair had to split up. Inevitably, the Romeo would come between them.

I liked Romeo-Dylan. If I could get my brain to cooperate with me, I was planning to *really* like him. He seemed to like me back.

But he clearly liked Dylan too. And she didn't have a hopeless crush or the lingering memory of an ex standing between her and him.

109

Some contestants' relationships had been damaged forever by that *Marry Me, Juliet* season. Friends never spoke to each other again. Sisters cut each other off.

If Romeo-Dylan came between me and Dylan, I didn't know what I would do.

No, I realised suddenly. There was something I could do. If Romeo-Dylan looked like he was coming between me and Dylan, all I had to do was leave.

It really was that easy. If I had to – if it looked like Dylan was falling hard for him – I could just pull the ripcord, head down to the Convent, wait for it all to be over, and then resume being friends with her on the other side.

Of course, I might feel differently in a few weeks' time, I thought, as we reached a big marquee and the crew started fussing around us. If my plan worked too well and I somehow fell madly in love with Romeo-Dylan, things would probably become a lot less clear.

'Turn this way, love,' a make-up artist said to me. 'We just need to give you a few touch-ups before we start shooting.'

'Just a few touch-ups' was a lot more involved than it sounded, especially given the ratio of hair and make-up people to contestants. They spent about twenty minutes working on the eight of us who were on the group date. Murray was there too, typing notes in his phone, scribbling on a clipboard, and talking to the crew. 'Kanda!' he said at one point, summoning her. She spoke to him briefly, then disappeared and came back wearing a new shirt. It was apple green, very different from the deep purple one she'd been wearing.

Lily was wearing a dress in that same shade of purple. *How dare you wear my colour?* I remembered.

Huh. Was Murray trying to protect Kanda, or was he just as scared of Lily as the rest of us?

Well, not all of us, I thought, glancing over at Dylan, who was laughing with one of the make-up artists. Some of us didn't put up with bullshit.

Dylan caught me looking at her and winked.

Oh dear. I should not have found that wink as sexy as I did.

I was giving myself a very stern lecture about how I was a new, improved Mandie who absolutely *was not allowing this to happen* when filming started. 'Welcome to your first group date!' Z announced.

I'd been so busy giving myself the Mandie 2.0 talk that I'd totally missed that Romeo-Dylan had turned up. He was standing beside Z, wearing a more casual outfit than the night before, jeans and a teal polo shirt. He had his hands clasped in front of him, making it *very* apparent that he had the arms of a Greek god.

I focused on those arms, which were 1) undeniably sexy, and 2) a much, much safer thing to find undeniably sexy.

'As I'm sure most of you are aware, the first date of *Marry Me, Juliet* is always a photo shoot,' Z said. 'We've done a lot of themes in these shoots over the seasons. Our Romeos and Juliets have been photographed as everyone from Johnny and Baby to Sid and Nancy to . . . well, Romeo and Juliet.'

We had to stop for a few moments and go back, because none of us laughed hard enough at the joke.

'But this year's theme might be my favourite one of all,' Z finally announced. 'Famous love triangles!'

'Technically we're in a love tridecagon right now,' Romeo-Dylan said. 'Yes, I did have to go and look up the word for a thirteen-sided shape, thank you for asking.'

We had to stop again and film a bigger laugh reaction.

'. . . but I thought love triangles might be slightly more manageable,' he went on. 'I'm new to this Romeo business. I've got to ease into it.'

He had a bit of a sheepish expression on his face, and I noticed his thumb and middle finger tapping together. I felt bad that we hadn't laughed harder at his joke the first time. If I'd been in his shoes, and a bunch of people had to order all my girlfriends to find me funny, I'd have wanted to disappear into the ground.

I managed to catch his eye and give him what I hoped was an encouraging smile. His expression didn't change (not that much, anyway – the laugh lines around his eyes might have deepened a little, but I might have imagined it), but a few moments later, his fingers stopped tapping.

'There are eight of you on this group date, which means we'll be shooting four love triangles with our Romeo Dylan,' Z said. 'Naya and Kanda, you two and Dylan JM will be playing Archie, Betty and Veronica.'

'I'm going to apologise in advance for how I'll look in a red wig,' Romeo-Dylan said. 'I doubt it's going to be pretty.'

'We'll cope with our pain somehow,' Naya said.

Romeo-Dylan smiled at her. His laugh lines definitely deepened this time. He really did have kind eyes.

'Kumiko and Parisa, you and Dylan JM are going to recreate the iconic film *The Graduate*, and play Ben, Elaine and Mrs Robinson.'

Parisa did not look pleased. I'd found out during the Great Shopping List Saga that at thirty-eight, she was the oldest woman in the Villa. It looked like the show had already decided on the narrative they'd build around her.

What were they going to build around me and Marija? They were obviously going to pair Lily and Dylan together – that combination promised classic *Marry Me, Juliet* drama – but all Marija and I had linking us was that we were both blonde.

. . . which probably meant we'd be the montage girls. They'd skim right over us when this episode aired – look, there's the Romeo with two blonde bimbos, nothing interesting to see here, and—

'Marija and Lily Fireball, you'll also be recreating an iconic film with our Romeo – *My Best Friend's Wedding*!' Z said. 'Which leaves Amanda and Dylan G, who'll be doing something a little bit different. You'll be teaming up with Dylan JM on one of the most famous love stories in history: *Pride and Prejudice*!'

7

I haven't read *Pride and Prejudice*. I tried to, when we studied it at school, but I couldn't really get into it. I just watched the Keira Knightley version and had some profound emotions about her cheekbones.

I didn't remember much about it (apart from the cheekbones), but I did remember that it was about a bunch of sisters, so when we got to wardrobe it was a big surprise that, instead of being handed one of those dresses with the waist right up under the boobs, they handed me a three-piece suit. 'Dylan G, you'll be playing Lizzy Bennet,' the wardrobe lady said, thrusting an armful of cream-coloured fabric in Dylan's direction. 'Dylan JM will be Mr Darcy, and Amanda, you're Mr Wickham.'

Dylan started laughing. 'Sri Lankan Darcy, Samoan Lizzy, and tiny blonde femme Mr Wickham,' she said. 'This is going to be the most interesting *Pride and Prejudice* in the history of time.'

Our shoot was the last of the four. I wasn't sure if this was for ~drama~ reasons or just because our make-up was the hardest to do and they needed to get the easy ones out of the way first. 'What's Mr Wickham's deal?' I asked Dylan as we sat next to each other in the make-up tent. 'What kind of energy do I need to bring?'

'Hold still,' the make-up lady said. She was fixing a very thin pencil moustache to my upper lip. A few stray dark hairs fell on the cover-up I was wearing over my shirt and waistcoat.

'He's a fuckboi,' Dylan answered. 'He spends the whole first part of the book flirting with Lizzy—'

'That's you?'

'Hold still!'

'That's me,' Dylan confirmed. 'But Mr Wickham doesn't have any money, and neither do I, so his attention wanders.'

This was ringing some Keira Knightley memory bells. 'Because he needs to marry rich?'

'Exactly. He's a gold-digger. Which is fine, you've got to respect the hustle – but then it turns out he's got a nasty habit of seducing teenagers.'

The make-up lady finished with my moustache. 'So I'm the villain,' I said.

'You end up seducing my baby sister and Mr Darcy wins me over by bullying you into marrying her,' Dylan said. 'It's very hot of him.'

'Well, we all know that's the hottest quality a man can have,' I said. 'Making a fuckboi marry your sister.'

'Speaking of hot, bow chicka wow wow, Mandie!' Dylan said, as the make-up lady whisked my cover-up away. 'You make a very hot dude.'

I looked at myself in the mirror. She . . . wasn't wrong.

My hair was pinned up and covered by a top hat. They'd given me sideburns – blonde ones, so you couldn't really see them that well – but darkened my eyebrows and given me the dark pencil moustache, adding some definition to my face. I didn't know where they'd found an old-timey three-piece suit in size pixie, but it fit me perfectly, the waistcoat cut close to my body, a silk cravat tucked into it.

'I understand why my baby sister gave in to your charms, Mr Wickham,' Dylan said, brushing aside one of the curls they'd carefully draped over her forehead. 'I'm only amazed I managed to resist you.'

Parisa stormed into the make-up tent behind us. 'I can't believe they made me do that,' she fumed, yanking off her leopard print jacket and throwing it on the ground. 'I'm a scientist. I'm a marathon runner. I'm a mother. I'm a goddamn *person* – and all they want to reduce me to is my *age*?'

'Dylan G, Amanda, you're up!' a PA called from the front of the tent.

I looked at myself in the mirror again, in my old-timey drag king get-up, and a nasty suspicion began to grow in my mind.

They'd set up our shoot to look like one of those quaint tea shops where they serve you scones on plates covered in doilies. There was a little round table, covered in a long lacy tablecloth. There were two chairs next to it, the kind that probably had some proper furniture name but which I could only describe as 'old-fashioned'. There was a fancy teapot and two delicate china teacups on the table. Next to them was a three-layer cake tray, filled with eclairs and petit fours.

'Do we get to eat the desserts?' Dylan asked.

'Not while you're in costume!' one of the wardrobe people said, horrified. 'We don't have a backup. If you get anything on that dress before the shoot, Murray will murder you, me, and everyone here.'

We had to wait for Romeo-Dylan, who was still getting changed after his last shoot. 'Do you think Lily was Julia Roberts or Cameron Diaz?' Dylan said.

'Hmmm?' I said, tugging at my waistcoat.

'Do you think Lily was Julia Roberts or Cameron Diaz?' Dylan repeated. 'In their *My Best Friend's Wedding* shoot?'

'Oh. Julia Roberts, surely.'

'See, I thought that too,' Dylan said, 'but then I also don't see her letting someone else wear a wedding dress.'

'Good point.'

'You okay, Mandie?'

I think they've put me in this outfit because they're going to out me, I wanted to say. *They're going to make the fact that I'm bi my whole storyline, the way they're making Parisa's age her storyline.*

But there were cameras everywhere, and on the off chance the show *wasn't* about to out me, I wasn't going to do it myself. 'Yeah, fine,' I said. 'Just nervous. I haven't read the book. I don't know what I'm doing. I feel like I've turned up to class but I haven't done the homework.'

'You'll be fine,' Dylan said. 'Big fuckboi energy. That's all you need to know.'

I took a breath and let it out slowly. 'Big fuckboi energy. Right.'

'Here's an idea,' she said. 'Just channel your ex. That ought to do it.'

'Jac wasn't – Jac isn't—'

Cameras. Everywhere.

'– a fuckboi,' I finished weakly.

'Hi ladies!' Romeo-Dylan said brightly, breezing into the room. 'Let's get this show on the— oh, Amanda, look at you!'

He put his hands on his knees and doubled over, wheezing with laughter. 'I'm sorry,' he said. 'When I suggested *Pride and Prejudice* for this shoot, I thought they'd make you Miss Bingley.'

'Who's Miss Bingley?' I asked.

'Another villain,' my Dylan said. 'She's rich and mean and chasing after Darcy and constantly sabotaging people. You would have been all wrong as her. You're clearly a Jane.'

'Oh, good call, Dyl!' Romeo-Dylan said. 'You're absolutely a Jane, Amanda.'

'And Jane is . . . ?' I asked.

'My sister,' Dylan explained. 'Not the one that Mr Wickham ends up marrying. A different one. Jane is the love-liest girl in the world.'

'Jane's very sweet and very nice,' Romeo-Dylan said. 'Wouldn't hurt a fly. Would probably let a fly hurt her.'

So . . . a doormat. They both thought I was a doormat.

Don't be a doormat, Mandie, Jac had said to me once in exasperation. I'd been refusing to pick a restaurant to eat at in case I picked the wrong one, trying to turn the conversation around so she chose instead. *You know what you want. Just say it.*

She was right. I did know what I wanted.

I wanted to be in control of what I did and what happened to me. And that meant I didn't want to be a doormat.

I gritted my teeth. Dylan wanted me to channel my ex? I was going to fucking well channel my ex.

'Not today,' I said, smiling Jac's little sexy half-smile, the one that had driven me wild whenever she turned it on me. 'Today, I'm a fuckboi.'

It would have been such a great moment if we hadn't had to go back and do it again, because we weren't allowed to swear.

They started the photo shoot with the Dylans sitting at the little table, looking into each other's eyes over the eclairs. I was in the background, arms crossed, mostly turned away from them, looking back over my shoulder.

The position gave me a great view of what an incredibly stunning couple they made. Dylan was facing away from me, but I could see Romeo-Dylan smiling as he looked at her, those little crinkles forming at the corners of his kind eyes. *Can we eat the cakes?* I saw him mouth to her, saw her shoulders move ever so slightly as she laughed.

They were perfect.

Before Jac, I'd been part of a perfect couple too. I'd had a perfectly sweet, perfectly nice boyfriend called Mark, who, sure, hadn't exactly set my world on fire, but who I could have been happy with. Especially when you considered that I wasn't the kind of girl who set anyone's world on fire either.

Then along came Jac.

My breath still caught in my throat when I thought about the first time we'd met. It had been at a wedding for one of Mark's friends. I'd been standing at the bar. She'd walked up and ordered a whiskey, looked over her glasses at me, smiled that sexy little half-smile, and said, 'Hey.'

And it was all over. No more Amarkda. No more perfect couple. Jac had cut me away from Mark as precisely as if she had a scalpel, and my universe had exploded in flames.

I wasn't a doormat today. I was a Jac, and I was in control, and that meant no perfect couples that didn't include me.

'Hey,' I said, walking up behind Dylan and putting my hand on the back of her chair. 'I believe that's my date to the ball you're flirting with, Mr Darcy.'

If the show really was planning to out me as bi, they were going to have a field day with this.

But Jac wouldn't give a shit. In some weird alternative universe where she'd found herself on *Marry Me, Juliet*, she would have screamed *I'M GAY* so loudly in Romeo-Dylan's face the first time they met that his ears would still be ringing from it.

Straight shoulders. Half-smile. Wear the suit, don't let the suit wear you. *Be Jac be Jac Jac Jac Jac.*

'Oh dear,' Romeo-Dylan said, standing up, his eyes

crinkling even further as he tried not to laugh. 'I do hope you're not going to cause a scene, Mr Wickham.'

'Damn straight I'm going to cause a scene,' I said. 'I'm going to, um –'

What did old-timey people do when someone tried to steal their girlfriend?

'– duel you,' I said. 'Let's have a duel, Mr Darcy. For Lizzy.'

Dylan broke into peals of laughter.

'What?' I said, turning around. 'Did I get it wrong? Do they not have duels in *Pride and Prejudice*?'

'Oh, Mandie,' she said, wiping tears from her eyes, 'you're the most adorable person to have ever lived.'

Adorable is a word for puppies and small children.

I gritted my teeth.

'Fun idea, but we can't do a duel,' Murray said. 'We don't have the props. How about we settle for you two staring intensely and competitively into each other's eyes instead?'

'I'm a foot taller than her,' Romeo-Dylan said. 'Won't I just look like I'm bullying her?'

'Sit down, Romeo,' Dylan told him. 'Mandie, you come closer to me. Put your hand on the table on top of mine.'

She pulled at my hand. Her fingers were warm. I hoped she couldn't feel how much my palms were sweating.

'Now, glare down at him,' she said.

I thought about the look that used to come into Jac's eyes whenever she'd had to deal with her homophobic Aunt Beverley, and tried to turn it on Romeo-Dylan.

It took about three seconds for him to burst out laughing, so hard that the make-up person had to rush in and touch up his face. 'I'm sorry, Amanda,' he said, still wheezing. 'It's just – you might be the least menacing person in the world.'

I caught myself right before I spiralled. I was not going to take it personally. Being bad at being Jac did not make me pathetic. It was not an insult, and I was *not going to take it personally*.

'You hold on just a minute there, sir,' Dylan said. 'Look at her! Look at this Mr Wickham, all sexy and mysterious and fascinating! You should be terrified of her! She could totally steal your girl.'

DO NOT TAKE THAT PERSONALLY EITHER, MANDIE MITCHELL. SHE IS YOUR FRIEND AND SHE DOES NOT MEAN IT LIKE THAT.

'Mandie, look at me,' Dylan said. 'Practise on me first. Show me your intimidating glare.'

I did what she said, because it was the only thing I could do. I turned towards her, looked right into her eyes.

Oh nooooooo.

My breath caught in my throat. My blood pounded in my ears. I was fixed in place, transfixed by her, completely unable to move.

But the magic didn't go both ways. Underneath my hand, I felt her fingers twitch.

'That's a little more bedroom eyes than intimidating glare, but you know what? Go for it,' she said lightly. 'Fun new take on *Pride and Prejudice*: now Darcy and Wickham are into each other. It's like a sexy "I hate you, you're a terrible person, but I really want to very slowly and meaningfully unbutton your waistcoat" kind of thing.'

Romeo-Dylan laughed. I made myself laugh too, a second too late.

After the photo shoot, Romeo-Dylan got to pick one of us to spend some extra time with. I don't know if anyone else was surprised when he picked Dylan, but I certainly wasn't. How could he not?

Once we'd shot that little scene, we all got hustled off to film in-the-moment interviews (ITMs, the crew called them). 'All right, Amanda,' Murray said. 'Same deal as always. Full sentences. The audience won't hear my question, just your answer.'

I nodded, scratching at the corner of my lip. The emotional rollercoaster I'd just been on had made me break out in a sweat, and the moustache was starting to itch.

'Talk us through the shoot today,' Murray said. 'What did you think when you got handed the costume?'

'I don't know what I thought.'

'Amanda. Full sentences.'

'I don't know what I thought when I got handed the costume,' I said. 'Just that it was, uh, an interesting choice.'

'What did it feel like, taking on that Mr Wickham character?'

'It's always fun, playing dress-up,' I said vaguely. 'Why not go for it, you know?'

We continued on like that for another half an hour or so. Every question Murray fed me seemed designed to prompt an answer like, *well, I date women too, so pretending to feud with the Romeo over a fair maiden came naturally to me,* and every answer I gave was something boring and generic like, *I had a good time and costumes are fun and why not roll with it?*

I could sense Murray getting frustrated with me. But I was determined to stick to number 9) on my list and make good choices at least once today. I might be a deeply impulsive person, but even I wasn't going to out myself on national television without thinking about it first.

I was surprised to see Dylan in the kitchen when I finally got free of a) Murray and b) the moustache. 'Hey,' I said. 'You're still here! Aren't you supposed to be having one-on-one time?'

'Later tonight,' she replied. 'Ol' Romeo had to go do something first. Shoot an interview, probably.'

'Cool,' I said.

Dylan was dressed for her one-on-one in a swishy dark blue maxi dress that showed off her arms. Her hair was down from the *Pride and Prejudice* updo, spilling over her shoulders, held back by a pink headband. She looked beautiful. It was a big, big problem.

'Earth to Mandie,' she said, snapping her fingers.

'Sorry,' I said. 'Just drifted away for a second. It was a big day. I know it wasn't even that long a day really, but . . .'

'I get it, I get it,' Dylan said. 'It's the emotional energy. It's a lot.'

'Yeah.'

'Our groceries came while we were on the group date,' she said. 'I just threw about a third of a bag of oven chips in.

I figure I need to carbo-load to have enough energy for this one-on-one thing tonight. Want to help me eat them? Carbs always make me feel better.'

I shook my head. 'I'm okay,' I said. 'I think I might take a walk outside. Before it gets too dark.'

'Don't fall in the lake.'

'I'll try my best,' I said. 'Enjoy your date. If I don't see you before.'

'Thanks,' she said. 'I will. Hard not to, with that man. Look what he did for me.'

She unfolded a serviette, revealing three eclairs.

'He made Murray save them for me,' she said. 'Isn't that sweet?'

'Yeah,' I echoed, remembering the way Romeo-Dylan's eyes had creased in the corners as he'd smiled at Dylan across the table, the most perfect couple in the world. 'Super sweet.'

The sun was setting as I tramped through the gardens. I didn't go far. I'm a rule-follower, and I took Suzette's warning to heart. But even going only a little way showed me just how big the property was.

The Juliet Villa was on the top of a hill, sloping gently down towards the lake we weren't allowed to drown in. If I squinted, I could make out another, smaller house down the bottom of the hill. That must be the Convent. I hoped Cece was doing okay down there.

There were rose gardens on two sides of the Villa, one surrounding the pool, the other planted in long lines, like grapevines. At the front was the long entranceway where our limos had pulled up on the first night, now with significantly fewer lanterns and chandeliers. On the other side were walls and walls of hedges.

I'd only ventured in a little way before I realised that they weren't just random walls of hedges. It was a maze.

I glanced up at the sky. It was getting darker. I should go back.

But the cool evening breeze felt nice on my face, blowing some of that nervous sweat away, so I went a little further.

What was I going to do?

The breeze might feel nice, but it didn't have any answers for me.

I trailed my hand against one of the hedges. Someone had told me once that you could always find your way out of a maze if you just put one hand on the wall and followed it faithfully. It might lead you down a few dead ends, but as long as you followed the wall, you'd get out eventually.

Pity I didn't even know where the wall was these days. I was just flailing around, hoping that someone would take my hand and lead me along the right path.

Whenever I had a problem, Jac had always had a solution. 'Okay, here's what you need to do,' she'd say decisively when I told her about some issue with the guys at work or some drama with my friends, or even when I couldn't decide what to make for dinner. Then she'd give me clear, concrete advice. Sure, it wouldn't always *work* (she'd never come up with anything even close to as effective as the Mummy Mandie strategy), but she'd always sound so certain, and even if the advice turned out to be garbage, it still helped me figure out what I needed to do.

For a moment, I wanted her here so badly.

Babe, I've got a problem, I'd say to her. *A few problems.*

She'd lean back against the opposite wall of the maze and cross her arms. *Hit me.*

I'm on Marry Me, Juliet, I'd say. *I like the Romeo, but I really* like *my friend. Who's straight. And also dating the Romeo, who seems to be pretty into her. Also no one knows I'm bi. Except the whole crew. I think, anyway. And if I don't out myself, then chances are they will.*

Easy solution, Jac would say. *Don't be on* Marry Me, Juliet. *What the actual fuck, Mandie? Don't you have any self-respect?*

Even imaginary Jac could make tears spring to my eyes.

I wiped them away. Crying wasn't useful. Jac had said that once – more to herself than to me; she'd been trying to pull herself together after her grandpa had died – but I'd been in the room.

She'd been wrong then, but she was right now. Crying over her *again* wouldn't do anything but get me sucked right back down into the quicksand.

You shouldn't be here.

I sighed and leaned back against the hedge. The twigs dug painfully into my back, but I let them. It was easier to feel something as uncomplicated as 'ouch' than it was to feel everything else.

The Jac in my mind might be cruel, but she was also right. I was in no fit state to be here.

'You shouldn't be here!'

127

Wait. Those words didn't come from imaginary Jac.

That was . . . Murray?

I took a few steps towards his voice and peered around the corner. 'Why not?' Lily demanded.

She was standing behind him, in her dark purple dress from earlier, hands on hips, as he tried to string some fairy lights up a trellis. They were in a clearing in the maze – the centre, maybe? – and there was a couch set up, covered in velvet cushions in deep jewel tones. There was a low coffee table in front of it with a green shopping bag sitting on top, a bottle of champagne poking out of it.

'Because I'm busy!' Murray said, trying to loop the fairy lights around the top of the trellis and failing. 'The Dylans are going to be here soon, and I've got about an hour and a half's worth of set dressing to do.'

'I didn't know this kind of menial labour was part of your job.'

'It isn't,' he growled. 'But the network's cut our crew numbers to absolute shit this season. We've all got to help out. Which is why I don't have time to talk to— don't touch that!'

Lily was taking things out of the green shopping bag. 'If you need help, then I'll help,' she said, her voice calm and even.

'You don't know what you're doing.'

'Murray, you know better than anyone that I can assemble a cheeseboard.'

Murray made a noise in the back of his throat.

'Don't try that with me,' Lily said. 'I'm not scared of you.

What kind of cheeseboard do you want? Simple and clean, or a real cheese extravaganza?'

There was a long pause before Murray answered. 'Extravaganza,' he said. 'Dylan G's a frontrunner. We want this one-on-one to have a real cornucopia feel. Abundance. Overflow.'

He took a few steps in my direction, towards another one of his green bags. I slipped away, frightened he would see me. Unlike Lily, I *was* scared of him.

I headed back through the maze towards the Villa, walking fast to beat the darkness, trailing my hand against the hedge again.

What the hell was Lily's deal? Did she and Murray already know each other? They must, right, if he was letting her assemble a cheese platter for a date and casually telling her that Dylan was a frontrunner?

Frontrunner.

I stopped for a second, closed my eyes, and took a deep breath. This was not news to me. Anyone with eyes could see Dylan was a frontrunner for Romeo-Dylan's heart.

There was a big difference between knowing something yourself and hearing someone else say it, though.

Ugh. This really was some classic Mandie nonsense. Here I was, taking my first newborn deer-style steps back to normalcy after Jac, and now I was going to lose my perfect rebound man and my hopeless crush *to each other*.

Dylan was just coming out of the Villa as I got back. 'Hey,' she said brightly, her hem swishing around her heels. 'How was your walk?'

But Carrie had appeared beside her, and I didn't have a chance to answer. 'No time for talk,' Carrie said. 'We've got to get you to your one-on-one time. Dylan JM has an early start tomorrow, so we can't keep him up too late.'

'Catch you later, Mandie,' Dylan said to me, and then she and Carrie were gone.

I made myself paste on a bright smile for the rest of the night. I didn't tell anyone about seeing Lily and Murray in the maze. If I was going to keep myself un-outed, the last thing I needed to do was get a producer off-side.

Besides, the only person I really wanted to discuss it with was Dylan.

Instead, I made polite, chatty conversation over dinner. I listened to Naya and Kanda tell everyone about the chaotic disaster that had been their Archie photo shoot and laughed in all the right places. I mediated a dispute about the chore wheel. I even read out the card for the single date the next day ('Roses are red, blue is the sea, I like to go sailing, join me, Jess D?').

I didn't think about Dylan and Dylan, out there in the garden. I didn't let the word *frontrunner* bounce around my mind like an old-school screensaver. I didn't even listen to Jac when her mean whispers tried to break into my thoughts.

Okay, fine. I did *all* those things.

But I tried not to. I tried to make my mind clear and empty and just have a nice night.

It wasn't until later that night, after Dylan had come home wearing one of Romeo-Dylan's necklaces and we'd filmed the obligatory sofa scene ('Did you kiss?' Jess K had demanded, and Dylan had refused to answer, which we all knew meant yes), that it all finally came crashing through.

The lights were out. I was lying in my bunk, staring at a ceiling I couldn't see, even though I could reach out and touch it if I wanted to. I could hear the murmur of whispered conversation between Naya and Jess K, the rustle of linen as Marija rolled over, the gentle, even breathing of Dylan below me.

I was surrounded by people. There was no getting any time alone in the Villa. But something about the darkness made it easier to feel like you had some privacy.

The darkness let me reveal some truths to myself, but they only made things more complicated.

1) I might be on the way to getting over Jac, but her voice was still so, so loud in my head.
2) Romeo-Dylan might be my perfect rebound, but he was very into my best friend.
3) Said best friend was the *very best* friend I could ever hope for.
4) Try as I might to pretend otherwise, I was so deeply, profoundly, and unhealthily into her it hurt.

8

If it had been a normal season of *Marry Me, Juliet*, these four realisations might have made me leave. 'I'm sorry,' I'd say to Romeo-Dylan. 'I can't accept your necklace. I have feelings for someone else, and it's not fair for me to take the place of another woman who might have a real chance with you.'

He'd understand. We'd hug it out. 'Amanda, this is the end of your journey,' Z would say solemnly. 'We wish you well on your road to love ahead.'

Some of the other women would offer me goodbye hugs. Dylan's would be the tightest of all. 'I'll call you the second I get out of here,' she'd whisper in my ear. 'We'll go for drinks, okay?'

She would, and we would, often. If she didn't have Romeo-Dylan she'd find another equally hot and charming man soon afterwards, but we'd stay friends. Good friends. I'd come out to her at some stage. She'd be fine with it. I wouldn't tell her about my crush on her, not until much later. A speech at her wedding to Romeo-Dylan or whoever she ended up with, maybe. 'Dylan and I met on *Marry Me, Juliet*,' I'd say, 'and [insert extremely hot man's name here], you're lucky she's straight, because when I first met her? I would have married that Juliet in a heartbeat.'

In that future, I could leave the Villa and go home. Go back to my teenage bedroom at Mum's place, lick my wounds, let my crush on Dylan fade away, and get on with the serious business of building a new life for myself post-Jac. That way, when I finally met Dylan for those drinks, I'd be a better Mandie. A proper Mandie. Mandie 2.0, all the way out of the quicksand.

But if I did any of that on this season, I'd just end up stuck down at the Convent, waiting for the six-week shoot to end. I'd be in exactly the same situation as I was now – crammed into a house full of other women – except without my friend. It would be Mandie's Childhood Bedroom: The Sequel.

So when Romeo-Dylan offered me a necklace at the next ceremony, I didn't hesitate. 'Of course I'll accept your necklace,' I said, and lifted up my hair so he could fasten it around my neck.

He got it first try this time. He was getting better.

'Kanda, I'm so sorry,' Z said, 'but this is the end of your journey. We wish you well on your road to love ahead.'

I felt a pang of guilt when Carrie led Kanda away. Maybe if I had done the noble thing and fallen on my sword, she and Romeo-Dylan might have ended up together.

133

But then I thought about the serviette full of eclairs. The way Romeo-Dylan's eyes had creased in the corners as he looked at my Dylan. The way they'd looked together in those *Pride and Prejudice* clothes.

All I'd taken from Kanda was a few extra days in the Juliet Villa. I'd probably be at the bottom of the hill with her soon enough.

'I'm a bit bummed Kanda went,' Dylan said, as we took off our make-up in the bathroom after the Necklace Ceremony.

'Hmmm?' I said, halfway through peeling off one of my fake eyelashes. 'Why?'

'Because she was in the other bedroom,' Dylan said, dabbing at her face with a cotton pad. 'Which means she was in the other bathroom.'

'I wonder what it's like in the Convent,' I said, peeling off the other eyelash. 'It doesn't look very big. It can't have more than one bathroom. It might be okay now, but when we get deep into the competition and nearly everyone is down there, it'll be a nightmare situation.'

Dylan shuddered. 'Let's hope we never have to find out.'

I didn't say anything. What was there to say? At least one of us was going to experience the Convent sooner or later, and it was almost certainly going to be me.

Someone hammered on the bathroom door. 'Hurry up!' Lily yelled. 'Some of us have skincare routines to do!'

'All of us have skincare routines to do!' Dylan yelled back, before turning back to the mirror and making a face. 'Why couldn't it have been her who went?'

I opened my mouth, stopped, thought for a moment, then

turned the tap on as high as it could go in case someone was listening. 'I think Lily's a producer plant,' I whispered.

Dylan paused, halfway through wrapping her hair up in a silk scarf. 'What?' she whispered back.

I told her what I'd seen in the maze. 'Sorry I didn't tell you before,' I said, 'but it's so hard to get you alone without the cameras or a million people around.'

A muscle had started twitching above one of Dylan's eyebrows again.

'Hey,' I said, 'I really am sorry.'

Because I was looking at her in the mirror, I could *see* her pull herself back together, the same way I did sometimes. 'I'm not mad at you, Mandie,' she said. 'Of course I'm not.'

Lily pounded on the door again. 'Hurry up!'

'Are you mad at her, then?' I said. 'It makes sense to me, actually. Surely no one could be such a cartoon mean girl by accident.'

'It's not that either,' she said. 'I just . . . fuck, I hate feeling like a chess piece.'

'What do you mean?' I asked, flipping my head over, tying my hair into a topknot, and then straightening back up.

'We're not people in here,' Dylan said. 'We're puppets. They're pulling our strings and making us dance so they can put on their big show, and there's nothing I – we – can do about it.'

She threw all her stuff back into her make-up bag and zipped it, so forcefully I was worried it would break. 'You're the only thing in here I know for sure is real, Mandie,' she whispered, meeting my eyes in the mirror.

Dylan's face was drawn the next morning after her daily phone call with Noah. 'Is everything okay?' I asked her, as we sat down on the sofas for the next group date card reveal.

'Noah's good, he's fine,' she confirmed, squishing in close to me so Parisa could sit beside her. 'I'm just – ugh.'

'What?'

'Nothing,' she said. 'Nothing new, anyway. It's just hard, being away from him.'

She sighed. 'He started crying on the phone. My ex made some off-the-cuff comment about how fun it was to have Noah living with him and his wife, and Noah interpreted that to mean that he'd be living there forever now, and he was like, "Mummy, why don't I live with you now, don't you love me anymore?"'

'Oh God, Dylan,' I said. 'That's brutal.'

'I've explained to him so many times that this is just temporary, that I'm just going away for a little while so I can be home with him more often,' she said. 'So many times, Mandie. But I don't know how to make him believe me. And the mum guilt is piling on top of the nurse guilt, and . . .'

Her voice trailed off. I reached over and squeezed her fingers. 'I'm sorry you're going through this,' I said. 'I wish there was more I could do to help.'

She squeezed back. 'Just keep telling me that I'm in the right place,' she said. 'That I'm doing the right thing.'

'You're in the right place,' I told her. 'You're doing the right thing.'

She let her head fall onto my shoulder. 'Maybe if I can work out how to believe you when you say that to me,' she said, 'I can work out how to make Noah believe that I haven't abandoned him.'

My name wasn't on the next group date card ('Roses are red, bright is the sun, if you want to find love, how far will you run?'). Dylan's wasn't either, which I was surprised about, but it made sense the next day, when Marija read out the single date card. 'Roses are red, Darth Vader's a villain,' she said, 'I've found an oven, bake with me, Dylan?'

'Oh my God, you're going to the Romeo Residence!' Belinda squealed. 'You lucky bitch.'

'Congratulations, Dylan,' Lily said coolly. 'The Romeo wants you to do menial labour for him. How sweet.'

'Menial labour *with* him,' Naya said. 'There's a difference.'

'Maybe you'll have a sexy food fight,' Jess D said.

I thought of Dylan in an apron with flour smeared along a cheekbone. I would have had to sit down, if I wasn't already sitting down.

'Ew,' Lily said. 'If someone got food in my hair, I would literally kill them.'

'Well, it's lucky you're not going on this date, then,' Dylan snapped.

'Please. I would be offended to be on this date. This girl does not belong in the kitchen.'

Lily and Dylan started to snipe at each other again. *What do you mean you don't belong in the kitchen, Lily?* a braver version of me would have said. *I saw you set up that cheeseboard the other night.*

I didn't, though. I wasn't tough like Dylan. Whether Lily was a producer plant or not, the last place I wanted to be was in her crosshairs.

'Have a good day, Mandie,' Dylan said, hugging me before she left for her date. 'If we make anything edible, I'll try to smuggle some back for you.'

I almost asked her to put in a good word for me with Romeo-Dylan. I might not be in Lily's crosshairs, but given I hadn't seen him since the last Necklace Ceremony, I was beginning to worry I was in his.

The fact that he hadn't invited me on any of the dates for this episode stung, if I was being honest. I'd started off so strong, getting the first necklace. Sure, being with Dylan on the photo shoot date probably hadn't helped my cause – who wouldn't be comprehensively outshone by her? – but I hadn't expected to fall off his radar *quite* so fast.

. . . then again, I was easy to let go of. Jac had proven that.

But I didn't want him to let me go. I was steadfastly ignoring the main reason why – acknowledging it would not serve me or either of the Dylans – but it was still a fact, and that meant I had to do something about it.

'I need to look really hot tonight,' I told the wardrobe lady before the next Last Chance Party. 'Like, really hot. Can you help me?'

'Of course, doll,' she said, patting me on the shoulder. 'I've got you.'

Dylan was nearly finished with make-up by the time it was my turn to go in. She let out a low whistle when I sat down next to her. 'Excuse me, babe alert!' she said. 'Fuck, Mandie. You're a total smokeshow.'

'So are you,' I said.

It was the absolute truth. She was in a burgundy dress, slit high on one side, with a plunging neckline. The half-heart pendant of Romeo-Dylan's necklace (of course Dylan got a necklace on her single date, as if that was ever in doubt) sparkled gold in her cleavage.

'Yeah, yeah, whatever, I look fine, but you look *incredible*,' she said. 'Don't get me wrong, you look super cute in those pastels they keep putting you in, but you should wear black more often. It suits you. Like, it *really* suits you.'

The make-up artist had already started on my face, but even underneath the first layer of make-up, I could see my cheeks turn bright red in the mirror.

'Well, I haven't seen Romeo-Dylan for days,' I said. 'I've got to make an impression tonight, or I'm on the chopping block for sure.'

Dylan snorted. 'Please. You're not going anywhere.'

'I might be,' I said. 'My personality obviously hasn't been doing much for him, so all I've got left is pretty.'

'Mandie!'

'What?'

'Don't talk shit about yourself like that,' she said. 'You've got so much more to offer than pretty.'

I shrugged.

'That man out there would be lucky to be with you,' she said. 'Any man in the world would be lucky to be with you.'

I did not let the words *What about any woman?* come out of my mouth, which felt like an enormous achievement. Big enough to go on the list, even. *10) I can restrain my impulses if I really try.*

'And even if you didn't get a necklace, that wouldn't say anything about you,' Dylan said. 'All it would mean was that you and he weren't the right match. There's no shame in that.'

It was strange, how I almost believed her. I'd heard those kinds of words over and over again from my friends and from Mum when Jac dumped me – *it's not about you, Mandie, you just weren't right for each other* – and they'd done exactly nothing to stop me spiralling into a pit of despair and self-loathing.

Maybe it hadn't just been that sparkly green dress from the First Night Party. Maybe Dylan really was magic. Maybe that was why being around her had such a profound effect on me.

'Dylan!' one of the PAs called. 'Out of the make-up chair! We need to get the next girl in!'

'Next *woman*!' she called back, standing up.

Then she bent low, her lips almost brushing my ear and consequently almost giving me a heart attack. 'Remember,' she whispered, 'if he let you go, it'd be his loss, not yours.'

'Are you cold?' the make-up artist asked. 'You're shivering.'

'Oh – um – no,' I said. 'I'm fine.'

Dylan left. I let out a long breath and pulled myself back together. 'Sorry,' I said to the make-up artist.

'No problems,' she said. 'Just don't want to get eyeliner all over your face. You look so gorgeous tonight. I'd hate myself if I ruined it.'

She was right. Wardrobe and make-up had done right by me. I did look gorgeous.

Even in the darkest depths of my post-being-dumped spiral, my appearance was the one thing in which my confidence had never wavered. I was pretty enough for Jac to spot across a crowded wedding and decide to steal away, even if she ultimately decided she didn't like anything else about me. I might not have a lot of hidden depths, but I gave very good surface.

I hoped the surface would be enough tonight. That my face and my hair and this killer black dress would be enough to convince Romeo-Dylan to keep me. That I could at least dazzle him enough with my appearance to distract him from my lack of substance.

No. Mandie. Stop. Quicksand.

I ran through my list in my mind and focused on number 6. I was good at making friends. I'd done it with Romeo-Dylan on the first night. All I had to do tonight was remind him of what a nice, easy, friendly dynamic we had. Didn't the best relationships start with a solid basis of friendship? I could totally do this.

. . . if I could just psych myself up to go and talk to him.

When I finally got out of hair and make-up, Dylan had been pulled away to do an ITM, so I was on my own. I got myself a glass of champagne from the bar, took a long swig, found a quiet spot near the hedge maze, away from everyone, and tried to give myself a pep talk. *Just do it,* I ordered myself. *What's the worst that could happen?*

141

What was I so worried about? The stakes weren't even that high! I would interrupt his conversation, and Romeo-Dylan would probably say, *Sure, let's talk*. Maybe, *Give me a few minutes to wrap this up and I'll come find you*, at the absolute worst.

We'd sit down. We'd talk. He was nice. It would be fine.

Amanda, I really don't see this going anywhere, he'd say. *I'm looking for a deeper connection. You're nice, but there's not that much to you*.

Tears would well in my eyes. *Please, we need to be adults about this*, he'd say.

I tilted my head back and looked at the night sky. *Stop being ridiculous*, I ordered myself.

'What are you doing?'

Lily Fireball was standing at the entrance to the maze. She was in dark green tonight, almost the same colour as the hedges, but the giant gold necklace around her neck made her stand out. It was shaped like a snake, with a twinkling green gemstone as an eye. Subtle.

'What are you doing?' she repeated, arching an eyebrow. 'Are you lost? Party's that way. You know, where all the cameras are?'

'I know,' I said, a little too defensively.

She arched her eyebrow even higher.

'I know,' I said, more firmly. 'I'm just . . . preparing myself. I want to go and talk to the Romeo.'

'What's there to prepare?' she said. 'You just sashay up to him and say, "Can I steal you for a second?" It's not complicated.'

142

'I—' I hesitated.

'Are you worried about it being awkward? They make it that way on purpose, because they want to start fights.' She arched her eyebrow again. 'You don't want to get in a fight?'

'Not especially, no,' I said.

She smiled, a glint in her eye. *Then you're in the wrong place, little girl,* I expected her to say.

But, 'Smart,' she said. 'Wifey like you, you should stay clear of the drama.'

I blinked. 'Wifey?'

'A wife-type,' she said. 'Sweet, nice, good girl. Perfect for marrying.'

'I know what a wifey is,' I said. 'I've watched this show before.'

'Then why am I here giving you Interrupting 101?' Lily said. 'Go talk to him.'

There were so many things I wanted to ask her. *Why are you being nice to me?* for one. *Are you some kind of plant?* for another.

But most of all, *You think I'm a wifey?*

'Go!' she said. 'Get out of here! He's with Marija now. She's a wifey too, she won't start shit with you. Shoot your shot.'

I went. I was too scared of her to do anything else. Fear was a powerful motivator.

Romeo-Dylan was sitting with Marija in a little bower in the trees, near the start of the hedge maze. He was holding both her hands. She was saying something to him, although I wasn't close enough to hear what. He was listening intently, his head cocked very slightly to one side.

143

It was one of the few times that I hadn't seen him smiling. It wasn't like he was *frowning*, exactly, but there was an intensity to him that I hadn't seen before.

'Go on!' someone hissed.

I turned. Murray was behind me with a cameraman.

'Go on!' Murray repeated. 'Talk to him!'

There was no wussing out now.

I took a deep breath and pretended I was Jac. I was at that wedding, and I'd spotted a hottie across the room. Maybe they were with someone right now, but not for long . . .

'Hi,' I said, smiling my brightest, widest, pearly-white smile. 'Can I steal you for a second?'

'Absolutely, Amanda,' Romeo-Dylan said, smiling up at me. 'Marija, it was lovely chatting to you, all right?'

He leaned in and kissed Marija on the cheek. 'Thank you,' he said to her.

'Thank you for listening,' she said.

It took a few minutes before I could actually sit down with Romeo-Dylan. They had to film Marija getting up and walking away a few times, and then me sitting down a few times. Considering the height of the heels I was wearing, it was a bit of a glute workout. If Lily was right – if I was a wifey, one of the contestants destined to go deep in the competition – my arse was going to look great by the time filming ended.

The serious look on Romeo-Dylan's face hadn't gone anywhere. 'Hey,' I said, 'are you all right?'

'Not yet!' Murray barked. 'We're not ready for you to talk!'

We had to sit there in silence as they fiddled with more things around us. They were having some problem with the sound equipment, and they were frantically trying to troubleshoot.

'Seriously, though,' I whispered, touching a finger gently to the back of Romeo-Dylan's hand, 'are you all right?'

'Amanda!' Murray snapped.

Romeo-Dylan didn't say anything, but he met my eyes, gave me a flicker of a smile, turned his hand over so he could catch my fingers, and squeezed them gently.

It wasn't particularly romantic. It was the same kind of hand squeeze I'd had from a bunch of the guys at work, when I'd given them some Mummy Mandie common sense advice about their love lives.

But it made me feel better just the same. If I could make *him* feel better when he was down, even if it was just in a weird maternal sort of way, then I might be worth keeping around.

Wifey.

I could be with this man. I could see it. Only dimly, only vaguely, sure, but it was not outside the realms of possibility that I could be with this man.

'All right,' Murray finally said, what felt like an hour of awkward silence later. 'We're ready.'

'And rolling,' the director said. 'In three, two . . .'

'Are you all right?' I asked. 'You look so serious. You're usually so happy and smiley whenever I see you.'

'I'm all right,' Romeo-Dylan said. 'It's just that being the Romeo is harder than I thought it'd be, you know?'

'I see how you got confused,' I said solemnly. 'It sounds *super* easy to have eleven girlfriends at the same time. An absolute piece of cake.'

He laughed. 'I missed you these last few days, Amanda,' he said.

'Really?' I asked.

'Really,' he confirmed.

I believed him. His eyes were honest as well as kind.

Wifey.

Me and him. Him and me.

Definitely . . . maybe?

'Well, you'd better keep me around then,' I said, smiling my brightest smile again and hoping like hell I'd done enough.

I had. This time, anyway.

'Amanda, I want to know if your heart is the other half of mine,' Romeo-Dylan said, holding my hands and looking into my eyes. 'Will you take this necklace and commit to finding out with me?'

'Of course I will,' I said. 'Thank you.'

There was a knowing smirk on Lily's face as I walked back to the bleachers. *Told you that you were a wifey.*

I fingered the half-heart pendant. I'd got the second necklace of the ceremony. Another early necklace – a classic sign that the Romeo was really into you.

God, it felt good to be liked.

You rely too much on validation from other people, Jac whispered in my mind.

Well, I have to, I wished I'd said to Jac. *I never get it from you.*

At the end of the ceremony, only Marija and Jess K were

left standing, waiting for the final necklace. I was a little surprised that Marija was one of the last two, given Lily had said she was a wifey too, but not very. Romeo-Dylan had looked so serious after they talked. They'd probably had some momentous conversation that would end up being a big part of the episode. Murray or Suzette or someone had probably made him leave her until last. It was ~drama~, yet again.

'Juliets, this is the last necklace for this evening,' Z said. 'If you don't receive it, then I'm sorry, but your journey ends here.'

Romeo-Dylan picked the necklace up. He took a deep breath.

'Jess K,' he said.

I blinked in surprise.

'Marija, I'm so sorry,' Z said, 'but this is the end of your journey. We wish you well on your road to love ahead.'

Marija burst into tears.

'Hey, hey, hey,' Romeo-Dylan said, striding up to her. 'I'm sorry, Marija. I'm so sorry.'

She wrapped her arms around his neck and sobbed into his shoulder. He held her for what was probably a few moments but felt more like a few minutes as she cried. 'Can I walk you out?' he asked, when she finally pulled back.

She nodded. The cameras crowded around them as they left the Necklace Ceremony room.

'Is that it?' Parisa asked. 'Are we done for the night?'

'Not yet,' Suzette said. 'Once Dylan JM's done with Marija, we'll get him up here to finish off the shoot. You can take five, though.'

I sank down, sitting directly where I'd been standing on the bleachers. Dylan sat down beside me. 'My calves are killing me,' she groaned, kicking her heels off and digging her fingers into her ankles.

'Yeah,' I agreed vaguely. 'Ow.'

She poked me in the shoulder. 'What's this about?' she asked, gesturing at my face. 'You're all serious.'

'Oh, nothing,' I said. 'I'm just surprised Marija went. Sad, I guess.'

'Really?' Dylan said. 'I know she sleeps like two inches away from us, but I didn't think you were that close.'

'It's not that,' I said.

I couldn't exactly tell her what Lily had told me about Marija and I both being wifeys, not with everyone around us, so I hedged. 'She was just so similar to me,' I said. 'Blonde. Nice. If he doesn't like her, then that doesn't bode well for me.'

'First of all, you and she are completely different,' Dylan said. 'Secondly, it's like I told you. If he's not into you, it's his loss. You're amazing.'

I shrugged.

'Mandie,' she said, grabbing my arm, 'you're amazing. Tell me you know that.'

I was saved from having to answer by Suzette. 'All right!' she called. 'That elimination was rough for Dylan JM, so he's not coming back tonight! Get back to your places so we can film our outro with Z. If we get this done quick, you can all be in bed in half an hour.'

It took longer than half an hour, of course. Even if Lily hadn't got into a fight with one of the other women (Heather, this time), sending all the cameras crowding around, there were still ITMs to film and dresses and necklaces to return to wardrobe and the complex bathroom schedule to negotiate so we could all take off our make-up.

But Dylan didn't let it go.

'Tell me you know that you're amazing,' she demanded, closing the bathroom door behind her. 'Say it. Say "I'm amazing".'

I started taking some of the bobby pins out of my hair. 'I'm amazing,' I repeated.

She snorted. 'How about like you mean it?'

I took some more pins out and didn't say anything.

'Mandie,' she said, 'you're amazing.'

I met her eyes in the mirror. 'Thank you for saying that,' I said. 'Really.'

You rely too much on validation from other people.

'You think I just go round telling people they're amazing?' she said. 'It's true, Mandie. I think you're great.'

My lip started to tremble. I quickly grabbed a make-up wipe and scrubbed at my lipstick so she wouldn't be able to see.

'I know we haven't known each other that long, but you're one of my favourite people,' she said. 'You're kind, and you're funny. And you're an incredible listener. There aren't a lot of people with your high level of tolerance for "this is what my kid said today" talk.'

I grabbed another make-up wipe and started taking off my mascara so she wouldn't see the tears beading in the corners of my eyes.

'Plus, you have extremely good opinions about the *Real Housewives of Auckland*,' she said, turning around and leaning against the second sink. 'It's rare to find someone who has such good and correct takes.'

I bit my lip. *You cry too easily.*

I tried my hardest. Not again not again *not again.*

'Oh, Mandie,' Dylan said, as the tears started running down my cheeks.

She pulled me to her, the same way that Romeo-Dylan had pulled Marija to him downstairs. 'If I'd known *Real Housewives* made you so sad I never would have made you watch it with me.'

I tried to laugh at the same time as I was sobbing and nearly ended up choking.

She didn't let go. She just kept stroking my hair. 'Who did this to you?' she said. 'Who made it so hard for you to hear nice things about yourself? To think nice things about yourself?'

I didn't say anything. I *couldn't* say anything.

She sighed. 'If I ever meet that fucking shithead ex-boyfriend of yours, I'm going to kick him in the nuts so hard they come out his nose.'

'Girlfriend,' I whispered.

'Hmmm?'

I pulled back. 'Girlfriend,' I repeated. 'Jac. Not my ex-boyfriend. She's my ex-girlfriend.'

There was a pause. Not even a heartbeat. The space between heartbeats, maybe. The briefest instant.

'She's still a shithead, though, right?' Dylan said. 'Because I'm still intending to kick her extremely hard for doing such a number on you.'

9

'Okay,' Dylan said, the next day. 'The girlfriend thing. I have a couple of questions. Is that all right?'

It was early in the morning, the sky still pink and silver from the sunrise. We hadn't exactly agreed that we'd get up with the sun, but it had somehow happened anyway. Quietly, as the other three women in our room slept, we got dressed, went downstairs, grabbed breakfast and went outside.

There weren't any camera crew around yet, but there were cameras mounted in nearly every room downstairs, and mics hanging from the ceiling. There was almost nowhere we could go without being seen and without being heard, and it meant the world to me that Dylan hadn't said a single thing until we were outdoors and well clear of the Villa, outside the range of prying ears and eyes.

'Of course,' I said. 'Ask away.'

'Don't worry. I'm not going to ask you anything weird or gross.'

'Oh, then I'm sorry,' I said. 'I'm only prepared to answer weird and gross questions. No others. They're the only kind I like.'

She snorted. 'Ha ha,' she said, tapping the end of my nose with her finger. 'Cute.'

I took a bite of my cereal, doing my best to ignore how much I liked that casual, easy, intimate little gesture.

'No, it's more logistical questions,' she said. 'Some things I wanted to check. You're not out on the show, right?'

I shook my head. 'I know there have been queer Juliets before,' I said, through my mouthful. 'And, like, more power to them, but it always seems like it's made their lives *super* unpleasant, you know?'

'God, yes,' Dylan said, taking a mouthful of her own cereal. 'Like when Crystal S came out last year and Brandi started that whole "Oh, ew, I don't want to sleep in the same room as her, what if she's *in love* with me?!" bullshit.'

'Or like three years ago when Gracie came out to Andrew and then he just casually outed her to all the women in the Villa without asking her, and those twins – what were their names? They started with M?'

'Madison and Mackenzie.'

'Yes! Them. Remember how they sat her down and were all like, "Gracie, you need to remember how conservative Andrew is, his family would never accept someone like you"?'

'Even though they were clearly trying to get him to be in some weird incest throuple with them.'

I sipped at my coffee. 'Then there was Taylor as well. I felt so bad for her. First, her Romeo was clearly angling for a threesome, and then she went on *Juliet on the Beach* and got in that love triangle with Penny and Seth and they gave her the worst edit in the world.'

'Ah yes,' Dylan said. 'Pansexual Taylor, Evil Slut Queen, Ruiner of Lives.'

'I remember watching an Insta Live Taylor did where she talked about all the death threats and hate mail she got,' I said. 'I'm not ashamed to be bi. At all. I've been out to most people in my life since I was a teenager, and it's honestly not that big a deal. But . . . if I can avoid getting death threats and hate mail, then I'd like to. Maybe that makes me weak or spineless, but—'

'Hey,' Dylan said. 'I would never think that. You know I would never think that. Right?'

'Thank you.'

'I mean it,' she said. 'You're not weak. You're not spineless.'

'I guess we'll see,' I said, trying to keep my voice light. I put my coffee down on the ground beside me, afraid my hands would shake and I would spill it. 'I'm about ninety-five per cent sure production knows I'm bi. If I don't out myself, they might do it for me, just to create some drama.'

Dylan exhaled. 'I wish I could tell you that they wouldn't do that, but we both know they would.'

'I know,' I said. 'I did my best to scrub my social media, but it wouldn't take much digging to figure it out. Like I said, I've been out to pretty much everyone for pretty much ever. It's not a secret.'

'Can I ask you another question?'

'Of course.'

'If it's not a secret,' Dylan said, looking over at me, 'then why didn't you tell me?'

I picked up my coffee and took another sip, just to give myself time to think of a good enough answer.

'Well, I didn't want to be out on the show,' I said eventually. 'Like I said. Just trying to avoid . . . you know. Everything.'

'I get that,' she said. 'But you know you could have told me, right? There's no universe where this would make me think about you any different.'

'I know,' I said.

She didn't say anything. She just kept looking at me.

'I wish I had a good answer for you, Dylan,' I said. 'I wish I had some clear-cut thing that I could point to, like, "Oh, I didn't tell you because an ancient witch put me under a curse to never let me speak of it."'

That drew a snort of laughter.

'It wasn't that I thought you'd react badly or weirdly or anything,' I said. 'Or that you'd out me on purpose. Although you remember how Taylor got outed on her original season, right?'

'Where she told her friend in front of the cameras and then producers *absolutely* leaked it to the Romeo? Of course I do,' Dylan said, taking a swig of her coffee. 'I promise I'll never talk about this when there's even a tiny chance there are cameras and mics around, okay? I wouldn't do that to you.'

'I know you wouldn't,' I said. 'Although it probably doesn't matter now. I'm almost positive they already know.'

'For what it's worth, I don't think man-Dylan would be a dick about it,' she said. 'It wouldn't be an Andrew and Gracie situation or anything.'

I nodded.

'And if it got out to the rest of the women in the Villa, I'd have your back.'

I nodded again.

'Is there –' she hesitated. 'Is there any other reason you didn't tell me?'

Mandie 1.0 would have cracked. *If I told you, you might ask me how I feel about you, and I might tell you, and then I might I lose you.*

But Mandie 2.0 could restrain her impulses, if she put her mind to it. 'It just never really came up,' I said, taking another mouthful of cereal. 'I left it too late after we met, and it's an awkward thing to shoehorn into conversation, you know? Like, we're messaging about *Real Housewives* or whatever, and what am I supposed to do? Just be like, "Oh, by the way, just FYI, I'm bi."'

'You could have.'

'I know. I'm sorry. I wish I had a better explanation for you. It's just . . .'

'Hey,' she said. 'You don't need to apologise, Mandie. I'm the one who's out of line. I'm the last person who should be making people feel shitty for not revealing things.'

I wanted to ask what she meant, but she reached over and took my hand. She folded her fingers through mine and squeezed tight, and I forgot how to breathe.

'I'm glad you told me now, though,' she said softly.

'I'm glad I told you too.'

That was true. I was glad.

Or I would be, if there was room for anything else in my brain besides her fingers wrapped around mine, her eyes looking into mine.

In the early morning sun, she was radiant. The light caught notes of gold in her hair. She had a kind of Medusa power over me, which was lucky, because if I'd been able to move, I would have reached out and traced a line down her face.

She licked her lips. My eyes flickered to them involuntarily.

Oh no. Had she caught me—

'Amanda!' Kumiko yelled from the Villa. 'Are you out there? We need to do the shopping list for this week!'

'Coming!' I called, scrambling to my feet, and I ran away before Dylan could ask me any more dangerous questions.

By the time we were summoned to the couches for the next group date card reveal, I'd been through:

1) Another intense round of political negotiations over the shopping list;

2) Hair and make-up (my rotation partner this time was Jess K, which meant I'd also been through a long lecture on keto and why we'd made all the wrong choices in doing the shopping list); and

3) An ITM with Murray about who I hoped would be on the group date card. ('I really hope I'm on the card today, I need some more time with the Romeo!' I'd said in the

brightest voice I could muster, hoping that my wild eyes would read as 'enthusiastic' and not 'unhinged'.)

It hadn't changed anything. My heart was still beating a million miles a minute. I was still playing the moment in my head over and over again.

Her hand in mine.

The sun in her hair.

Her licking her lips.

My eyes flickering to them.

Between the hair and make-up rotation and ITMs and Dylan's daily phone call with Noah, I hadn't been able to speak to her since. I felt like I was teetering on the edge of a cliff, unsure if she was going to catch me or shove me off.

'Roses are red, a fire does burn,' Jess D read off the date card, 'things that are lost can one day return.'

Dylan was sitting next to me on the couch. The whole side of my body that was brushing against her felt hot. Could she feel it?

Her licking her lips.

My eyes flickering to them.

'What does *that* mean?' Belinda wondered aloud.

'Is one of the Convent girls coming back?' Jess K asked.

'It'd have to be Marija, right?' Naya said. 'It seemed so obvious that he liked her. He got rid of her out of nowhere.'

'And she was so upset when she left,' Kumiko said. 'He might have felt bad.'

'Maybe it's – whatshername,' Parisa said. 'The one that fell in the pool and fainted. He definitely felt bad about that.'

'It better not be her,' Lily said. We were all squished together on the couches, but she still somehow found room to lean back and spread her arms out along the top, crossing one ankle over her knee. 'Unless she wants another dunking.'

'Lily, don't start,' Dylan said.

'What are you going to do about it?' Lily said.

'I'm not going to let you casually threaten people like it's nothing,' Dylan said. 'It's not okay.'

Lily smirked. 'All right, hero.'

Dylan flinched. I wanted to reach out to her, but I managed to restrain myself.

She couldn't have missed my eyes flickering to her lips. Surely.

'Can we just read the names on the date card?' Kumiko said. 'Have this fight on your own time, you two.'

Once again, I wasn't on the date card, but Dylan was. She, Naya, Belinda, Jess K and Lily traipsed out of the Villa and off down the hill. She waved goodbye to me, perfectly normally. I waved back, probably normally. *It's all right,* I tried to tell myself, *it's fine, you're overthinking things, settle down.*

It didn't work. My stomach was a mess of bubbling questions and feelings.

I tried desperately to think about something else. Anything else. I helped Parisa make an eggplant stew for lunch. I mediated when Heather complained about it. I volunteered to do all the dishes, scrubbing the stew pot to within an inch of its life.

Her lips. My eyes.

My chore on the wheel this week was cleaning our bathroom, so after I finished the dishes, I got to work and started scrubbing. I put my whole self into it, getting right into the grout, wiping the shower door carefully clean so there were no streaks on the glass.

I was good at cleaning. It was one of those 'nice hand-writing' level good things about myself – i.e. too small to count for much – but it was still satisfying. It cleared my mind and made me feel calmer.

Usually.

Her lips. My eyes.

I wiped down the mirror and got rid of all the tooth-paste flecks before going over it with a microfibre cloth. The Mandie in the mirror's hair was falling down from her messy ponytail, and her cheeks were flushed with exertion. One strap of my dove-grey singlet top had fallen off my shoulder. I looked like I'd just rolled out of bed with someone, and they'd messed me up *real* good.

I could see it. Lying on top of the covers with her. One of her hands in my hair, pressing her lips to mine, the other pushing the strap of my shirt off my shoulder. She'd kiss her way down my neck, bite gently on that soft place where neck and shoulder met. *I wish you'd told me sooner,* she'd say, *because we could have been doing this sooner.*

I leaned close to the mirror and blew hard, letting the fog cover my reflection.

My eyes had flickered to her lips.

But it had been because she'd licked them.

Probably because they were *dry*, Mandie, geez.

She'd been holding my hand, though.

Because she was being a supportive friend! Hadn't I done that for some of the guys at work before?

. . . granted, on at least one occasion that had led to them propositioning me, but that absolutely hadn't been what Dylan was doing. Everyone came out on their own timeline and in their own way and all, but hard as I tried, I couldn't imagine a scenario where I said *I'm bi* to Dylan, and she didn't say *me too* back to me if it were true.

I'm the last person who should be making people feel shitty for not revealing things, she'd said. Which could mean . . .

No. Dylan might have some skeletons in her closet, but she wouldn't hide in there with them, not from me. If she were into women, she would have told me.

I wiped down the mirror with the microfibre cloth again and looked into Mirror Mandie's eyes, giving her a stern lecture. *She is straight and she is your friend and you are not going to sabotage your friendship by reading things into it that aren't there,* I told her. *Get it together.*

I practised doing normal, casual faces in the mirror. 'Hey!' I said to my reflection, smiling and waving. 'Welcome back! How was your date?'

It looked and sounded neither normal nor casual.

I sighed, pulled my singlet strap back up my shoulder, and started polishing the taps. At least I'd hit a new break-up milestone. This was the first sexual fantasy I'd had in a very long time that wasn't about Jac breaking down the door at Mum's place and begging me to take her back.

It was late when Dylan and co finally came traipsing back from the group date. They looked bone tired, and they were all covered in mud and – blood?

'Oh my God,' I said, rushing up to Dylan, my angst momentarily forgotten as the splatters of blood on her shirt performed an emergency full system override on my brain. 'What happened? Are you okay?'

'It's not my blood,' she said wearily. 'It's Belinda's.'

I'd gone straight to Dylan, but Parisa, Kumiko, Jess D and Heather were all clustered around Belinda. 'Holy shit,' Jess D said. 'Belinda, you need to go to a dentist.'

'I can't,' Belinda said. 'If I leave, I can't come back.'

Dylan sagged back against the kitchen island, fingers digging into her temples.

I immediately activated Mummy Mandie mode. 'Sit down,' I told her, nudging her towards one of the bar stools. 'I'll make you a cup of tea.'

'Are you making tea, Amanda?' Naya said. 'I'd love one, if that's all right.'

'Sure.'

'Me too,' Jess K said.

'Okay,' I said. 'Almond milk for you, right? Regular for you, Naya?'

They both nodded.

'Anyone else?' I asked.

'I'm having the first shower,' Lily announced, and waltzed away.

'You should have a shower too,' Parisa told Belinda. 'You might feel better if you clean up.'

Belinda nodded. As she left the room, escorted by Parisa and Jess D, I noticed that her lip had a big cut in it and one of her front teeth was badly chipped.

It was her week to clean her bathroom. I made a mental note to take that task over for her.

I busied myself making tea for everyone. Dylan was sitting on the bar stool I'd nudged her towards, slumped over the island, head resting on her forearms. There was dried mud in her hair.

'Hey,' I said, touching her hand gently and putting her mug down on a coaster next to her. 'Tea.'

She made a noise of acknowledgement, but didn't look up.

People slowly started to drift away. It was a nice night outside, so Naya and Jess K took their tea out there. Lily came back down a while later, clean and dressed in a dramatic satin robe (she had an apparently endless collection of them, I had no idea how she'd managed to pack them all) and went outside too. The women from the other bedroom headed upstairs, probably so they could fuss over Belinda, which left Dylan and I alone in the kitchen.

'Hey,' I said. 'Tell me what happened.'

She made a noise which could have been a moan, a groan, or the word 'no'.

'Your tea's getting cold.'

Another noise, much the same as the first one.

'Dylan, talk to me,' I said. 'Don't shut me out. Please.'

She looked up. Her eyes met my eyes.

My heart began to beat faster again.

But if she felt it too, she showed no sign of it. 'I'm sorry, Mandie,' she said. 'I know I'm being rude. It was just . . .'

Her voice trailed off. She buried her face in her hands and let out a muffled scream.

'Is there anything I can do?' I asked.

She took her hands away. 'No,' she said. 'I've just got to . . .'

'Sit with it?'

She smiled, just a little, and her shoulders relaxed, a little more. 'Yeah,' she said.

Then she reached up and patted her head experimentally. 'If you are in the market for something to do, you could help me get all this shit out of my hair.'

'Sure,' I said. De-mudding someone's hair was a very safe, very appropriate, very Mummy Mandie kind of task. 'Lily and Naya and Jess K are all outside. Our bathroom's free.'

We went upstairs. There was a little monitor room down the hall from our bedroom that always had at least one production assistant in it, and he was very nice to me when I tapped on the door and asked if I could borrow a stool. I put it in front of the sink in our bathroom and sat Dylan down on it, closing the door behind us.

'Ooof,' I said, studying her hair. 'What were you even doing today? Mud wrestling?'

She snorted. 'Not that far off.'

I started picking the larger clumps of mud out while she told me about the nightmare that had been their group date. They'd played a game called Love Jockey Hockey against the women from the Convent. It was basically hockey but using plastic flamingos instead of sticks and a heart-shaped puck instead of a normal one, played while wearing giant satiny jockey shirts.

'I know the producers are always telling us they're running on a skeleton crew missing half its bones, but surely they could have come up with something better than that,' I said, gently picking out another clump of mud. It broke apart into a spray of dirt. 'That sounds like the kind of idea you scribble down quickly in the middle of the night, and then in the morning you look at it and it says something like "cheese bus".'

'A cheese bus is a million times better an idea than Love Jockey Hockey,' Dylan said. 'I would totally ride the cheese bus.'

'Maybe that's something that Mandylan Project Management can work on when all this is over,' I said, smiling at her in the mirror.

She smiled back, but only weakly. 'Maybe.'

I loosened another clump with my fingernails. 'So what happened to Belinda?' I asked. 'Flamingo to the face from one of the Convent girls?'

'I think so,' Dylan said. 'Or it might have been the puck. It was a bit of a scrum. I didn't really see. But . . .'

She leaned forward, resting her elbows on the edge of the sink and pressing her head into her hands again. 'Fuuuuuuuck,' she groaned.

'Oh, Dylan,' I said helplessly.

She didn't take her hands away, but she met my eyes in the mirror, looking at me from between her fingers. 'I don't want to be a nurse anymore, Mandie,' she said. 'Not wanting to be

165

a nurse is the whole reason I'm here. So why does it feel like this when they don't let me help?'

'They wouldn't let you help Belinda?'

'No,' she said. 'Not really. I mean, I did some emergency first aid on the field, but that red-headed medic turned up pretty quickly and shoved me out of the way.'

'I'm sure he looked after her.'

'That's part of the problem, though!' she said. 'He didn't! If he did, she wouldn't be here! She needs to go to a dentist! But she can't. The only exemptions they have are for hardcore medical issues. They might be able to get her one, but they'd have to send a staff member with her, and then neither she nor the staff member could come back because of the bubble, and then the skeleton would be missing even *more* bones, and . . .'

She muffled another scream in her hands. 'I hate this place, Mandie,' she said. 'I hate how artificial it is. I hate the rules. I hate how little power I have. I hate how there isn't a single fucking thing I can do to change it.'

'You could leave,' I blurted out.

She looked up.

I was immediately horrified that I'd said it, that my impulses had got the better of me, but I couldn't stop talking. 'I know you like to be in control of things,' I whispered, reaching over and turning on the tap as hard it could go in case someone was listening. 'I know how hard it must be, having your control taken away. But you've still got control over that. You can leave.'

She didn't say anything.

'Sure, I know it's not the same as on a regular season. You can't just go home. You'd have to go to the Convent. But it would only be for a few weeks, and there wouldn't be any of the pressure down there that there is here.'

'Wouldn't you miss me?' she said, offering me another weak smile.

'Of course I would!' I said. 'But—'

I tried. I really tried not to say it.

'I could go with you,' I said.

She shook her head immediately. 'No.'

I tried to bite this back too, but Mandie 1.0 had the reins now, and she was not letting them go. 'I mean it,' I said. 'I like man-Dylan a lot, but you're more important to me. If you decided to go, I would go with you.'

'No, Mandie,' she said softly. 'Besides, I like him too.'

Those words cut much deeper than they had any right to.

I busied myself with her hair again. I didn't dare look at the Mandie in the mirror, terrified that what I was feeling would be clear in my expression.

'Though he was fucking useless today,' Dylan said, her tone more conversational. 'He disappeared at the first drop of blood.'

'Oh no!' I said, making myself laugh. 'Who would have thought such a big strong man would be scared of a little blood?'

'I know, right?' she said. 'I know he's got the whole sweet and gentle cinnamon roll thing going on, but come on, dude, really?'

'Tell me more about the game,' I said, resolutely ignoring the sick, hot feeling building in my stomach, forcing myself to sound conversational. 'Tell me about the Convent women. I take it he didn't bring any of them back, or they would have been breaking down the door demanding bathroom time by now.'

Later, when we were done, and I'd returned the stool to the monitor room down the hall, I came back into the bathroom to do my night-time skincare routine. There was dried mud and dirt all over my nice clean floor.

10

I barely slept that night. I stared up at the ceiling, only just visible in the darkness. I reached up to touch it a few times, to remind myself that it was still there, that I was still here, in my top bunk, not careening out of control.

Beneath me, Dylan's breath was slow and even. If she was sleeping okay, after the day she'd had, I shouldn't be worried. Hadn't our conversation ended up being totally normal and fine?

I couldn't believe I'd said that to her. How had I let the phrases *you could leave* and *I would go with you* come out of my mouth?

Everything anyone had ever said to me about not thinking ahead collapsed in on me all at once. I turned over onto my stomach, pressing my face into my pillow. I wanted to scream into my hands, the way Dylan had, but I wasn't brave enough. If I woke anyone up – if I woke *Dylan* up . . .

I'd basically propositioned her. She either hadn't noticed or was pretending she hadn't noticed so I could save face, but that was what had happened. It was the worst idea in the world but I'd done it anyway. Because I never, ever *thought*.

The first fight I'd ever had with Jac had been about this. *So when did you decide that you were going to run off with me?* she'd asked.

We'd been in bed, her head resting on my shoulder. I was playing with her hair, tracing the line where the longer part of her hair met the buzz of her undercut. *I don't know,* I'd replied. *I don't know that I did decide. It just happened.*

She sat up. *What do you mean, it just happened?*

You blew me away, I said, sitting up too. *You came up to me at that wedding and it was like my brain short-circuited.*

You were with Mark for, what, two years?

Two and a bit, yeah.

And you left him, she said, grabbing for her glasses on the bedside table and putting them on, *on impulse?*

For you, I insisted, reaching out to her.

She shoved my hand away. *You didn't even know me,* she snarled. *Is that really all it takes for you to fall for someone, Mandie? Someone to walk up to you and give you the tiniest bit of external validation? Then you're just 'no thoughts, head empty, it's you now, fuck everything else'?*

Tears welled up in the corners of my eyes, just like they had that day in bed with Jac.

She'd been right. She hadn't been kind, but she'd been right. Because here I was, doing exactly the same thing all over again. Dylan had told me I was cool and interesting and fun to talk to, and how had I reacted?

No thoughts. Head empty. It's you now. Fuck everything else.

Fuck the fact I'm not over my ex. Fuck the fact that we're both here dating the same man. Fuck the fact that we're friends and you're straight. It's you now.

You know who thinks like that? Jac had said. *Children.*

I am not a child! I'd protested.

Then why do I feel like I've lured you into my van with a lollipop? she'd snapped. *Seriously, Mandie, do you think at all about the consequences before you do things?*

I bit down on my pillow. *I am not a child,* I recited to myself. *I am not a child I am not a child I AM NOT A CHILD.*

There was a rustle of bedcovers. I froze, terrified it was Dylan.

But Dylan's breath was still slow and even beneath me. I turned my head to the side slightly, just in time to see Lily's satin robe trailing behind her, briefly illuminated as she slipped quietly out the door.

I was scratchy-eyed and sleep-deprived the next morning. I drank two cups of coffee at breakfast instead of one, but all it did was intensify the scratchiness, making me feel like the nerves behind my eyes were made of wire. Heather and Naya got into an argument over who had the right to the last of the frozen berries (one of the most precious commodities in the Villa), and I was snappish with both of them when I waded in to mediate. To put it mildly, I had not woken up as my best self.

And so of course, when we sat down on the couches to hear who had today's single date . . .

'Roses are red, I've been to Uganda,' Kumiko read, 'we can't go that far now, but come with me, Amanda?'

'What?' I said, blinking, as some of the other women politely applauded. 'Really?'

'I can't believe this,' Heather said, sinking back into the couch. 'I've had one date with him. One! A group date! And it was that sucky obstacle course date!'

'Just be grateful you didn't have to play Love Jockey Hockey,' Naya said.

'Don't tell me what I should or should not be grateful for,' Heather said. 'I don't appreciate being told how to feel.'

'I'm not telling you how to feel!'

'Yes, you are!'

'Amanda, you'd better hurry,' Kumiko said, turning the card over. 'This says he'll be here to pick you up in fifteen minutes.'

'Oh God,' I said, jumping up. 'Okay.'

'Seriously,' Heather groaned. 'What's Amanda got that I don't? We're basically identical! Why her and not me?'

'She's a nice person?' Dylan said.

'If you like her so much, why don't you marry her?'

A sudden wave of nausea rose up in my belly.

'What are you, five?' Dylan snapped back. 'Come on, Mandie. I'll help you get ready.'

Given my mental state, this didn't seem like a particularly good idea, but there was no easy way to say no.

Dylan and I were both quiet as we went through my suitcase together, trying to pick out a good date outfit. 'I wish he'd told me what we were doing,' I said at last. 'I don't know what I'm supposed to dress for.'

'Men,' she said. 'They never think of these things. Try this one?'

She handed me a black T-shirt with a scoop neck. I peeled off the one I was wearing and put it on. 'Okay?' I asked.

'Hmmm?'

She was staring at me with a kind of stricken look on her face, like I had a massive food stain on my shirt. I looked down.

'Not that one,' she said decisively. 'That one's all wrong.'

She grabbed another T-shirt from my suitcase and shoved it at me, a frilly lemon yellow one with cap sleeves. 'Give this one a go.'

I took the black shirt off and pulled the lemon one on. 'Better?' I asked.

'Better,' she said, tugging at one of the sleeves so it sat straight. 'You look adorable. Cute as a button.'

Adorable. A word for puppies and small children.

'Here's hoping man-Dylan likes his women adorable,' I choked out.

'Who wouldn't?' she said, tapping my nose with her finger. 'But be careful today, all right?'

I was still reeling from the nose tap, so it took me a second to realise what she'd said. 'What do you mean, be careful?'

'He's an easy man to like,' she said. 'Just . . . try not to get carried away, okay?'

Is that really all it takes for you to fall for someone, Mandie? Someone to walk up to you and give you the tiniest bit of external validation?

'I won't,' I said tightly, around the giant lump that had appeared in my throat.

'Good,' she said, straightening my other sleeve, her fingers deft and gentle when they brushed my skin. 'The last thing I want for you is to walk right out of one heartbreak and into another.'

I didn't say anything.

'Oh, shit, babe, that came out wrong,' she said. 'It's not that I think he won't like you. It's just—'

'That he'll probably like someone else better?'

She hesitated.

'Like you?'

'No, no, no!' she said. 'That's not what I'm saying at all!'

'It's okay,' I said, looking for an elastic to tie my hair back, more as an excuse to turn away from her than anything else. 'I know you're the frontrunner, Dylan. I know he likes you. And you like him.'

'Mandie—'

'I forgot to tell you,' I said, scraping my hair back into a ponytail, totally unable to make Mandie 1.0 shut up. 'At the last Last Chance Party? Lily told me I was a wifey. Can you believe that? Of course, it's probably not true, given she said Marija was a wifey too and she got cut, like, five minutes later, but even if it is, you don't need to worry. I like him, sure, but if this ends up with you and him together, I wouldn't dream of getting in the way.'

'Mandie, can you listen to me? Please?'

I stilled.

'This isn't about me and him,' she said. 'It's not about me. It's not even really about him. It's just – you.'

'What about me?'

She swallowed. 'I'm sure you'll have a lovely date today,' she said. 'You're lovely. He's lovely. Of course it'll be lovely. But . . . keep your guard up. Don't forget there are still ten women in the game.'

'Trust me,' I said. 'There's no way I could forget that.'

'I'm not trying to be a bitch and undermine you or anything,' she said. 'I just don't want you to get hurt.'

She tucked a wayward piece of hair into my ponytail. 'You're the last person I would ever want to get hurt,' she said.

'I doubt it'll get that far,' I croaked, using every ounce of my energy to sound reasonably normal while her hands were *touching my hair.* 'He probably won't like me that much anyway.'

'Shut up, of course he will,' she said. 'You're Jane Bennet, babe. You're hot and sweet and generous.'

'Stop.'

'Absolutely not. You're amazing. You're the most organised person on the planet. You remember exactly what kind of milk everyone takes in their tea, even if it's a kind of milk I haven't heard of. You let me complain and cry on your shoulder all the time. You—'

'No, really, please, stop!'

175

I wiped furiously at the tears starting to fall down my cheeks. 'I need you to stop,' I said.

'Oh God, Mandie, I'm sorry,' she said. 'I didn't mean to make you cry.'

'I know I'm a crybaby,' I said. 'I'm sorry.'

She bit her lip, clearly biting back words with it.

'I know you're just trying to be kind,' I said. 'But I can't hear this right now, Dylan. Please.'

She looked at me for a second that felt like an hour.

The air in the room felt all hot and thick. It was hard to breathe, let alone speak.

'Of course, babe,' she said. 'Whatever you need.'

It took me longer than the fifteen minutes of getting ready time I'd been allotted to calm myself down, fix my mascara, and deliver several long lectures to myself about how I wasn't doing this anymore, I wasn't going to be this person anymore, and I *was* going to get myself under control.

This meant we started out the date with Murray annoyed at me. He only got more annoyed when it took us eight takes to shoot my entrance into the date (i.e. me walking down the stairs to Romeo-Dylan). 'Go back, do it again!' he barked. 'Slower, Amanda! This is your girl-coming-down-the-stairs-after-a-makeover-in-a-teen-movie moment!'

'Sorry about him,' Romeo-Dylan murmured to me, when I had finally descended the stairs to Murray's satisfaction. 'He's definitely not getting enough sleep.'

'It's okay,' I whispered back. 'It was my fault.'

'Moving outside!' the director called.

We turned to walk out the front door, Romeo-Dylan's hand feathering over the small of my back.

'Not like that!' Murray said. 'She's not your elderly aunt! Hold her hand!'

Sorry, Romeo-Dylan mouthed to me again, as he complied.

His fingers felt strange, twined through mine. His hands were warm. His palms weren't sweaty. He didn't hold too tightly or too loosely. As far as hand-holds went, it was perfectly pleasant.

But it wasn't like sitting under that pink and silver sunrise sky. Her taking my hand. Our eyes meeting. Her licking her lips, and—

Then Romeo-Dylan and I walked outside, and one of the greatest things that had ever happened to me took place.

Maybe I really could make this work with Romeo-Dylan. Maybe he and I could be perfectly happy together after all, if it meant I could keep *her.*

'Oh my God,' I breathed.

'I thought you might appreciate it,' Romeo-Dylan said.

'Can I touch her?'

'Of course.'

I let go of his hand and walked towards her. God, she was gorgeous. She might be the most gorgeous thing I'd ever seen. Was this what it felt like to have a religious experience?

'I don't get it,' Heather said. The other women had followed us outside, I registered dimly. 'It's just a car.'

'Shut your mouth,' I said. 'This isn't just a car. This is a Lamborghini Aventador SVJ Roadster.'

I ran my hands reverently over the hood. 'Oh my God, I'm shaking,' I said. 'I don't want to get smudges on her.'

'I'm sure we can get it washed,' Romeo-Dylan said, chuckling.

We would do no such thing. If she got smudged, I would look after her myself, showing her the care and reverence she deserved.

'Can you start the engine?' I asked.

'I thought you might like to drive.'

'Oh, buddy, I am one hundred per cent driving,' I said. 'But will you start her up for me? I want to listen to her.'

'She is *so weird*,' I heard one of the other women – Belinda, maybe? – say as Romeo-Dylan obediently hopped into the driver's seat.

I couldn't even begin to care. 'Ready?' Romeo-Dylan asked.

I walked around the car and knelt down next to one of the back wheels. 'Absolutely.'

'What are you doing?'

'Lambos are mid-engine cars,' I said. 'She's built to go fast. If you want a car to go fast, you don't put the engine in the front. You put it in the middle behind the driver. Balance her out. Otherwise you get all these issues with braking and torque and understeering, and—'

Romeo-Dylan looked like he might be about to fall asleep.

'– and you can't possibly want to know any of this,' I said. 'Just start her up.'

'Here we go,' he said, turning back to the steering wheel.

'Sing for me, baby,' I said, stroking the car. 'Go on, girl.'

He turned her on. She purred for me, and for a moment, just a moment, I understood why the guys at work gravitated so hard towards those calendars of beautiful girls draped over the hoods of beautiful cars. She was a beautiful girl, and if I'd been alone with her, I – well, I don't want to say I would have come on the spot, but I would have been significantly turned on. *Significantly.*

But I wasn't alone. So, reluctantly, I peeled my ear away from her beautiful body. 'You have made my day,' I told Romeo-Dylan. 'My month. My year, even. Possibly my life.'

'I'm glad,' he said, the corners of his eyes creasing again as he smiled at me. 'I'm a bit worried about the rest of the date, though. Surely it can only be a disappointment from here.'

It wasn't a disappointment. It was perfectly nice.

Strike that. It was better than perfectly nice. I got to drive a *fucking Lambo*. 'You're so beautiful,' I crooned to her, stroking her dash. 'You're such a beautiful girl.'

Romeo-Dylan made a noise in the back of his throat that I thought was a laugh.

'You're very beautiful too,' I said, patting him on the knee and then putting both hands back on the steering wheel.

His response was *definitely* a laugh.

We were under strict orders from Murray that we were not, under any circumstances, allowed to get out of the car until we reached our final destination. 'The second you put a toe on the ground outside the property, the bubble is broken and the whole show is fucked,' he growled at us. 'You see a crash on the side of the road? Someone else's problem. You see a granny who needs help crossing the street? Fuck Granny. You see a leprechaun promising to show you the pot of gold at the end of the rainbow? You run him over.'

'Murray, we've got it,' Romeo-Dylan said. 'We won't get out of the car.'

'I'm trusting you two,' he warned. 'The whole fate of this season is in your hands. So if you fuck it up—'

'We're not going to fuck it up!' Romeo-Dylan said. 'Are you feeling all right, Murray? You're even snappier than usual.'

Privately, I didn't think the problem was going to be stopping the car. It was going to be resisting the urge to put my foot to the floor to see how fast she could really go. I knew for a fact she could go from zero to a hundred in less than three seconds, and zero to two hundred in less than nine. I was *itching* to see what she could do.

Alas, absolutely obliterating the speed limit while being filmed for one of the most popular TV shows in the country probably wasn't the best idea. Not if I wanted to keep my licence, anyway.

If it weren't for the lipstick cameras mounted in the car, though, it might have been one of the safest possible times for me to push the beautiful girl to her limits. The long straight road we were driving down was deserted.

We passed through a small town. It was basically deserted too. Not, like, zombie-movie deserted – there were a few people walking up and down the street, some in activewear, some with dogs. A couple were carrying grocery bags, and as we drove past the supermarket, I saw that it was open. So was the pharmacy next to it.

Nothing else was, though. Shops, cafes, bars, all the usual places people went – all closed.

'It's sad, isn't it?' Romeo-Dylan said softly. 'I understand why the lockdown's necessary, obviously, but it's still hard to see everything like this.'

'Yeah,' I replied.

'That said, I don't think my mother's ever been this social in her life,' he said. 'She's pretty outgoing at the best of times, but now with Zoom and Houseparty and everything, she can catch up with the whole world. I saw her diary once and nearly had a panic attack.'

'My mum's the same,' I said. 'She's got six regular Zoom chats on the go. All different, too. There's one for bridge, one for sewing, one for bowls—'

'How do you do Zoom bowls?'

'As far as I can tell, they mostly just complain about the fact no one's mowing the bowling greens.'

He chuckled. 'Turn here,' he said, pointing to a side street.

Romeo-Dylan directed me to the other entrance to the Juliet property, down at the bottom of the hill, and we eventually pulled up near the edge of the lake. 'I'm sorry the driving part of our date isn't longer,' he said, as we got out. 'If they weren't so uptight about the filming schedule I would totally try and get you more time with the car.'

'That's all right,' I said, even though I could gladly have driven around for at least a thousand more hours. 'I'm just honoured I got to meet her.'

I leaned down and pressed a kiss to the driver's side door as Murray and the crew pulled up behind us. 'You be good for Mama,' I whispered to her. 'I'll see you again someday, okay?'

Romeo-Dylan was clearly trying not to laugh as I straightened up. 'You'll probably hate me for this,' he said, 'but when they asked me what kind of car I wanted for this date, all I said was that I wanted a red one.'

'Look, that's totally valid,' I said. 'Colour is important. I too am a basic bitch who likes a red car.'

'You know,' he said thoughtfully, 'I've been called a lot of things, but I don't think anyone's ever called me a basic bitch before. Thank you for the new experience.'

'You're welcome,' I said. 'Welcome to basic bitch club.'

'ITMs!' Murray barked. 'Dylan, you first. Amanda, you wait over there.'

To my chagrin, one of the crew drove my beautiful baby away, so all I could do while I was waiting for my ITM was wander about near the edge of the lake.

It was a beautiful view. If I looked up the hill, I could see the Juliet Villa, bright and white in the sun, the hedge maze a dark smear of greens and purples running away from it. Across the lake, I could see the bobbing boat that was the makeshift Romeo Residence. Romeo-Dylan had taken Jess D sailing on it for her date, and while she hadn't gone into his actual private quarters, he'd told her that's where he was living.

Beyond the boat was the Convent. I could see it better down here than from the top of the hill. It was two storeys tall, but small, with a wraparound verandah. I could just make out two figures sitting on the front lawn, although I was too far away to tell who they were.

The Villa still felt packed, even though a) it was huge and b) we were losing women all the time. They must be crammed into the Convent like sardines.

You could leave. I would go with you.

The two of us, crammed into that tiny house together. Pressed against each other, skin to skin. Her hand, tangled in my hair. My fingertips, trailing over the beautiful lines of her body.

Shhhh, I'd whisper into her mouth. *You have to keep very quiet, or someone will hear us.*

Okay, she'd breathe back.

I'd take it as a challenge. Her breath would catch. She'd lick her lips and I'd lean in, lick them for her, and her breath would catch again, and—

'Amanda!' Murray yelled. 'Look alive!'

I jumped as Romeo-Dylan touched me on the shoulder. 'Tag,' he said. 'You're it.'

I hoped like hell that if the camera had picked up any of that fantasy on my face, they'd assume I was still thinking about the car.

The first part of my ITM was easy. Murray asked me a bunch of questions about what it had felt like to see the car, touch the car, drive the car. If there was one thing I was comfortable monologuing about at great length and in extremely full sentences, it was incredible and exquisite and magnificent and possibly magical sportscars. 'God, she's a beautiful girl,' I enthused. 'I've never seen such a beautiful girl in all my life.'

'You've used that phrase a few times,' Murray said, leaning back in his chair. 'Beautiful girl.'

My heart thudded so hard to the ground I was amazed it didn't come rolling out of the leg of my jeans.

Why did I never learn? Why, why, *why* did I never think before I said anything?

'That's just how we talk about cars in the industry,' I said. 'I bet Dylan JM talks the same way about boats. Don't you call boats "she"?'

Murray raised his eyebrows at me.

I glared back at him.

He didn't waver. He had dark circles under his eyes the size of small planets.

'I'm not doing it,' I said. 'I'm not saying it. I know what you want, but – no.'

'Ladies,' he said to the cameraperson and the soundie, without breaking eye contact with me, 'Amanda and I are going to sidebar for a minute. Take five.'

He led me a little way away, towards a small grove of trees. 'So—' he started.

'I'm not doing it, Murray,' I said. 'I know you know I'm bi. I'm not an idiot. But I'm not doing it. I'm not coming out on national television.'

'Fair enough.'

I blinked. 'What?'

'If you don't want to come out, I'm not going to make you do it.'

'But you'll have someone do it for me, right?' I snapped, folding my arms. 'How long is it going to be before your little plant stands up and announces, "Guess what, Amanda likes girls!" to everyone?'

'What do you mean, my little plant?'

'I know about Lily.'

'What do you think you know about Lily?'

'I know – I know –'

I stopped. *I know she sneaks around at night in dramatic dressing gowns* was nothing. Neither was *she called me a wifey* or *I saw her set up a cheeseboard for you one time*.

'Lily's not a plant,' Murray said. 'Trust me, if I was going to plant someone, I'd pick someone I could actually control.'

I hugged my arms tighter around myself.

'I'm not going to out you, I'm not going to make someone else out you, and I'm not going to make you out yourself,' Murray said. 'I know what's happened to other Juliets who've come out on the show before. I'm not going to make you do anything you're not comfortable with.'

'Okay,' I said, unsteadily. 'Good. But then . . . what was all that about? The beautiful girl stuff?'

'I'm just throwing you some balls,' he said. 'It's up to you which ones you catch.'

I had no idea what he meant.

'But I need you to catch some of them,' he said. 'You're not giving me what I need at the moment, Amanda. Can you do a couple of things for me?'

'I don't know, can I?' I said. 'What are they?'

185

'I need you to give me a story,' he said. 'If it's not going to be the "I also date women, are you cool with that?" story, that's fine, but I need something. You started off really strong with the whole "I'm broken-hearted, I need to get over my ex, I'm here to find love again" angle, but it's completely fallen away since the first night.'

It seemed impossible that he could think that. Couldn't he tell how much Jac still whispered in my ear?

'Remember, this is reality TV, not reality,' Murray went on. 'Fuck the truth. This is about stories. You want to do well, you've got to give me the ingredients to turn you into a character.'

'How do I do that?'

'You're in the perfect position to do that!' Murray said, an edge of exasperation coming into his voice. 'You've got the whole intimacy portion of your date ahead! Tell him your sob story! Hell, tell him any story, just make it *a* story.'

'Okay,' I said slowly. 'I can do that.'

'Second thing,' he said. 'Stop making heart eyes at Dylan.'

'Isn't the whole point of this show that I make heart eyes at Dylan?' I said. 'I'm on a date with him. A date where he let me drive one of the most beautiful cars in the world! How do you expect me *not* to make heart eyes at him?'

'Amanda,' Murray said, 'you know perfectly well which Dylan I mean.'

'So tell me why you became a mechanic,' Romeo-Dylan said to me, as we sat on artfully arranged cushions on the deck of his boat, a cheeseboard and a bottle of champagne in front of us. 'How did you get interested in cars?'

'It was because of my dad,' I said. 'He was a big car guy. He loved them. When I was a little kid, we lived in this house with three bedrooms. One was my parents' room, one was my room, and one was Dad's home office, and it was absolutely *plastered* with pictures of cars. He also liked red ones, you'll be pleased to know.'

Romeo-Dylan smiled and squeezed my hand. It didn't feel quite right, his fingers laced through mine, but it gave me something to hold onto.

'When I was about seven, he brought home this old broken down 1968 Pontiac Firebird,' I said. 'It was a wreck of a thing, really. It didn't run, it was covered in rust, it was missing probably three quarters of the parts it needed . . . it was a mess. My mum was furious. I remember her yelling at my dad, being all, "Why did you buy this piece of crap? Do you think money grows on trees?" and he was like, "Honey, this is one of the finest muscle cars ever made, and when I fix her up, she'll be worth more than money."'

The boom mic above us dipped lower. I tried to ignore it, focusing on the space between Romeo-Dylan's eyebrows.

He was a handsome man. I liked him so much.

His eyebrows weren't a patch on hers, though.

'So he got to work, fixing her up, and I helped,' I said. 'At the beginning I'm sure I got in the way more than being any actual help, but after a while, I turned into a proper little grease monkey. "Give me those tiny steady hands, Mandie," he'd say to me. He had arthritis in a few of his fingers, so I used to help him with all the jobs he couldn't do.'

'Did you finish the car?' Romeo-Dylan asked, squeezing my hand again.

'I did,' I replied. 'He didn't. He died when I was twelve. Cancer.'

'I'm sorry,' he said. 'I don't know what I would do if I lost either of my parents.'

'It's awful,' I said. 'You get used to it in time, to having this hole in your life where they used to be. But it never goes away.'

'I can't even imagine.'

'My mum never remarried. Never really dated again. When Dad died, that was the end of her love life.'

I took a deep breath, then a sip of my champagne. Then another deep breath.

None of this was a lie, not even a little. But Murray and I had decided to tell the story this way, to make this leap, so even though it was the truth, I felt dishonest.

'That's not what I want, though,' I said.

'What do you mean?' Romeo-Dylan asked.

I chanced a look into those kind eyes. 'Before I came here,' I said. 'Not that long before, actually, I lost a partner. Someone that I loved.'

'Oh God, I'm so sorry. What happened?'

'Whoa whoa whoa, not like that!' I said. 'Nothing tragic, nothing dramatic. We just broke up, that's all. But I took it hard. I'm still taking it hard, to be honest. It hurt me really badly.'

'Break-ups suck.'

'But I don't want to hurt forever,' I said, pitching my voice low, soft. 'I don't want there to be a hole in my life. I want to find love again. So . . . here I am.'

'Here you are,' he echoed.

He was still looking into my eyes. His fingers twitched under mine.

Should I lean in? Go for the kiss? Or should I wait for him to do it?

I'd just about decided to go for it when Romeo-Dylan turned away abruptly. 'Amanda, I've had the most wonderful day with you,' he said, fiddling with something beside him. 'It was so much fun, seeing you absolutely delighted by the car. Then tonight, when you opened up to me, that really meant a lot. You were really vulnerable with me. Really showed me who you are. I'm really grateful you did that.'

'I'm *really* grateful you listened.'

If he'd clocked my gentle ribbing, he didn't acknowledge it. 'Which is why I'd like you to stay,' he said, producing a necklace. 'Amanda, I want to know if your heart is the other half of mine. Will you take this necklace and commit to finding out with me?'

'I'd love to,' I said. 'Thank you.'

I turned and moved my ponytail aside. He fastened the necklace. It took him two tries this time. His fingers were a little shaky.

Those same fingers were shaky on my cheek when I turned back around. Out of the corner of my eye, I could

189

see Murray. He was holding his phone up, screen sideways, the words *KISS HER* emblazoned across it.

Romeo-Dylan's Adam's apple bobbed as he swallowed. He stroked a strand of my hair back, then rested his hand gently against my jaw, barely touching me, thumb and middle finger tapping together twice behind my ear before he stilled them. *Can I?* he asked me with his eyes.

I nodded, ever so slightly.

The kiss was . . . nice.

It had been so long since I'd kissed anyone other than Jac. It was good to know that she hadn't ruined me for all other people. It felt pleasant, Romeo-Dylan's lips on mine. I enjoyed the moments when we broke apart but were still close together, breathing each other's air, before our lips brushed together again.

It reminded me of kissing my ex-boyfriend Mark. It didn't blow my mind. It didn't rock my world.

But it was nice. You could do a lot worse than nice.

There was no beautiful Lambo to take me home. After we did another round of ITMs, Murray drove me back up to the Villa on a golf cart. 'Good job,' he told me gruffly. 'It's good to know one of you can actually take instruction.'

I wondered if he was talking about Lily. It didn't seem wise to ask, though.

Production had made sure all the other women were sitting on the couches in the living room when I came back in. I took Murray's *tell-a-story* directive to heart and did my best to regale them with all the events of the day (including, I'll be honest, probably a lot more details about the car than anyone gave a shit about).

'Did you kiss?' Naya asked.

I bit my lip and didn't say anything.

'They totally kissed!' Naya said. 'Look at her turning red!'

I looked at the floor, mostly so I didn't accidentally look at Dylan and give the game away. Murray might have promised not to out me, but if I looked at her, surely someone would see *it was the wrong Dylan* written all over my face.

Naya followed me into the bathroom when I went in to take off my make-up – 'Tell me more about the kiss,' she demanded – so Dylan and I didn't do our usual night-time ritual together. 'Hey,' I said to her, as I came out of the bathroom, and 'Hey,' she said as she went in, but that was about all the interaction we had.

I was grateful. There might not be cameras in the bedrooms or the bathrooms, but if my heart eyes were so obvious that Murray had clocked them, other people would notice soon too – if they hadn't already.

How on earth was I going to get that under control? Not talking to Dylan was not a sustainable solution. Even if I was willing to just cut her out of my life – which I was not! not a chance! – there was no way I could do that in an environment like the Juliet Villa.

But however I did it, I had to get it under control. The last couple of days had been such a dangerous backslide. I'd let Jac's voice in. I'd let a whole bunch of negative self-talk in. I'd let my friendship with Dylan get all strange and weird, because I'd let all those dangerous fantasies in, those tantalising thoughts that maybe, just maybe, she might feel a little of what I felt about her.

Here was what I was not doing anymore:

1) Any of that.

Here was what I was going to do instead:

1) Keep it together.
2) Make good choices.
3) Restrain my impulses.
4) Stay the fuck out of anything that even *looked* like quicksand.

Maybe also *5) Kiss Romeo-Dylan again.* I probably wasn't going to end up with him, but he was nice. Kissing him had been nice. Kissing him again could absolutely be a distraction from everything – else. If I accidentally made heart eyes at Dylan, I could just pretend I was actually thinking about Romeo-Dylan, and claim she just happened to be standing in my line of sight.

Ugh. Murray would be fooled by that for exactly no seconds.

I climbed into my bunk and curled up under the dark green bedspread. I was exhausted, physically and emotionally. The heart-eyes thing would have to be a tomorrow problem. I'd work out how to deal with it then.

There was something hard under my pillow.

I reached under and pulled out a stack of cards, held

together by a rubber band. *For when you need a little reminder that you're amazing,* a note on the top read. *D xxx*

I took the rubber band off and set the note aside. *I am strong,* the first card read.

I flipped through the stack. *I am kind. I am confident. I am clever. I am brave. I am beautiful. I am capable. I am Queen Shit.*

Oh God.

I turned to the last card. *I am enough.*

Dylan came out of the bathroom. 'You like them?' she asked, bending down to get something out of her suitcase. 'They're affirmation flashcards. I know hearing a bunch of compliments all at once like I dropped on you this morning was overwhelming, so I thought this might help. You can sort of drip-feed them to yourself when you need a little pick-me-up. As many or as few as you want.'

'Dylan, they're – they're –'

They weren't nice, that was for sure. No word had been invented that could adequately describe how I felt.

'Thank you,' I said at last. 'I love them.'

'They're all true,' she said. 'This is who you really are, Mandie. Don't let anyone ever convince you otherwise.'

I just nodded. If I tried to speak, I might just vomit up my heart, right at her feet.

'Don't cry again!' she said hurriedly. 'I felt terrible about this morning.'

'I'm sorry,' I said. 'I cry too easily. I know that.'

'Hey,' she said. 'Cards. This is your one warning. Every time I hear you talking shit about yourself from now on, you'll have to drop and give me twenty affirmations.'

I laughed weakly.

'I really am sorry about this morning,' she said. 'Nothing came out the way I wanted it to. I put my foot so far in my mouth I practically swallowed my leg.'

'S'okay.'

'Did you have a good time on your date?'

'Yeah,' I managed. 'Yeah, it was . . . nice.'

'Good,' she said. 'Anyway, good night, babe.'

'Night,' I said.

I flopped back against my pillow, nearly hitting my head against the roof in the process, clutching the cards to my chest.

A list. She had written a list of nice things about me and put them on cards, so I didn't forget a single one of them. A *list*.

Don't make heart eyes at Dylan.

I was in so much trouble.

11

'Welcome to today's group date!' Z said. 'All nine of you have been invited along to spend some time with Dylan today.'

We all cheered and applauded. It was our third week on the show, and we were well-rehearsed by now. The producers hardly ever had to make us reshoot our reactions.

(Well, except for during the last Necklace Ceremony, where Jess K had been eliminated. She'd been one of Lily's few friends – was 'friends' the right word? 'allies'? 'hench-women'? 'people she wasn't actively trying to make cry'? – in the Villa, and Lily had pitched an absolute fit about it. Murray had made us shoot that bit four times, for the opposite reason we usually had to reshoot things: Lily's reaction was way too big, rather than way too small.

'You'd think a plant wouldn't fight with him so much,' Dylan had said as we took our make-up off in the bathroom together. 'He says she isn't a plant,' I'd replied, and she'd snorted and said, 'Yeah, sure, Murray, cool story bro.' I'd felt stupid for believing him, and she'd noticed and said, 'Babe, thinking the best of people isn't a character flaw; go look at your affirmation cards,' and I'd had to bend over and pretend I was having trouble tying my hair into a topknot so I could take a few deep breaths.)

'Today, you will be divided into three groups,' Z said. 'You're here to win Dylan's heart, so you're going to build a love machine and throw your hearts right at him.'

Romeo-Dylan looked appropriately embarrassed by the phrase 'love machine'. I focused on him, so I wouldn't look at my Dylan. I was trying so, so hard not to make heart eyes at her. I'd done a pretty good job over the past few days – Mandie 2.0 was back in control – but the easiest way to avoid it was still just . . . not to look at her.

I knew what her expression would be, though ('Love machines? *Love machines?*'). Biting back my laugh took a lot of effort.

Z explained the rest of the rules. Each team would have twenty plushie hearts, and once they built their love machine, they had to use it to fire them into a pool. 'You'll be divided into groups of three,' Z said. 'Group one will be Parisa, Jess D and Kumiko. Group two will be Naya, Heather and Belinda. That leaves group three: Amanda, Dylan G and Lily Fireball.'

My eyes went straight to Murray, who was standing a few metres away, out of camera shot. *Hey Murray, here's an idea*, a braver version of me would say to him. *If you don't want me to make heart eyes at Dylan, how about you don't put her right in front of me?*

But he wasn't looking at me. His gaze, like the cameras, was tracking Lily Fireball as she strode over towards us. 'You better not get in my way, bitches,' she said, flicking her hair over her shoulder. 'Or there'll be hell to pay.'

'Did you read some kind of book on how to be a cartoon villain?' Dylan said. 'Watch too many Disney movies and imprint on the wrong characters? What is this whole persona you're doing?'

'Your worst nightmare,' Lily said, smiling widely and batting her eyelashes.

Luckily for Dylan's blood pressure, Z started talking again. 'The winning team will get a little after-party with our Romeo, and then one lucky lady will get some additional one-on-one-time. You all know that time with the Romeo is the most important thing you can have if you want to keep developing those connections, particularly as we approach the halfway mark of the season, so, Juliets: make today count!'

A cameraman trailed behind Lily, Dylan and I as we traipsed over to the pieces of our love machine. It was marked by a sign with a big red number 3 on it, planted slightly crookedly in the ground.

There was a set of instructions on top of the machine components. I picked them up and scanned through them quickly. 'All right,' I said. 'This doesn't look super complicated. If we just lay out the pieces by number, then—'

'Get out of the way,' Lily said, ripping the instructions out of my hands and giving me a paper cut. 'I'm going to take charge on this project. You two will only slow me down.'

'Um, Amanda's a mechanic,' Dylan said, snatching the instructions back. 'If anyone's going to take the lead, it's going to be her.'

Lily turned her terrifying gaze on me. 'Are you a mechanic for love machines?'

'No,' I said, sucking my cut finger, only barely resisting the urge to back away. 'Obviously not.'

'Then give me that!' Lily tore the instructions out of Dylan's hand. 'I'm amazing at IKEA flatpack furniture. I'm going to nail this.'

'IKEA?' Dylan said. 'Really? You think building a couple of Billy bookshelves stands up against her being an actual mechanic?'

'I don't think about her much at all,' Lily said coolly.

'Hey, both of you, how about we calm down?' I said, suddenly understanding why I'd been paired with them. They were the drama. I was the buffer. 'This isn't helping. We're never going to win the extra time if we don't get this done.'

'I bet boy-Dylan thinks about her, though,' Lily said, ignoring me. 'Thinks about that big smooch he planted on her the other day.'

'Lily, please,' I said.

'*Lily, please,*' she said, in a high-pitched girly voice. 'Can't we just all be *friends*? Can't we just all be *nice* and *kind* and *sweet*?'

Dylan stepped in front of me. 'Don't,' she said to Lily, an edge in her voice.

'And here comes our hero,' Lily said, switching into

a David Attenborough voice. 'Rushing in to save the damsel in distress.'

'How hard did you practise being like this before we got here?' Dylan demanded. 'How much time did you spend looking in the mirror and thinking of bitchy things to say? Did you have a training regime? A coach?'

I gave up. If Murray had wanted an actual buffer, he should have picked someone with more authority and the ability to take control of a situation.

At least Lily making fun of me for being childish had merely stung, instead of taking all the wind out of my sails. Maybe that was growth, or maybe I'd learned not to listen to anything she said. Either was a net positive.

I knelt down next to the pieces of the love machine. There was no chance of reclaiming the instructions from Lily, but I'd spent most of my professional life fiddling around with machinery. I could figure this out.

At least Dylan and Lily weren't the only ones fighting. Group two was around the corner from us, but I could hear Naya and Heather screaming at each other from here.

I sorted quickly through the pieces and started assembling. I made a couple of wrong turns at first, because I expected the machine design to be sensible, but once I realised that a) it was just a catapult, and b) it was pointlessly complicated, it started going a lot quicker.

'How are we going, ladies?' Romeo-Dylan asked, walking up to us. 'Or should I say – lady? You seem to be the only one working on this, Amanda.'

'Well, machines are my thing,' I said. 'Do I have to use all the pieces we've got here? Or am I allowed to improvise?'

'I don't know,' he said, looking genuinely surprised. 'Good question.'

'Please let me optimise this,' I said, putting my hands together like I was praying to him and his Greek god biceps. 'You're the Romeo. You make the rules. Please. Let me fix this.'

'Who am I to stand between an artist and her art?' he said. 'Optimise away.'

'What are you *doing*?' Lily demanded, suddenly appearing behind me. 'You're doing it all wrong, stupid! Those pieces are supposed to go in first, and you haven't even touched them!'

'Lily—' Romeo-Dylan started.

'Don't you call her stupid—' my Dylan was saying.

But none of it mattered, because Lily had already kicked the machine apart.

I can probably count the number of times I've been really, truly, genuinely angry in my life on one hand. Annoyed, sure. I get annoyed all the time. But actually, properly *furious*?

'Lily,' I said, standing up slowly, 'walk away. Now.'

That infuriating smirk spread across her face. 'Or what?'

'Else.'

'Oh no,' she said. 'I'm so scared.'

My fingers curled into fists. I wanted to punch that smirk right off her face.

There were two hands on my back. Both Dylans. 'Don't cry, Amanda,' Romeo-Dylan said. 'It's just a silly game.'

'I'm fine,' I said, blinking furiously, wishing like hell

that I didn't cry when I was angry. Stupid traitorous body. 'Or I will be, once someone gets Lily out of my sight.'

'It's Lily Fireball.'

'Shut up!' Dylan and I exclaimed at the same time.

'Tell you what,' Romeo-Dylan said. 'Lily, how about you come with me for a while, and we'll leave Amanda and Dyl to finish this off.'

'Absolutely not,' Dylan said. 'She's not getting alone time with you. She doesn't deserve that.'

I recognised the look on Romeo-Dylan's face. I wore it myself on the regular. I call it 'oh no, there is no way here to make everyone happy'.

(I never said it was a *catchy* name. I'm a mechanic, not a poet.)

But even my niceness had its limits. 'I don't care what you do with her,' I said, kneeling back down in front of the wreckage of the love machine. 'Just get her the fuck away from me.'

I didn't realise until much later that they didn't make me reshoot for swearing.

'What the hell?' Dylan demanded, when Z announced that Parisa, Kumiko and Jess D had won the challenge. 'They only got eight hearts into the pool. We got seventeen! That's more than twice as many!'

My rage had subsided enough for me to feel some pride at that. The love machine I'd built was clearly the best one of the bunch. By far.

'Ah, but we never said that the team who got the most hearts into the pool would be the winners,' Z said. 'Little did you know that while you were building your love machines, one of our Romeo Dylan's best friends was watching your every move.'

'Who?' Kumiko asked.

'How?' Naya asked.

'Dylan JM's friend was the one responsible for picking the winning team today,' Z went on, ignoring them. 'But because they're his friend, they were also looking for red flags – for women who might not be right for our Romeo. And I'm sorry to say, they spotted one.'

That could mean literally anyone on my team. My whole body went cold for a moment.

It wasn't any of us, though. 'Heather, your heart isn't the other half of mine,' Romeo-Dylan said. 'We're on very different pages, and I don't think it's right that you continue on this journey.'

'What?' Heather exclaimed. 'This is bullshit. *Bull. Shit!*'

'I wonder what she did,' I said a while later, as the five of us who hadn't won trudged back up the hill to the Villa.

'Hmmm?' Dylan said.

'Heather,' I said. 'I wonder what she did.'

'Oh,' Dylan said. 'Probably something racist, knowing her.'

'What?'

The answer came from an unexpected source. 'She was super racist,' Lily said.

'Thank you!' Naya said. 'I thought I was going crazy for a while there. I'm so glad it wasn't just me.'

'I was making toast one morning and she was all like, "Oh wow, I didn't think you people ate normal people breakfast!"' Dylan said, putting on a high-pitched voice.

'What did she think you ate?' Naya asked.

'No fucking clue,' Dylan said.

'She asked me if I felt bad that my people had spread the virus around the world,' Lily said.

'She did not!' Naya exclaimed.

'She did,' Lily said. 'Then I told her I was Vietnamese, and she was like, "So? It's all the same, isn't it?"'

'Fucking hell,' Dylan muttered.

'What did you do?' Naya asked.

Lily smirked that familiar smirk again. 'Don't you worry,' she said. 'I got my revenge.'

'I feel bad,' I told Dylan as we were taking off our make-up that night. 'I didn't see any of that stuff Heather did. I feel like a terrible ally.'

'It's a lot easier to spot when you've spent your whole life hearing it,' she replied. 'Besides, it wasn't like she was doing it when everyone was around. It was always little comments, slipped in here and there, usually when there was no one else in the room.'

'I still should have realised she was the literal worst, though,' I said. 'I'm sorry.'

We left the bathroom, and Naya ducked in after us. With Jess K and Marija both gone, Lily was the only other person left in our bedroom, but she'd mysteriously disappeared again, so Dylan and I were alone. 'Just so you know,' I said, as we walked over to our bunk, 'if there's another Heather – if you need me to use my white privilege to call someone out – I'll do it.'

'Mandie, it's cool,' Dylan said. 'Put your guilt away. I don't need a hero. I can handle the Heathers of the world.'

'I know you can,' I said. 'Doesn't mean I can't help, though.'

I climbed up onto my bunk. 'You've spent enough of your time in here standing up for me and making my voice heard,' I said. 'The least I can do is the same for you.'

'Thanks, babe,' she said, patting my hand. 'You're a great friend.'

I refused to let myself hear a single negative thing in that statement. I'd been giving myself some extremely stern talking-tos in the few days since the Great Affirmation Flashcards Oh God My Emotions incident, and this was what I had decided:

1) Those flashcards had been an absolutely top-notch friend gesture from her.
2) That was because she was an absolutely top-notch friend.
3) That friendship was, far and away, the most important thing to me.
4) I wasn't going to jeopardise it by making heart eyes at her.
5) Even if I did sometimes wonder what sounds she would make if I touched her just the right way.

It wasn't because it was what Murray wanted me to do. It was because it was what I needed to do. No matter what happened in the Villa, I wanted to keep my absolutely top-notch friend Dylan in my life.

'You too,' I said, patting her hand back.

'I don't know if I was a particularly good friend today,' Dylan said, leaning her chin against the post at the end of my bunk. 'I'm sorry about letting Lily get under my skin like that.'

'Oh, because she didn't get under my skin at all,' I said. 'I was completely cool and calm and collected the whole time.'

She chuckled. 'That ruled, actually,' she said. 'I love mad Mandie. You were like this tiny avenging angel.'

'Right up until I started crying.'

'You are not the first woman in the world to cry when they get angry,' Dylan said. 'I used to be exactly the same. I trained myself out of it, because it's really not good to burst into tears in a hospital whenever someone makes you mad, but it's definitely not just you.'

I grabbed my pillow, put it at the foot of my bunk, and flopped down on my stomach, leaning my arms on it so I could face Dylan properly. 'Jac always told me I cried too easily.'

'Can I ask you a question?' Dylan asked, curling her fingers around the bedframe.

'Of course.'

'What did you actually like about Jac?'

I blinked.

'She sounds like a nightmare,' Dylan said. There were no cameras or mics in the bedroom, and Naya was in the shower, so we were safe, but she still lowered her voice. 'Everything you tell me about her makes me want to run her over.'

'She wasn't a nightmare,' I said. 'She could be mean sometimes. Cruel, even. But she wasn't a nightmare.'

I tried to find the best way to say it. 'She wasn't an easy person,' I said at last. 'But that was one of the things I liked about her, because the reason she wasn't easy was that she was always so certain. She knew what she liked. She knew what she didn't like. She knew what to do, no matter the situation. She knew who she was, and she wasn't going to change, not for anyone.'

I hugged my pillow closer. 'It was really powerful, being one of the things that Jac liked,' I said. 'It was even more powerful, being one of the things she loved. The first time she told me that she loved me, I thought I was going to explode. I've never had so many feelings at the same time.'

Dylan leaned against the bedframe, a slight furrow appearing between her perfect eyebrows.

'Of course, when she decided she didn't love me anymore, I also had a bunch of feelings,' I said. 'I'm still having a bunch of feelings. I don't know when I'll stop having a bunch of feelings. I'm kind of sick of it, to be honest.'

'They'll stop.'

'Are you sure?'

'Well, not as sure as Ol' I Know What I Know Jac, but pretty sure,' Dylan said. 'That's what happened with me when my marriage broke down. It hurt and it hurt and it hurt for a long time. I couldn't tell you exactly when it stopped hurting.

But it did. There's still a twinge sometimes, an old ache that flares up, but . . . it'll go away in time.'

'You know what was really comforting about Jac, though?' I said. 'She'd be able to tell me exactly when. She'd look at her diary, and she'd make some calculations, and she'd be like, "Mandie, this will stop hurting on May the second at 3.18 pm," and she'd be so sure about it.'

'Would she be right about it, though?'

'God, no. She was wrong about shit all the time. But that certainty she had . . . it was like a drug.'

'I'm certain about one thing,' Dylan said. 'She was wrong about you.'

It was suddenly a little hard to breathe.

Friend. Friend. She was my friend. That was enough. That was plenty.

Stay on the solid ground. STAY OUT OF THE QUICKSAND.

'Not about the crying thing,' I said. 'She was right about that. I do cry too much.'

'Even a broken clock can be right twice a day,' Dylan said. 'Maybe some of the shit she said had a grain of truth to it. Although I'm not willing to concede the crying thing. You're allowed to cry.'

'Okay.'

'I know she's the little voice in your head that whispers nasty things to you,' she said. 'But no one who saw you build a perfectly functioning catapult today out of random pieces of machinery could ever think you weren't the absolute best.'

Dylan's fingers, still clasped loosely around the bedframe, brushed mine. Then her pinkie finger curled around mine, like we were making a pinkie promise.

In that moment, I was conscious of three things:

1) Dylan's face was very close to mine.
2) Some inconsiderate person had sucked all the air out of the room.
3) I was going to kiss her.

There was not a single other thought in my mind. No thoughts. Head empty.

She was so close. I was going to take a deep breath, fill my lungs with the little oxygen left in the room, and then I was going to kiss her.

But the door to the bathroom swung open and Naya came out, dressed for bed, a silk scarf around her hair. 'Fuck, today was unpleasant,' she said, flopping down on her bunk.

Dylan found her voice first. 'I think it might have been worse than Love Jockey Hockey.'

'I wouldn't go that far,' Naya said. 'Nothing in the world will ever be as bad as Love Jockey Hockey. Where's Lily?'

'No idea,' Dylan replied.

'We need to put a bell on her or something,' Naya said. 'I heard you got in her face today, Amanda.'

'We, uh, had some words,' I managed to say.

Dylan was still so close to me. Our pinkies were still linked. If this were a movie, she would have jumped twelve feet away from me the second the bathroom door had banged open, but she hadn't moved at all.

'Good for you,' Naya said. 'Although she was nice enough later. I've never seen you two actually be civil before, Dylan.'

Dylan rolled her eyes. 'She only puts on the Disney villain act when the cameras are around. It annoys the shit out of me.'

She disentangled her hand from mine and sat down on her bunk. She and Naya kept talking, but I was only half-listening. Quarter-listening, really. Maybe only eighth-listening.

It wasn't just me. This wasn't all in my head.

I wasn't Jac-sure. But I was pretty sure.

I'd been about to kiss Dylan.

And Dylan had been about to kiss me.

12

We had a rare day off the next day. 'We would have been shooting the Last Chance Party and the Necklace Ceremony, but because Heather got canned at the group date yesterday, we don't need to,' Suzette told us. 'So the crew will be taking a well-deserved break today, and you ladies can too.'

'Can we see Dylan JM?' Parisa asked.

'He's taking a day off too.'

'Can he take a day off with us?'

'Let the man rest,' Suzette said. 'Most of you are only filming properly three or four times a week. He's filming pretty much every day. He could use some peace and quiet.'

'I get that,' Parisa said, 'but I just feel – and so do most of us – that I haven't had any time with him. How are we supposed to fall in love with him without spending time together?'

'I hear you, Parisa, I really do,' Suzette said, 'but any time you spend with him needs to be on camera. Today, we're resting. If you and Dylan G want your phone calls, now's your chance. Come with me.'

I didn't wait for Dylan to come back from talking to Noah. As soon as I found an opportunity to slip away, I went outside. It was a beautiful day, and some of the other women were talking about having a picnic next to the pool, which sounded lovely – or would have, if things weren't so *loud* in my head.

I headed out to the maze instead, trailing my left hand against the wall and letting it take me down whatever pathways and dead ends it wanted. It knew what it was doing. It would get me somewhere.

I didn't know what I was doing, though.

What I'd been positive – well, almost positive – fairly sure of? – last night seemed ridiculous in the light of day. I might have wanted to kiss Dylan, but there was no way she wanted to kiss me.

I knew Dylan liked me. Dylan might even love me. Those affirmation flashcards had been such a beautiful act of love. Jac and I had dated for well over two years and she'd never once done anything so loving for me.

That didn't mean Dylan was attracted to me, though. It was my poor, lonely, affection-starved brain playing tricks on me again, like it had that morning when we'd sat outside and watched the sunrise. I just . . . wasn't her type.

Because there was no getting away from one simple fact: if Dylan was attracted to women, she would have told me by now.

I came to the end of the hedge maze long before I reached the end of the maze in my mind. Although it probably hadn't taken me the fastest way through, that piece of advice about picking a wall and following it worked. I'd solved it.

It had spit me out about three quarters of the way down the hill. I wasn't exactly close to the Convent, but I was closer than I'd ever been before. I could see that all the windows were open, upstairs and downstairs, including a set of French doors that opened onto the verandah, letting the lovely day's fresh air in – and probably the smell out. Despite our cleaning roster, the Villa was starting to smell pretty lived in, so things must be twice as intense in a place as small as the Convent.

Three women were outside doing yoga – Kanda, Marija, and one of the women who'd been eliminated on the first night, whose name I couldn't remember. I thought about walking down and saying hello, but decided against it. Murray would definitely be mad if I crossed the still-in-the-game/gone-from-the-game Juliet streams.

Murray. God. I was doing such a bad job of not making heart eyes at Dylan. I was lucky there were no cameras in the bedroom. Screw mad, he'd be *livid* if he saw how we were last night.

Instead of walking down towards the Convent, I headed across the hill, trailing my hand along the outside edge of the maze. Maybe I could follow it to the corner and then walk back up the hill to the Villa, instead of having to go through the maze again to get home. Or I could walk around the hill, come back up the driveway, and give everyone a bit of a scare by knocking at the front door. *Oh my God, it was all a lie!* someone would squeal. *It's Z with a date card!* Sure, it wouldn't be a *great* practical joke, but when you didn't have access to any outside entertainment, your standards really dropped.

It was a beautiful clear day, and the lake was shining silver in the sun. Romeo-Dylan's boat was tied up to the jetty, bobbing gently. There was a golf cart parked nearby, like the ones the crew zipped around in. Romeo-Dylan's big day off clearly wasn't as Day Off-y as Suzette had suggested.

I stopped, one hand still on the hedge. If I squinted, I could just make out two figures on Romeo-Dylan's boat, sitting on the deck.

Murray, maybe? One of the other producers? Z?

There was a thought. Where were they keeping Z? Given how intense they were about the bubble, he had to be somewhere on the property.

Maybe Romeo-Dylan and Z were roomies. Maybe they had bunk beds down there in the cabin, just like we had in the Villa, and now they were sitting out on their shared deck together.

If that was true, I hoped they were filming it for the *Marry Me, Juliet* website. That would be hilarious bonus content, seeing Romeo-Dylan and Z fall over each other and argue about whose turn it was to make dinner and fight over the wardrobe space for their incredible suit collections.

But it probably had its upsides. For Romeo-Dylan, anyway. It must be really tough and really lonely, being the star of the show. He could probably use a friend.

Oh my God. Was Z the mysterious friend who'd been watching us and judging us in the love machine date?

I tried to figure it out if it was possible, and I was almost positive it was. Z had done the little introductory spiel on the group date, but then he'd disappeared until right at the end, when he came back for that snap elimination. He could totally have been sitting in some secret room with a million screens, watching us all.

I squinted hard at the two people on the deck, wondering if I was right. Was Z the one who had somehow decided that Kumiko and Parisa and Jess D's love machine was better than my extremely elegant catapult? Just because they hadn't had an all-out shitfight while they were making it?

But then one of the figures on the boat stood up and walked towards the railing, and all my Z conspiracy theories were driven right out of my head.

What the fuck was *Dylan* doing on Romeo-Dylan's boat?

There were trees spilling down the hillside towards the edge of the lake. I stole through them, wincing every time a stick cracked under my feet, as though the Dylans might somehow hear me.

The trees didn't go all the way to the waterline, but they came close. I did my best to conceal myself behind one of the larger ones, grateful that I was a) a tiny enough person that hiding behind a tree was a legitimate option for me, and b) wearing relatively muted colours.

Unlike Dylan. That orange dress – the same one she'd been wearing the day we met – was practically hi-vis.

Romeo-Dylan had joined her, and they were standing

together at the railing. I wasn't close enough to hear what they were saying, but they were clearly deep in conversation as they looked out over the water. Romeo-Dylan was leaning casually forward, his hands folded loosely together, occasionally glancing up at her. Dylan was standing tall, but even from here I could tell – somehow? from her shoulders, maybe, or her posture? – that her fingers were clenched tight around the rail.

Romeo-Dylan straightened and put his hand on Dylan's back.

I could feel that hand on my back, as firmly as if it was shoving me to the ground and holding me there.

Because she was turning to face him, leaning into his hand. They were close now, so close together, Romeo-Dylan looking into Dylan's beautiful eyes and her looking back, and then her arms were around him and his were around her and they were hugging each other like they never, ever wanted to let go.

I felt so stupid I could vomit.

Whatever it was I thought I'd felt last night, I was absolutely kidding myself.

Dylan wasn't the least bit interested in me. Not even the tiniest bit.

And neither was Romeo-Dylan, for that matter. I was nice and unthreatening enough to keep around – a wifey on paper – but that was all. I was vanilla ice cream: inoffensive enough to keep in the mix until you'd got rid of all the flavours you didn't like.

Neither Dylan was into me. Because – as should have been obvious all along – the only people the Dylans were into were each other.

13

Lily got the next single date ('Roses are red, clowns are so silly, I know you like fire, make one with me, Lily?'). She got in everyone's faces about it and was, in general, really fucking annoying, but try as she might – and she truly did try! – she couldn't get a rise out of Dylan.

I wished she had, to be honest. 'God, Lily Fireball is so irritating' was one of the few genuinely safe topics Dylan and I had to talk about.

It wasn't like I started *avoiding* Dylan. As we'd all well and truly found out over the course of the pandemic, you can't avoid someone you're locked down with. Especially not when you share a bunk bed with them.

But I made a point of spreading my time around. I got in a yoga routine with Kumiko. I asked Jess D to teach me how to bake. I even tried to go jogging with Parisa.

'You know she runs marathons, right?' Dylan asked, when I collapsed on the floor, unable to move.

'Nnnngggghhhnnngghhh,' I replied.

She laughed and sat down beside me. 'And her legs are about three times as long as yours. No wonder you couldn't keep up.'

'It was stupid,' I said. 'I know.'

'Don't make me get the flashcards.'

'I said *it* was stupid, not I was stupid,' I replied.

I sat up gingerly and tried to touch my toes. My legs screamed in protest.

'I can give you a calf massage, if you want,' Dylan said. 'I've got some physio training in my bag of nurse tricks.'

'It's fine,' I said. 'Don't worry about it. I'm being a wuss. I just need to stretch.'

It wasn't a lie. I was being a wuss. The thought of Dylan's fingers on my body – even if they were digging painfully into my deep tissue – was more than I could stand.

I didn't tell her I'd seen her on the boat with Romeo-Dylan. I wanted to. I'd planned to, even, as I'd gone back up the hill that day.

But when I finally got an opportunity, later that night, I chickened out.

I wasn't exactly *afraid* of what she was going to say. I knew what she would say. I'd always known, if I was honest with myself. I would ask her what the deal was, and she would sigh, and say something like, 'What he and I have, it's something really special.'

Well, she probably wouldn't use those exact words. I couldn't imagine that phrase coming out of her mouth. But that was what she would *mean*. Her and Romeo-Dylan, together. Me, a third wheel at best.

So no, I wasn't afraid of what she was going to say. But that didn't mean I wanted to hear her say it.

'You okay?' she asked. 'You've got that thinking line between your eyebrows.'

'Oh, fine,' I replied. 'Just wondering what the next group date will be, that's all. They'll have to come up with something pretty special to be worse than Love Jockey Hockey and the love machines.'

'I'm going to be having screaming nightmares about Love Jockey Hockey for the rest of my life,' Dylan said. 'I don't know what could possibly be worse. It'd have to involve broken bones, at a bare minimum.'

I was glad I didn't have to find out. There were five names on the next group date card ('Roses are red, violets are blue, when Cupid comes calling, is his aim true?'), and mine wasn't one of them.

Dylan's was, though. Of course it was. 'Have a nice day, Mandie,' she said. 'I might be missing an arm or a leg or possibly my head the next time you see me.'

'Try not to die,' I said, in my sunniest, most nothing-is-wrong-why-would-you-think-that tone.

Jess D, Lily Fireball and I were the only ones left in the Villa. Lily immediately disappeared. 'Want another baking lesson?' Jess D asked.

'Sure,' I replied. I didn't particularly *like* baking, but the

218

process was calming, and it sure as hell beat moping around on my own, drowning in my feelings.

We'd produced some cupcakes by that evening, when the rest of the women, minus Naya, came trooping back in. 'Naya won the one-on-one time with Dylan JM,' Kumiko explained. 'She'll be back later. Maybe with a necklace.'

'What was the challenge?' I asked, offering around the tray of cupcakes.

'Archery,' Kumiko said, taking one. 'Classic *Marry Me, Juliet* shit. The targets were heart-shaped. The arrows were pink. They made Z dress in a toga with a little gold crown.'

'Seriously?' Jess D said.

'It was a laurel wreath,' Belinda said, snagging a cupcake.

'It was a two-dollar headband masquerading as a laurel wreath,' Dylan said. 'These are good, Mandie.'

'It was all Jess,' I said, offering the tray to Parisa.

'So how did they judge it?' Jess D asked. 'Was Dylan JM's mysterious friend back?'

'Nope,' Parisa said. 'It was a basic competition. Naya shot the closest to the bullseye—'

'Also heart-shaped,' Kumiko said.

'– so she won the date,' Parisa finished, popping the last morsel of her cupcake into her mouth. 'Thank God.'

'What do you mean, thank God?' Jess D asked.

'Well, we all know what would have happened if Dylan JM got to pick his own winner,' Parisa said.

'Do we?'

'Oh, come off it, Jess, you know what I'm talking about,' Parisa said. 'He would have picked Dylan G. Like he always does.'

Dylan swallowed. 'Excuse me?'

'It's obvious you're his favourite,' Parisa said. 'He always grabs you at Last Chance Parties. You never have to steal him. You've been on every single group date—'

'Not every single one!' Dylan protested. 'There was one I didn't go on.'

'Oh wow, a whole *one*,' Parisa said. 'On top of that, you've got the one-on-one time in just about all of those group dates—'

'One. *One* of those group dates. The first one!'

'And Love Jockey Hockey,' Belinda said.

'That was group time, because our team beat the Convent team,' Dylan said. 'Which I spent most of trying to make sure you hadn't suffered some kind of permanent facial injury, Belinda.'

'You still managed to slip away with him for forty-five minutes,' Lily Fireball said, materialising smoothly from nowhere. 'Longer than any of the rest of us.'

'Don't you start, Lily.'

Lily raised an eyebrow. 'I'm just stating a fact. But how about we ask your little sidekick?' She turned to me. 'Amanda, do you think it's obvious that Dylan is the Romeo's favourite?'

My fingers were curled so tightly around the edge of the kitchen bench that my knuckles were white. How long had they been like that?

Everyone was looking at me. Including Dylan.

'Well?' Lily demanded.

'Yes,' I said. 'Yes, I think he likes her better than anyone else.'

That wasn't the end of the argument. It went on long after everyone had angrily eaten all the cupcakes. 'I can't believe you all think I'm getting special treatment,' Dylan said.

'We didn't say you're getting special treatment,' Parisa said. 'We said that he likes you the best.'

'In fact, you're kind of getting the opposite of special treatment,' Kumiko added. 'They've started keeping you away from him, because it's so obvious he likes you the best.'

'That's total bullshit.'

'No, it isn't.'

I slipped upstairs somewhere in the middle of the discussion. Well, it might have been the middle. It might also have still been the beginning. Neither side was giving ground, and I couldn't think of anything I'd like to do less than endlessly debate the subject of whether Romeo-Dylan liked Dylan best of all.

I went into the bathroom to take my make-up off. The splash of cold water on my face did nothing to erase the image of them standing on the deck, holding each other like they might never let go.

The door clicked shut behind me.

I looked up, and had to suppress a groan. 'I don't have the energy for this, Lily.'

'The energy for what?' she said. 'Taking your make-up off? I can tell. That falsie's dangling by a thread.'

I pulled the fake eyelash off. 'I'm tired. I just want to go to bed. So if you're going to hit me with your snarky little

221

comments, could you do them all at once? As some kind of monologue, perhaps?'

'Amanda,' Lily said, 'much as I appreciate this new spine you seem to have grown, I'm also tired. I also want to go to bed. Even I can't muster the energy for snarky monologues every second of the day. Do you have any micellar? I'm out.'

I passed her my micellar water.

'Thanks,' she said.

And then, for several minutes, we stood there in silence, taking our make-up off together. It was almost nice.

I twisted my hair up into a topknot. My elastic broke. 'Shit.'

'Here,' Lily said, passing me one of hers. 'It's the wrong colour, but it'll work.'

'Thanks.'

'They're wrong, you know.'

'What?'

'They're wrong,' she repeated. 'He doesn't like her the best out of anyone.'

A piece of hair fell out of my topknot and into my eyes. I tried to put it back in, and failed.

'They'd be a terrible match,' Lily said.

'If you think that, then you've never seen them together,' I said. 'They look perfect.'

'Sure, they look perfect,' Lily said. 'Doesn't mean they are perfect, though.'

'We're going to have to agree to disagree on this one,' I said, finally managing to get the rogue strand of hair into my bun.

'Are you going to give up on Dylan that easily?'

My eyes met hers in the mirror. I was almost positive I knew exactly which Dylan she was talking about.

'You're not the only person who's seen them together,' Lily said. 'Can you tell me, without a word of a lie, that you see any spark there? Any passion?'

'He gave her cake.'

'So? You and Jess gave everyone cakes today. Are you in love with everyone?'

'It was different,' I said. 'After the photo shoot date. He saw that she wanted the cakes in our shoot, and so he gave them to her.'

'He heard that you were a mechanic and he gave you a Lamborghini.'

'Come on, Lily, I'm not as stupid as I look. I know the producers plan the dates. Plus, they would have had to source that Lambo way before the bubble.'

'I'm not saying he doesn't like her,' Lily said. 'I'm sure he does. He's nauseatingly nice. He likes everyone. He even likes me.'

Did she have any proof of that?

'I just don't think he likes her better than he likes anyone else,' she said.

Is he sneaking anyone else down to canoodle on his boat, or just her? I wanted to snarl.

But even I wasn't foolish enough to reveal that kind of information to someone like Lily. 'Why do you care, anyway?' I asked instead.

One corner of her mouth curled up, her expression a subtler cousin of her usual smirk. 'I want things to be interesting,' she said. 'Things are going to be dull as hell if the next three weeks are just a grim progression towards Double Dylan.'

'You sound like Murray.'

I said it without thinking, and I regretted it immediately. Lily eyed me in a way that sent a cold trickle running down my spine.

Dylan was right. Murray had lied to me. Lily was a plant. She had to be.

But then she turned back to the mirror and the look was gone. 'He's not wrong,' she said airily. 'It's in everyone's best interests for this season to be interesting. If you want to get on *Juliet on the Beach* or make any money at all as an influencer, you need people to know who you are. Nobody's going to know who any of us are if they stop watching because we're too boring.'

'Is that why you . . . ?' I had no idea how to finish the question.

'Am the way I am?'

I nodded.

'Honey,' Lily said, 'this is who I am.'

'It's not, though,' I said. 'You're different in here to how you are out there. When the cameras aren't around, sometimes you're almost pleasant. When they're on, you're a monster.'

'Thank you.'

'That wasn't a compliment.'

'You,' she said, 'are more complicated than people give you credit for.'

I had no idea how to respond to that.

'And so am I,' she said. 'The monster and the person are both me, Amanda. I contain multitudes.'

'Are you . . .' I bit my lip.

'Am I what?'

'Are you worried?' I asked. 'You obviously know you're going to be the villain of the season. Are you worried about the reaction? The trolling? The death threats? Are you going to be okay?'

Lily met my eyes in the mirror, and for the first time, I saw her smile. Not a smirk, not a half-smile, not a sarcastic grin, but a proper smile.

'Thank you for worrying about me,' she said. 'That's sweet. But you don't need to. I know what I'm doing.'

She took a make-up wipe and rubbed it across her lips. Her lipstick came off in a red smear that looked for all the world like blood.

'I always know exactly what I'm doing,' she said.

I felt the exact opposite way. I had no idea what I was doing. Not even a little bit.

So I made a decision. The only one I could. The only one a person with any self-respect would make.

I was going to leave.

My hair and make-up partner for that night's Last Chance Party was Belinda. She was quiet, sitting in her make-up chair, looking at herself in the mirror, running her tongue over the edge of her broken tooth over and over again, so instead of talking to her, I planned what I was going to say.

I like you, but I think we both know there isn't a spark here, I'd say to Romeo-Dylan. *It's time for me to go.*

Of course, he'd say. *I'm so honoured I got to share that date with you, Amanda.*

He'd tell me he was sad. But then he'd let me go.

And I would go down to the Convent, away from both Dylans, and use the time to sort myself out. I wouldn't have to worry about dates and parties and one-on-one time and all the on-camera stuff we had to do. I could just spend three weeks pottering around at the edge of the lake and figuring out what to do with my life.

The Convent was full of women, so it wouldn't exactly be the ideal place for this, but I could practise being on my own. I'd bounced from Mark to Jac to the Dylans with only that brief period of wallowing in my childhood bedroom between them. I could use the time to reflect, rather than wallow. I could try and believe in my best features list. I could try and believe in my affirmation flashcards. I could try and actually become the Mandie 2.0 I kept pretending I already was.

I could finally do what Mum had wanted me to do: sit down and come up with a plan for what was next. Not a fantasy plan. A real one, with real steps, back towards solid ground.

The dress that wardrobe gave me for the Last Chance Party was dark, dark purple. It was long – so long that it even had a little train, which trailed behind me as I walked – but it was slit high up the front, high enough that if I sat wrong, it'd be extremely clear whether or not I was wearing underwear.

(I was, for the record. I was already going to get enough shit from the guys at work for being on this show. I hated to think how gross it would get if I flashed the entire nation.)

The dress was paired with strappy silver heels, which added several inches to my height, and accessorised with silver cuffs and dangly silver earrings. The make-up artist had given me a dramatic smoky eye.

It wasn't me at all, but I didn't care. I didn't want to be me tonight. I wanted to be someone braver than me. Someone bolder than me. Someone in control of her own destiny.

When I emerged from hair and make-up, Dylan was standing at the bar near the pool. 'Want one, Mandie?' she called, gesturing to the champagne.

I shook my head. There was such a cocktail of fears and feelings and frustrations roiling around in my belly that I already felt drunk, even though I hadn't had a drop.

'You sure?'

She was in white tonight. It was a cocktail dress, so it wasn't exactly bridal, but it was close enough that I could see it. Him, standing next to her in a tux. Her hands in his. The corners of his eyes crinkling as he looked at her. Her, winking back at him.

I could see it. Everyone else could see it. Lily apparently couldn't see it, but how stupid would you have to be to believe a word that came out of her mouth?

'Mandie!' Dylan waved her champagne flute at me again. 'You sure?'

My jaw had started to ache. I was clenching my teeth.

'Yes,' I said.

I should say goodbye to her. She deserved that. She hadn't done anything wrong. If anything, she'd done too many things *right*.

I walked away instead.

Belinda had got out of hair and make-up a few minutes ahead of me. She clearly hadn't wasted any time, because she was already sitting with Romeo-Dylan on a bench in one of the rose gardens.

I took a deep breath and then walked up to them. 'Sorry to interrupt,' I said, 'but can I steal you for a second?'

'I'm sorry, Amanda,' Romeo-Dylan said, looking up at me. 'Would you mind giving us a few minutes?'

'I – of course.'

I was thrown totally off balance. In all my psyching myself up for the conversation, I hadn't anticipated that I might not be able to have it immediately.

'No, it's all right,' Belinda said. 'I've said everything I needed to say.'

She stood up. 'It's been lovely getting to know you.'

'You don't need to lie to me,' he said. 'You don't owe me anything, Belinda. I owe you. I'm so sorry for – what happened to you.'

He gestured to her mouth. She reflexively covered it with her hand.

'Sorry,' he said again.

'It's all right,' she said, not taking her hand away. 'It wasn't your fault.'

'If there's anything I can do . . .' His voice trailed off. 'Like – your dental bills. I can pay those. Absolutely.'

Her head dropped. She was crying. 'There was only one thing I wanted from you,' she said. 'I wanted you to fall in love with me. And you haven't.'

Romeo-Dylan looked stricken. 'I – I—'

'Don't say you're sorry,' she said. 'You came here to find someone. It's not your fault it's not me.'

'Thank you,' he said. 'For being here.'

She nodded. They hugged. And then, pursued by one of the camera crew, Belinda left.

Leaving me to – do what, exactly?

Romeo-Dylan sank down on the bench again and buried his head in his hands. 'Fuuuuuuck,' he groaned.

'No swearing, Dylan,' Murray said. He was standing next to the remaining camera.

'Fuck off, Murray,' Romeo-Dylan said, without looking up.

He wasn't the only one who wanted to swear. I wanted to tilt my head up to the sky and scream FUUUUUCCCC-CCCKKKKK a thousand times louder than he had.

For once in my life, I'd made an actual, proper, adult decision. I'd made a plan, instead of acting on impulse. I'd thought about what I was going to say, and I was going to follow through.

But now what was I supposed to do? Sit down beside this man who'd just been kicked in the nuts and kick him again, just for good measure?

There was only one thing I could do, really. Only one way I knew how to handle this situation.

'Are you all right?' Mummy Mandie said, sitting down beside Romeo-Dylan on the bench and putting her hand between his shoulder blades. 'That was horrible.'

He looked up at me, wild-eyed. 'Was I – was I horrible to her?'

'No, no, of course not!' I reassured him. 'That's not what I meant. Just that it was a horrible situation. It's not nice, to be broken up with.'

'No,' he said faintly. 'It's not.'

He took his head out of his hands, but he stayed hunched forward, curled into himself. His elbows were resting on his knees, his hands hanging down between them, the thumb and middle finger of his right hand tapping together furiously. 'But that's what I'm doing,' he said. 'Every single time I come to one of these Last Chance Parties, that's what I'm doing. Breaking up with someone. Hurting them.'

'Hey,' I said. 'We all knew what we signed up for.'

'I thought I knew what I signed up for!' he said. 'But I never knew it would feel like this.'

He let out a long, shaking breath. 'I'd already decided what I was going to do,' he said. 'At the Necklace Ceremony tonight. I was going to eliminate Belinda. I was going to send her to the Convent anyway. So I should be relieved. She did the hard part for me. But instead I just feel . . .'

'How?' I asked, after he'd been silent for a few moments. 'How do you feel?'

'Guilty,' he said at last. 'I feel guilty. That I can't be everything to everyone. That I can't give everyone what they want. That I can't make everyone happy.'

230

'I'm not going to tell you that your feelings are wrong,' I said. 'They're your feelings. You can feel however you want to feel. But this show isn't about you making everyone happy. It's about you finding someone who makes *you* happy.'

I scooted a little closer. I kept my hand on his back, but angled myself in towards him, putting my other hand on his knee. 'I think you and I are quite similar, in a lot of ways,' I said. 'We're both people-pleasers. We want everyone around us to be happy. It hurts like hell when they're not.'

He let out another breath. 'Yeah.'

'The realisation that I wasn't making my ex happy – that I couldn't make my ex happy, no matter how hard I tried – that just about broke me,' I said. 'But it didn't. I survived. And you will too.'

'You remind me of someone,' he said suddenly.

'Oh?' I asked. 'Who?'

'I have this friend,' he said. 'A good friend. A close friend. Sometimes, it feels like I'm carrying the world on my shoulders, but when we talk, I get to take it off and set it down for a while. It helps me believe that things aren't as out of control as they seem.'

I thought of my Dylan. Of her hand on the base of my neck as I sobbed on the steps at auditions, of that text she'd sent me telling me to look at the best features list on my application, of the affirmation flashcards under my pillow. Of how every time someone cut me down, or I cut myself down, she'd build me back up. Of how she had my back, no matter what.

'I have a friend like that,' I said softly.

231

'You're totally different people,' Romeo-Dylan said. 'Nothing alike, really. But sometimes, when I sit down with you, it's a bit like sitting down with my friend. You make me feel calm, Amanda. You make me feel steady.'

I already knew I had no chance of winning *Marry Me, Juliet*. But if I did have tender little hopes that it might be me at the end, that would have been the moment I knew I was screwed. *You remind me of my friend* and *when I'm with you, the ground* doesn't *move beneath my feet* weren't exactly romantic declarations for the ages.

I wished I could be mad at him. If I could do that, then I could leave with no regrets, with no consideration for his feelings. It would still hurt like hell when he and Dylan ended up together, but it would be so much simpler if leaving was the emotional equivalent of throwing darts at a board with his face on it.

'I like you so much,' I said.

Romeo-Dylan's head snapped up, eyes wide.

Oh. Shit. No. That hadn't come out right. What had I said?

'I mean – you're so nice,' I babbled. 'Such a nice man. You deserve to find someone who makes you happy. And she's here! I know she's here. You *will* be happy.'

'Amanda, stop,' Murray said.

I wanted to sink into the ground.

'What we need is a response from you,' Murray said to Romeo-Dylan. 'She's told you she likes you. You can't just leave her hanging.'

Romeo-Dylan's finger and thumb had started tapping together again, faster and faster.

'Tell him you like him again, Amanda,' Murray said.

'Um, I like you,' I said.

'Properly!' Murray snapped. 'Like you did before.'

I swallowed. 'I like you so much,' I said to Romeo-Dylan.

My hands were still on him, one on his back, one on his knee. His whole body was tensed up, like a gazelle that might flee at any moment.

'I like you too, Amanda,' he said.

'More!' Murray demanded. 'You just told her a whole bunch of beautiful stuff before! Make it bigger! Make it better!'

I squeezed his knee, trying to give him whatever Mummy Mandie strength I had to get through this.

He closed his eyes for a second, took two deep breaths, then looked at me. 'I like you too, Amanda,' he said. 'I'm so glad you're on this journey with me. Every moment we spend together, I enjoy. You're such a beautiful, special person. I love the way I feel when you're around.'

I met his eyes. His creased at the corners as he smiled at me.

And—

And—

And—

'Come on, Dylan,' Murray snarled. 'Are you just going to sit there and stare at her?'

'I'm sorry,' I said. 'I should have said something. It was my turn to talk.'

'Amanda, you're fine. Dylan, pull it together,' Murray said. 'How many kisses do I need to coach you through?'

'Sorry, sorry, sorry,' Romeo-Dylan said, pulling away from me and running his hand through his hair.

'You're the one making it awkward for yourself, not me,' Murray said. 'You've done all the hard work creating the moments. Just fucking follow through! Make-up, can we get someone to fix his hair?'

'I can do it,' I said. 'Do you mind?'

'No,' Romeo-Dylan said.

I gently finger-combed his hair back into place. 'You don't have to kiss me if you don't want to.' There was no point in whispering – there was a boom mic directly above us, they could hear every word we said – but I did anyway. 'It's fine, I promise.'

He let out a long, shaking breath which I thought was part-laugh. 'You're sweet,' he said, 'but who wouldn't want to kiss you?'

'Let's get back to it,' Murray said. 'Take it from that bit about how she's beautiful and special and whatever, Dylan. Then fucking kiss her this time.'

'Is that okay with you?' Romeo-Dylan asked me. 'The same goes for you, you know. You don't have to kiss me if you don't want to.'

'Of course it's okay with her!'

Romeo-Dylan ignored Murray and kept looking stead-fastly at me. 'Do you want to?'

I thought about saying no. Should have said no, given he was probably going to be my best friend's boyfriend in three weeks' time. Would have said no, in almost any other circumstances.

But I recognised the feeling in his eyes. The feeling that you were on the edge of a cliff, and the smallest little thing might topple you over. The feeling I'd had for weeks and weeks after Jac had dumped me, the one that had seen me bursting into tears every five seconds.

I could say no, and it would be fine, but this sweet man had been through enough rejection for one night.

'Who wouldn't want to kiss you?' I said, stroking my thumb comfortingly across the back of his hand.

'Are you two done?' Murray said exasperatedly. 'Can we shoot this already?'

'Go,' I said.

'Rolling,' the director said. 'In three, two . . .'

'You're so beautiful and special, Amanda,' Romeo-Dylan said. 'I love the way I feel when you're around.'

His fingers came up to caress my cheek. I closed my eyes as his lips brushed against mine.

Like last time, it was nice. There was absolutely nothing wrong with kissing Romeo-Dylan. He was exactly what I'd hoped for in the limo, when I'd thought for those few moments that the Romeo was going to be Chris Gregory. Dylan Jayasinghe Mellor was a gentleman in the most literal sense of the word: he was a man who was gentle. There was a gentle something between us, solid enough that it would hurt when it ended, but only in a gentle sort of way.

In another universe, kissing him would have been exactly the right thing to do. It would have been an important step forward in me getting over Jac, even if he and I were never destined to be anything. He would have been the solid ground on which I landed, giving me time to brace myself before I leaped again.

He was the best rebound I could have possibly hoped for, and I'd messed it up.

When we broke apart, Romeo-Dylan leaned his forehead against mine for several long moments. 'You're such a beautiful person, Amanda,' he whispered.

'So are you,' I whispered back.

'I don't feel like it,' he said. His breath was shaky. 'Being here – being the Romeo – it's making me feel like such an arsehole.'

'Ahem.'

Dylan was standing about six feet away. She was backlit by the giant TV lights they were shining on Romeo-Dylan and me. In that white dress, she looked like an angel.

'If you're done,' she said coolly, 'they need us for filming, Mandie. Apparently Belinda left, so there's not going to be a Necklace Ceremony tonight.'

There might not have been a Necklace Ceremony, but filming took *forever*. Romeo-Dylan kept messing up his lines when he told us that Belinda had made the decision to leave and go to the Convent. Then they wanted to get reactions from everyone, positioning us in a bunch of different groups on the Necklace Ceremony bleachers. My feet ached in my heels, and sweat rolled down the back of my neck under the lights.

'Why do you think Belinda left?' Jess D asked, in one of the little reaction groups they put me in.

'Isn't it obvious?' Naya said. 'It's because of that conversation we had in the kitchen the other day. Why hang around when we all know who his favourite is?'

She nodded at Dylan, who was in a group with Kumiko and Parisa.

'It's pathetic,' Lily said.

'That's a bit harsh,' Naya said.

'No, it isn't,' Lily said. 'It's giving up. Why would you come on this show to give up?'

'Belinda was really struggling, though,' Jess D said. 'She was so self-conscious about her teeth.'

'Suck it up. Stick it out,' Lily said. 'Opportunities like this are so rare. Who would just throw it away?'

I wanted to believe it was a sign of growth that I didn't immediately say, *Oh, I was totally going to leave too, but I thought getting dumped twice in one night would be a bit much for one man to handle.*

It wasn't, though. It was mostly just that I was distracted.

There were a thousand thoughts bouncing around my head and crashing into one another, but I decided to focus on the simplest one: I was going to kill Murray.

Lily had been right when she said the next few weeks would be boring TV if it was just about the Dylans falling in love. The show needed conflict. It needed drama.

And I was the spanner production was throwing into the works.

Of course Murray had made Romeo-Dylan and I kiss, even though neither of us particularly wanted to. How long had he had Dylan waiting in the wings before he wheeled her out at the worst possible moment?

They'd done this kind of plotline before. A lot of times. It had been the foundation of that whole weird pairs season, but it happened all the time on other seasons, too. Two contestants would become friends, but then they'd get deep into the competition, they'd both develop feelings for the Romeo, and their jealousy would get in the way.

'This show actively hates women,' Jac had said, on one of the rare occasions she'd actually sat down and watched an episode with me. 'Pitting them against each other like this is bullshit.'

'Yeah, it's not my favourite part of the show,' I replied. 'But it'll probably be okay afterwards. They'll get over it as soon as they're out of the Villa. They'll be all over each other's Insta stories in no time, just you wait.'

The look Jac had given me had made it extremely clear that she would not be watching the Insta stories of any *Marry Me, Juliet* contestants.

She'd been right, though. Pitting Dylan and I against each other like this *was* bullshit. As for whether the show hated women . . . I couldn't speak for all women, but in that moment, it felt like it pretty actively hated me.

So I devoted my energy to actively hating Murray. I fantasised about finding my Lambo and running him over. It was safer than thinking about literally anything else.

It was nearly dawn by the time we finished filming. 'All right, ladies, you can grab a couple of hours sleep,' Carrie announced. 'Sorry it's not more, but tonight's shoot took longer than we thought, and we've got a big date tomorrow. Don't wrinkle those dresses – we're going to do ITMs for tonight in the morning, so you'll need to put them back on.'

None of us commented on the irony of in-the-moment interviews being filmed the next day. We were all well and truly used to it by now.

I knew there was going to be a fight for the bathroom, and that there was no way I would win that fight, so I sank down on the Necklace Ceremony bleachers and took off my heels instead. My calves, still aching after that jog (well, 'jog') with Parisa the other day, were screaming at me, almost as loudly as the braver version of me wanted to scream at Murray.

'Hey.'

I looked up at Dylan. 'Hey.'

Around us, the crew were taking down the lights, breaking down the set, so they could turn this room back into our living room. For once, they were paying no attention to us.

Which was a good thing, honestly. The awkward silence between Romeo-Dylan and I earlier had nothing on this one.

'Want to go for a walk?' she asked, after several excruciating moments.

'We're not supposed to go outside at night.'

'It's basically sunrise. If production has a problem with it, they can fight me.'

It was petty, but that was the thought that got me off my arse. I was very here for the concept of someone fighting production. Punching them, perhaps. Right in their scruffy, overtired, dad-meets-daddy face.

I looped the tail of my dress up over my arm and carried my heels as we walked outside. The dewy ground was freezing under my bare feet, but I didn't mind. 'My feet are cold' was such a simple, easy thing to feel.

'You've been avoiding me,' Dylan said quietly.

'No, I haven't,' I said. 'Tonight was just chaotic, with Belinda leaving and everything.'

'Not just tonight,' she said. 'For the last few days. Ever since the love machine day, when Heather got eliminated. You've barely spoken to me.'

'That's not true.'

'Then why do I miss you?'

I didn't know how to answer that.

We followed the outer wall of the maze down the hill. Dylan was closest to it, and she trailed her hand along the hedge. *You don't need to do that,* I thought about saying, *you only need to follow the wall when you're inside the maze,* but I didn't.

As we reached the maze's corner, the first rays of the sun were coming up over the lake. They turned the surface silver at first, and then, as the sun came up, a pale gold, then a deeper gold, with streaks of pink and purple.

We stood there a long time before Dylan spoke again. 'I miss you, Mandie.'

'I haven't gone anywhere,' I replied.

She was the one who had gone somewhere. I could just see Romeo-Dylan's boat, bobbing gently beside the jetty.

'I'm sorry,' I said.

'For what?'

I paused. There were so many things I wanted to say, and almost none of them were a good idea.

'For tonight,' I replied at last. 'The thing where Murray made you walk in on me and man-Dylan. I wouldn't have kissed him if I'd known you were there.'

'I don't care about that.'

'Oh. Okay.'

'No,' she said suddenly, turning to me. 'That's a lie. I do care about that.'

I opened my mouth to reply, although I had no idea what I was going to say.

But she grabbed my hand first. 'You feel it, right?'

'Feel what?'

She exhaled heavily and ran her free hand through her hair. It was almost exactly the same gesture that Romeo-Dylan had made when we were on the couch. They really were going to be perfect together.

'This thing between us,' she said. 'Please tell me you feel it too.'

The world stopped turning.

For a moment, everything was completely silent and still.

She took my other hand. My heels dropped from my fingers to the ground. The sunrise caught in her hair and painted the side of her face in delicate streaks of gold.

'Please tell me I'm not imagining it,' she whispered. 'Please tell me it's not just me.'

I didn't speak. I couldn't. For a long moment, I just looked at her.

Then, 'No,' I said. 'It's not just you.'

That was all it took for her to kiss me.

This kiss wasn't nice.

This kiss was terrifying.

This kiss didn't make me feel like I was on solid ground. This kiss was an earthquake, the ground breaking apart beneath my feet.

Our teeth clashed together. It was hard and fast and ravenous. One of her hands was fisted in my hair. One of mine was in hers. We couldn't get close enough, tongues and lips and teeth smashing together again, no time to breathe, no room for air, only her, only her, only her and the sounds she made as I kissed her, only her and the sounds I made as she kissed me, the feel of her skin against mine as we pressed together, not close enough, not close enough, the racing of her heart beneath my hand, the fire as my heart caught alight in my chest.

This kiss was a bomb, and it was exploding, breaking the whole world apart.

Which, in theory, sounds like everything you want from a kiss.

But my world had been blown up before.

'No!' I said, breaking away. 'No, no, no, Dylan. Wait.'

'Mandie?'

She looked so beautiful in the early morning light. Her hair was in disarray. Her lips were swollen. There were fading marks on her shoulder from where my fingers had dug into her skin.

What had just happened? What were we doing?

What was *she* doing, kissing me?

Something started to bubble up in my stomach, a volcano of panic and confusion and fear.

'No,' I said, and fled.

I didn't even realise I'd left my heels behind.

14

When you get angry as infrequently as I do, you get kind of rusty at it. It's like a muscle that's out of shape. You barely realise it's there. But then you use it, and it starts to ache.

It took me a long time to realise I was furious.

There was no time to go to bed before call time the next day. So I showered, did my best to unwrinkle my dress, put on my bubbliest voice and chatted to Murray about the Last Chance Party in my ITM. 'So what was it like when Dylan G interrupted your kiss with Dylan JM?' he asked.

'Oh my goodness, it was so awkward when Dylan G interrupted us!' I said, wishing there was a pie nearby that I could smash into his face.

I was mad at Murray for setting me up, for making Dylan walk in on the kiss, for all the little strings he kept pulling. That I knew. That wasn't news.

But that wasn't when I realised I was furious.

They'd flipped the order of the dates for this episode, so the group date was first, with the remaining seven of us lined up in front of Romeo-Dylan in one of the rose gardens. 'Today we're going to play a game that will help us find out who really knows Dylan best,' Z said. 'On the ground in front of you, you'll find a whiteboard and a marker. In Dylan's hands, you'll find a stack of questions.'

'They're not hard, I promise,' Romeo-Dylan said.

'Dylan's going to ask these questions, and you're going to write your answers on your whiteboards,' Z said. 'For every question you get correct, you get a point. The person with the most points at the end of the date will win the all-important single date.'

Romeo-Dylan smiled at us. I was mad at him too, although I knew it wasn't entirely fair. His job was to be a perfect Prince Charming who women wanted to be with, and all he was doing was exactly that. And who could blame him for falling for Dylan? I'd done exactly the same thing.

So that wasn't when I realised I was furious either.

It wasn't when Z announced the date's big twist – that we'd be competing in this trivia contest against *Cece*, of all people, who Romeo-Dylan had apparently found time to become friends with after she fainted on that first night. It wasn't when Cece managed to win the trivia contest either, giving her the next single date, even though she wasn't technically in the competition.

And it wasn't when we were trudging back up to the Villa after the date ended, cold and miserable, as everyone bitched about how unfair it was that Cece was going on a date with

Romeo-Dylan. 'What is this "friend" thing they've got going on anyway?' Jess D demanded.

'I know, right?' Naya said. 'Just how much time has he been spending with her if she can win a whole damn trivia contest about him?'

'Do you think he's going to invite her back into the Villa?' Kumiko asked.

'He'd better not,' Parisa said.

Dylan didn't say anything. I glanced sideways at her as we walked up the hill. She was looking straight ahead, stone-faced.

I almost realised I was furious then.

But Jess D started to cry – 'It's just so unfair!' she sobbed, 'I like him so much and I've been trying so hard and it's just *not working*!' – and I let Mummy Mandie come out of her box again, the fury shoved way, way down.

It wasn't until the next night that I finally realised.

'Since none of you are going on a single date this episode, we need to do something else with you,' Murray told us. 'So we're going to have a dinner party.'

'With Dylan JM?' Kumiko asked.

'No.'

'What, as a punishment? Because we haven't earned time with him?' Parisa said, folding her arms. 'Because none of us won that ridiculous trivia contest?'

'No,' Murray said. 'Because we gave him the day off. He's been filming every day, and he's exhausted.'

'Is he spending that time with *her*?' Jess D said. 'The fainter?'

'You'll be happy to know,' Murray said, 'that Dylan and Cece agreed on their date last night that it was best he spend the rest of this season focusing on his relationships, not his friendships.'

Lily snorted. Murray raised an eyebrow. 'Do you have something to add, Lily?'

'Not at all,' she replied sunnily. 'Why would I have something to add?'

He looked at her for a long moment. She looked back, unafraid.

'So Cece's not coming back,' Naya said. 'She's not back in the competition.'

'No, Cece is not coming back into the competition,' Murray said, dragging his eyes away from Lily. 'They're just friends. Can I get on with explaining this dinner party now?'

Production had placed a big box of questions in the centre of the dining table. 'They're compatibility questions,' Murray explained. 'Designed so we can find out exactly what you're looking for in a partner, and if that matches up with what the Romeo wants.'

'Does the person who's most compatible with him win anything?' Naya asked.

'They'll win the first chat at the Last Chance Party. A private chat, where no one can steal him away.'

Murray could claim all he wanted that this dinner party wasn't a punishment. It was absolutely going to look like a punishment when they edited the footage. They'd film some talking head with Romeo-Dylan where he said something like, 'When my friend Cece turned out to know me

247

better than my seven remaining Juliets, that really sent me into a tailspin. What if none of the women here are right for me?'

They'd show the dinner party, where we all looked like bad, terrible girlfriends who never listened to their boyfriend when he talked. They'd let the question hang in the air for a while, maybe an episode or two: were *none* of us compatible with Romeo-Dylan? Maybe he'd eliminated the wrong person! Maybe they'd even show some footage of him in the Convent, talking to Cece and the other women he'd let go, trying to work out if he'd made a mistake.

But then it would all turn out fine in the end. He'd go on another date with Dylan, and they'd be perfect together, and he'd say something like, 'I really feel like you *know* me, Dyl,' and she'd reply, 'Sorry I didn't know all that random trivia about you,' and he'd laugh and say, 'Knowing random trivia about a person doesn't mean you know them.'

Then they'd kiss.

I wondered if it was nice, when they kissed, or whether it was an earthquake.

I gritted my teeth and clenched my fists, dimly aware that something was simmering.

They'd laid out placecards on the dinner table where they wanted us to sit. I was between Lily and Parisa, across from Dylan. 'Are you open to changing the seating arrangements at all?' I overheard Lily asked Murray.

'No,' he said shortly.

'Shame,' she said. 'I could have done a much better job.'

He made a growling noise in the back of his throat.

They'd made us cook the dinner for the party, but they didn't let us eat it (not a punishment, my arse). 'Questions first,' Murray said. 'Then you can eat.'

'We're grown women,' Parisa said. 'We can do both.'

'No one looks good on camera with sauce on their face,' he said. 'And no one sounds good talking with their mouth full. Kumiko, you start.'

Kumiko reached into the box of questions. 'Name one thing you and Dylan JM have in common.'

'Subtle,' Lily said. 'I'll start. Dylan JM and I have nothing in common.'

'Then why are you here?' Parisa asked.

'Because opposites attract, obviously,' Lily replied, batting her eyelashes. 'Who's next?'

I was next to her, so everyone looked at me. 'We're, uh, both people-pleasers,' I replied.

I felt, rather than saw, Murray roll his eyes.

Parisa said something about how they both loved the outdoors. Naya said something about how they were both scared of heights ('Wish I'd known that yesterday,' she grumbled). Jess D struggled for a few moments, then said they both loved cheese, which drew a bit of a laugh.

Then it was Dylan's turn. 'We're both very clear about what we want,' she said.

My fingers closed tight around my fork, my knuckles white. The thing simmering inside me started to bubble more vigorously.

Jess D asked the next question. 'What's the worst thing a romantic partner could do to you?'

'Clearly a man wrote that question,' Kumiko said. 'How many kinds of abuse do you want us to list?'

'Let's modify it,' Jess D said. 'Outside of abuse or violence or anything straight-up illegal, what's the worst thing a partner could do to you?'

'Insist on joint bank accounts,' Parisa said. 'I made that mistake with my ex. It took me years to untangle it all.'

'That could fall under the abuse category,' Kumiko said. 'Spending your personal assets without asking, controlling access to accounts . . . that's financial abuse.'

'Okay, Miss Lawyer,' Parisa said. 'What's your answer?'

'Easy. Cheat.'

'Lie,' I said.

Everyone turned to look at me, including Dylan.

My fingers clenched even tighter around my fork, but I managed to keep my voice mild as I said, 'You can't be in a relationship with someone you can't trust.'

'I agree with Amanda,' Naya said. 'That goes for lying by omission as well.'

'Yes,' I said. 'Absolutely.'

'Making you feel small,' Dylan said. 'Making you feel worthless. Making you feel like you're nothing and no one without them.'

She was looking right at me. Could she *be* any more obvious?

'Depending on the situation, that could be abuse too,' Kumiko said. 'Emotional abuse is a very real thing.'

'Tell me about it,' Jess D said. 'I had an emotionally abusive partner a few years ago and they made me feel like a shell of a person. The amount of therapy I had to go through was wild. *Wild.*'

'I can't believe none of you have mentioned the obvious one.'

'And what is the obvious one, Lily?' Kumiko said.

'Die,' she said.

The table went silent.

'I'll ask the next one, shall I?' Lily said, sticking her hand in the box. 'All right, here we go. What's the sexiest quality a person can have?'

'Lily,' Murray said quietly.

She ignored him. 'Far be it from me to state the obvious,' she said, 'but the sexiest quality a person can have is to be good at sex. No one can be sexy if they're bad at it.'

'I don't think that's true,' Naya said. 'There are plenty of men I find sexy, and I have no idea if they're good in bed.'

'Dylan JM, for instance,' Parisa said. 'Sexy as hell! That smile! Those hands! The way he rolls up his shirt sleeves and gets his forearms out! I have no idea what he's like in bed, but that doesn't mean he's not sexy.'

'He's got to be good in bed,' Jess D said. 'He's so considerate. He'd be generous.'

'But what if you found out he was bad in bed?' Lily said. 'Would he be sexy then?'

'Lily, if you don't think Dylan JM is sexy, no one's forcing you to be here,' Kumiko said.

'That wasn't the question, though,' Lily said. 'It was "What is the sexiest quality a person can have?" The answer's in the question, people.'

'Competence.'

'Competence?' Parisa asked.

'Competence,' Dylan repeated. 'I've got two answers, but that's the first one. Competence is one of the sexiest qualities a person can have.'

'What do you mean?' Jess D asked.

'You know when people are really good at something?' Dylan said. 'It doesn't matter what it is. It could be, I don't know, flower-arranging. Singing. Dog grooming.'

'Sailing?' Kumiko said.

'Sure, sailing, whatever,' Dylan said. 'Like I said, it doesn't matter what it is. It could be simple. Tiny. When you see someone absolutely killing it at something they're great at, that's the sexiest thing in the world.'

You're an organisational machine.

Putting together that meal plan was like solving a fucking Rubik's cube.

No one who saw you build a perfectly functioning catapult today out of random pieces of machinery could ever think you weren't the absolute best.

My head was starting to ache from how hard I was gritting my teeth together.

'What's your second answer?' Parisa asked. 'You said you had two.'

'I don't quite know how to put the second one into words,' Dylan said. 'I don't think there's a word for the quality I mean.'

She leaned her elbows on the table and rested her chin on her hands. 'It's . . . listening, I guess?'

You're kind, and you're funny. And you're an incredible listener.

'Agreed,' Jess D said. 'Listening is sexy. That's one of the reasons I like Dylan JM so much. You can tell he's really listening when you talk to him.'

'But it's not just listening,' Dylan went on. 'It's listening, and hearing. Listening, and hearing, and understanding, and responding with kindness and compassion and generosity.'

You're Jane Bennet, babe. You're hot and sweet and generous.

The pot boiled over.

I slammed my fork down so hard my plate cracked. 'Excuse me,' I bit out, and left the room.

I went to the only place I knew I could be guaranteed alone time: the bathroom.

I sat down on the toilet lid, head in my hands, fingers clawing at my hair. The rage was permeating my whole body.

We had this heater when I was a kid. I think we'd inherited it from my grandparents, because it was very old-fashioned. It was electric, a wood-panelled box with a steel grate in front of the heating element. When you turned it on, the element went bright red, radiant with heat, so hot that you could see the air shimmer around it.

Modern radiant heaters have temperature control. There are safety rules and things, so you can only turn them up so high, the same way they build some cars with speed limiters. But this one was old, so you could really crank it. If you turned it up too high, it would start to vibrate. Dad used to love to turn it up too high – 'I run cold,' he'd say, putting his arthritic fingers so close to the red-hot part that it always amazed me he didn't get burned.

A few months after he died, I turned the heater on as high as it would go and curled up in a ball in front of it. It started to shake. So did I, crying.

But it got too hot in front of the heater, so I got up to open a window. I was halfway across the room when it exploded.

That was how I felt now. I was red-hot, the air bright and shimmery around me, shaking harder and harder, about to explode.

There was a tap at the bathroom door. 'Mandie?'

'No!'

'Mandie, please!'

'I said no, Dylan!'

'Mandie, just tell me what's wrong!'

I yanked the door open and pulled her in. I caught a glimpse of Suzette and a whole bunch of crew behind her before I slammed it again.

I turned the sink on, as high as it could go. 'Mandie—' Dylan started.

'Do you really want to have this conversation right now?' I hissed, turning the shower on as well. 'Seriously? With half the Villa outside the door?'

'Mandie, can you just look at me?'

I looked at her.

'I need to apologise to you,' she said. 'I'm sorry.'

The shower spray was soaking the cuffs of my jeans.

I folded my arms, digging my fingers into the flesh of my biceps.

'I know that just because you're into women doesn't mean you're into me,' she said. 'I just thought . . . the other morning, I asked if you felt it too. You said you did.'

'What the fuck, Dylan?' I snarled.

She looked at the ground.

'Of course I fucking felt it too,' I said. 'Do you know how confusing this has been for me? To have all these little signals from you? All these little moments? Having to constantly be like, "Calm down, Mandie, it's all in your head," when *it wasn't fucking all in my head*?'

'I know,' she said quietly. 'I'm sorry.'

'Why couldn't you just be up-front with me?' I said. 'How hard would it have been to tell me the truth? When I was like, "Hey, guess what, I date women," how hard would it have been to say, "Oh cool, me too."?'

She closed her eyes and bit her lip.

'You do, right?' I said. 'Or am I some straight-girl experiment?'

'Of course you're not an experiment!' she said, opening her eyes again. 'I'm not as experienced as you. I got married so young, and then I had Noah . . . I've kissed women, sure, fooled around with them, but I've never really dated a woman properly, never had a girlfriend or anything like that. But . . .'

'But you're bi.'

'I've never used the word,' she said. 'It's not a side of myself that I've had much of a chance to explore. But . . . yes. I'm attracted to women. Yes.'

'And it didn't occur to you to tell me this?' I bit out. 'When we were outside, and I was spilling my guts to you about Jac? When you were asking me all those questions about why I didn't tell *you* I was bi?'

She buried her face in her hands, digging her fingers into her temples. 'Fuck, I've messed this up so badly,' she said. 'I'm so sorry, Mandie.'

'Yeah, you have,' I said. 'At least Jac told me the truth.'

'No, she fucking did not!' Dylan said, dropping her hands. 'She told you horrible lies about the kind of person you are!'

'Don't,' I said shortly. 'I don't want to hear how great I am. I don't want another set of affirmation cards. If you believed any of that, you would have had enough respect for me to tell me the *fucking truth.*'

I blinked furiously. Why, why, why did I have to be one of those people who cried when they were angry?

'Mandie, I've gone about this so poorly,' she said. 'You deserve so much better. You mean the world to me, and—'

'No,' I said. 'I don't want to hear that either.'

'It's the truth.'

'Is it?'

'Yes!'

'Okay, fine,' I said. 'Leave with me. Go down to the Convent with me. Right now.'

Dylan froze.

'Well?' I demanded.

'I can't.'

'That's what I thought.'

The tears kept welling up. I wiped my hand angrily over my face.

'Mandie, it's not what you think,' she said. Tears were beading in her eyes too, and her voice was shaking. 'It's complicated.'

'No, it's not,' I said.

I leaned against the wall next to the shower. I was getting wet, but I didn't care. I just needed something to hold me up.

'It's this simple, Dylan,' I said. 'I believe you like me. I believe you are attracted to me.'

'Yes,' she said, a tear rolling down each cheek. 'Yes, Mandie.'

'But it is not fair of you to do this to me,' I said. 'It is not fair of you to make heart eyes at me, or to make those little comments at dinner, and it is definitely not fair of you to kiss me. Because what you actually want is him.'

She didn't say anything.

Maybe it was just because I was so unused to being exploding-radiant-heater angry, but the fact that she didn't say anything made me really happy.

At least she respected my intelligence enough not to deny it.

15

We didn't talk for a week.

I should have packed up, dusted off my 'I'm leaving' speech for Romeo-Dylan and gone to the Convent, but I didn't. I'd always thought of myself as a nice person, but that radiant-heater anger had burned away some layers and unearthed my petty bitch core.

I wasn't going to make this easy for her. I wasn't going to just go away. She was going to have to look at me and choose him anyway, and I hoped it made her feel *terrible*.

I played into it for Murray. 'Dylan G and I had a falling out,' I said in an ITM. 'We're not friends anymore.'

'Did your feelings for Dylan JM get in the way?'

'You could say that.

'Full sentences, Amanda.'

'Our feelings for Dylan JM came between us, but it wasn't just that,' I said. 'Dylan G just isn't who I thought she was.'

'Good job,' Murray said to me when we wrapped up. 'You've got a really strong narrative arc coming through now. It'll set you up well for the rest of the season, and give you a smooth shot onto *Juliet on the Beach* if you want it.'

I appreciated that he wasn't even pretending there was a possibility I was going to win. At least someone was being honest with me.

Production stood Dylan and I next to each other at the next Necklace Ceremony, probably hoping for some kind of showdown, but we didn't say a word to each other. I hugged Naya goodbye. So did Dylan. Our elbows knocked painfully together, but neither of us said anything, not even sorry.

Production also sat us next to each other on the couch for the single date card reading ('Roses are red, some salads are Caesar, I've kept you waiting, but date me, Parisa?'). 'I'm excited for you, 'risa, but the rhymes are getting worse,' Kumiko said. 'Caesar?'

'I don't know, my favourite's still when they rhymed "Amanda" with "Uganda",' Parisa said. 'Did we ever find out whether that was true? Has he been to Uganda?'

'Not that he told me,' I replied. 'I was too preoccupied with the car on that date to do any fact-checking.'

'He has,' Dylan said. 'When he was a baby.'

'What a shame for you that it didn't come up in the trivia game the other day,' Lily said.

I could feel Dylan beside me trying to control her irritation, but I didn't say anything to her, and she didn't say anything to me.

I suppose it was technically a lie that I didn't say *anything* to her for a week. 'Ladies, there will be no group date this episode,' Z announced. 'No Last Chance Party or Necklace Ceremony either. Instead, it's time for the dreaded Thunderdome date. Two women will be going on a date with our Romeo. One will get a necklace and return to the Villa. The other will go straight to the Convent.'

He laid the date card on the coffee table. 'Amanda,' he said, 'if you'd like to do the honours?'

I got up and slipped the card out of the envelope. 'Roses are red, a lock needs a key,' I read, 'it's time for a choice, Lily, Dylan G.'

Dylan exhaled and leaned back against the couch cushions. Lily laughed. 'This should be fun,' she said.

I was feeling a whole lot of emotions, but chief among them was relief that it wasn't me on the Thunderdome date card instead of Lily. The last way I wanted to be eliminated was with both Dylans grabbing me by the hair and rubbing their relationship in my face.

There were other emotions in the cocktail too, though. Anger, definitely, still. Fear, despite myself, that Dylan might not come back. And worse, hope that she wouldn't – that she and Romeo-Dylan *weren't* perfect for each other, that all this had been some horrible misunderstanding and there was hope for her and me yet.

Don't you have any self-respect? Jac whispered in my mind.

I cracked and said two words to Dylan just before she left. 'Good luck,' I muttered.

'Thanks,' she replied.

Then she and Lily were gone. Even though Parisa and Kumiko and Jess D were still in the Villa with me, it suddenly felt cavernously empty.

I went to bed early that night. It was the first time I'd taken my make-up off by myself in the whole four weeks I'd been on the show. Dylan and Lily were the only other people left in my bedroom, and neither of them were here. I was going to be alone with whichever one of them came back.

I closed my eyes and tried to force myself to go to sleep. I could feel the hard edges of the affirmation flashcards under my pillow. I traced them with the tip of one finger, over and over again, as I lay there for hours in the darkness, waiting for the bedroom door to open.

When it finally did, I allowed myself the quickest peek. It was Dylan silhouetted against the hall light.

Of course it was.

'Mandie?' she whispered.

I didn't respond.

After a moment, she sighed. The bathroom door clicked shut softly behind her.

I turned over so I was facing the wall and curled myself around my feelings, my knees almost touching my chin.

I could feel her eyes on me when she came out of the bathroom. She stood there for what felt like hours, looking at me.

I tried to keep my breath deep and even, hoping she couldn't hear my heart hammering in my chest.

Eventually, she exhaled. The sheets rustled as she got into bed.

Even when I heard her sobbing quietly into her pillow, I didn't say anything. I just pulled the doona tighter around me and tried not to cry too.

Dylan got the next single date. No one was surprised.

She came back with a necklace. No one was surprised by that either.

Kumiko, Parisa, Jess D and I went on the final group date of the season. ('Remember,' Z said, 'this is the last chance you'll have to spend time with our Romeo before the all-important final four stage! Make it count, Juliets!') We spent the afternoon frolicking around in the icy water of the lake. The four of us were shivering in bikinis, and eventually wardrobe made us wear pasties underneath because of all the visible nipples.

The date was made even harder by the fact that Romeo-Dylan was clearly distracted the whole time. He smiled and said nice things and he was very handsome in all his shirtless glory, but even when he was talking to you, it was obvious his mind was somewhere else.

'Are you all right?' I asked him, even though it was a stupid thing to do, because I knew exactly where his mind was and who it was on and I didn't want to hear about it.

There was something a little sad about the smile he gave me. 'You're one of the only people who ever asks me that,' he said. 'Thank you.'

He hugged me. I hugged him back. If I were better at being a petty bitch, I would have hated him, but I didn't. None of this was his fault, after all.

There was a necklace on offer on the group date, and he gave it to me. 'Being around this person always makes my day brighter,' he said. 'Amanda, I want to know if your heart is the other half of mine. Will you take this necklace and commit to finding out with me?'

It was easier to say yes than to say no, so I took it.

Don't you have any self-respect? Jac whispered again.

It wasn't even a case of not having self-respect at this point. It was active self-punishment. At the Last Chance Party, I watched the Dylans talk after she stole him for a second. His head was bent towards hers, their fingers laced together, knees touching. His necklace glittered around her neck.

I traced the line of my own necklace, and thought for a second about yanking it off and flinging it at their feet. *Not anymore,* I'd yell. *I'm done.*

'Stop fingering your necklace, Amanda,' Parisa said. 'You're rubbing it in.'

'Oh. Sorry.' I dropped my hand.

'What were you thinking about?' Kumiko asked. 'You were a million miles away.'

'My ex.'

Jess D raised her eyebrows. 'Your ex?'

'Not like that,' I said. 'When my ex broke up with me, it wasn't because there was someone else. I thought that made it harder. Like, I'm so terrible that you'd rather be alone than be with me? At least if there was another person I'd understand, you know?'

'It doesn't make it easier, though,' Parisa said.

'Not even a little,' I agreed.

The four of us watched the Dylans together for a long moment. Neither Dylan noticed.

'Is it weird that I miss Lily Fireball?' Jess D said. 'Sure, she could be annoying, but at least she never let us sit around like sad sacks.'

I'm not sure if Jess D saying she missed Lily counted as a wish exactly, but if it did, she got it. She was sent down to the Convent, leaving Parisa, Kumiko, Dylan and I as the official final four of the season.

'How do you feel about being one of the final four?' Murray asked me in an ITM.

'I feel great about being part of the final four!' I lied through my teeth. 'Dylan JM and I have built a really strong connection, and I'm excited to explore it further.'

Murray gave me a little *keep talking* gesture.

'Being here has helped me rebuild my self-confidence,' I said. 'I went through a tough break-up that shook me to the core. Dylan has helped me feel like I'm worthy of love again.'

He gave me a thumbs up. 'Normally, this is the part of the season where the Romeo would get to meet some of your friends and get an idea of who you are in the real world. We can't do that this year for obvious reasons, so how are you planning to communicate this to him?'

'I know that this season isn't a normal season,' I said. 'I know Dylan can't come home with me and meet my friends and see who I am in the real world. But that's the person

I've showed to Dylan. The real me, all along. There are no surprises with me. No hidden depths. What you see is what you get.'

Murray didn't answer.

I waited.

His eyelids drooped closed.

'Murray!' I said.

They snapped back open. 'Sorry,' he said. 'That was very rude.'

'I know I'm not the most interesting person in the world, and I know I don't always tell a story like you want me to, but I didn't think I was that boring.'

'It's not you, Amanda, it's me,' he said. 'I'm being pulled in about twenty different directions, and I'm not getting enough sleep.'

The bags under his eyes made it clear he wasn't lying (about this, anyway). 'Are you all right?'

'You don't need to worry about me. It's my job to worry about you. Tell me about you and Dylan G.'

I folded my arms.

'For fuck's sake, Amanda, you don't have to tell me the truth,' he said. 'I don't care what the truth is. I care about the storyline. You're in a feud, and rivalries are good TV. Give me something.'

'Fine,' I said, sitting up straighter. 'I hate how obvious it is that Dylan and Dylan are going to end up together. It's bullshit.'

Murray closed his eyes again, but this time it was in frustration. 'I know you know not to swear, Amanda.'

When Murray and I were (finally) done, Dylan was waiting outside to film her ITM. 'How was it?' she asked.

'Fine,' I said shortly. 'Have fun.'

I wondered what kind of things Murray was going to make her say about me, about our so-called rivalry. *It's cute, really, that she thinks she has a shot. Everyone likes vanilla ice cream, but no one chooses it.*

No. She wouldn't say any of that. Even if she was the kind of person who would say that, she was the frontrunner. She was getting the winner's edit. They'd focus on her saying all kinds of lovely stuff about her connection with Romeo-Dylan, and they'd edit me to come off looking like a jealous bitch who couldn't handle her friend's success.

Lily was gone now. They needed a new villain. Wifey-turned-monster was as good a narrative as any. My whole not-being-out-on-the-show plan would be for nothing. I might not get outed, but I'd get death threats anyway.

I went up to our bedroom. It was empty. Everyone who slept there except me and Dylan had been eliminated.

Fine. *Fine.* They wanted me to be the jealous bitchy one? I was going to be the pettiest little bitch in the world.

My suitcase was beside Dylan's, sitting at the end of our bed. I shoved all my loose ends into it and moved it over to the other side of the room, to the bunk where Lily used to sleep. I took some of my stuff and spread it across the bottom bunk, then threw my pyjamas on the top one. Then I climbed up onto my old bed, and even though it was tricky to do for a top bunk, I made it – perfectly, pristine, so it looked like nobody had ever slept there.

I hesitated when I pulled the affirmation flashcards out from under my pillow. *I am confident. I am capable. I am strong. I am enough.*

My fingers tightened around them. I wanted to keep them, so badly.

But no. I had my own list. I could make my own flashcards.

I left them on the pillow, climbed down, and went to have a shower before I changed my mind.

I washed my hair slowly, digging my fingers into my scalp. I took my time combing conditioner through it, letting the steady, orderly movement – a simple thing, an easy thing, something I knew how to do – calm my nerves.

Lily's conditioner was next to mine on the shower shelf. She must have been fuming when she got down to the Convent and realised she'd forgotten to take it.

What was it she'd said to me, that night we'd taken our make-up off together? That Romeo-Dylan didn't like Dylan the best out of anyone? That they had no spark? That they'd be a terrible match?

She'd be fuming again when she realised she was wrong about that. 'Oh, it's obvious the Dylans are going to end up together, whenever we talked Dylan JM would just *gush* about Dylan G,' Cece would tell her.

Then Lily would probably push her in the lake or try and drown her in a bathtub or something. Partially for old times' sake, but mostly because she was clearly someone who didn't like to be wrong.

I wrapped a towel around myself and stepped out of the bathroom.

'What the fuck is this?' Dylan snarled.

She was standing next to the bunk that had been Lily's. She nudged my suitcase with her foot. 'What the fuck, Mandie?' she repeated. 'Is this what it's like now? You can't even be within six feet of me?'

'It's nothing,' I said, pulling my towel tighter around myself. It felt like my voice should have come out all quavery, but it didn't. 'We're the only two left in here. There's no reason for us to be on top of each other.'

She threw my affirmation cards down at my feet. 'It's not nothing.'

I wanted to bend down and gather them up. I wanted to clutch them to my heart. I wanted to tell her what they meant to me, what *she* meant to me.

I dug my nails into my thigh and made myself stay silent.

'I know I've fucked everything up,' she said. 'But you're so important to me, Mandie. The thought of you and I being nothing to each other after this kills me. It *kills* me.'

My voice hadn't wavered, but hers had cracked. Her shoulders were shaking. She swallowed once, twice, convulsively, and then she buried her face in her hands and started to sob.

I tried.

I tried to restrain my impulses.

I tried to make a good choice, even though it was a hard one.

I tried. I tried. I tried.

I failed.

'You could never be nothing to me, Dylan,' I said, and held her tight as she sobbed into my shoulder. 'Never.'

I'm not sure how long we stood there like that. It was a bubble within our bubble, a moment that existed outside of the show, outside of the world, outside of time.

But she pulled back eventually. 'I have to tell you some stuff, Mandie,' she said hoarsely.

'Okay,' I said. 'Can I put some clothes on first?'

'No.'

I raised my eyebrows.

'Not like that!' she said hurriedly. 'It's just that if we stop now I'm going to lose my nerve because it's a big deal, telling you what I have to tell you, and – can I just tell you? Can I just tell you now? Please?'

'Come on,' I said, and led her into the bathroom.

We sat on the floor, leaning against the cabinet beneath the sinks, taps and shower running, steam misting the air, so there was no chance anyone could hear us. 'Okay,' I told her. 'We're alone. No one's listening except me. Say what you need to say.'

Dylan let out a long exhale. 'There are a few things I need to tell you,' she said. 'The first one is that I like you, Mandie. I like you so much. You're so important to me. I meant what I said. If we can't at least be friends after the show is done, it's going to kill me.'

'I like you too,' I said. 'A lot. Too much. Which is why I've been so upset.'

'That leads me to the second thing,' she said. 'Which is that I'm so, so, so sorry. Everything you said to me the other night after the dinner party was absolutely correct. I've been

269

horribly unfair to you. If you never want to speak to me again after this, it'll kill me, but I'll understand. I deserve it.'

She took another deep breath. 'I know I shouldn't have kissed you,' she said. 'I should have just shoved all these feelings down, pretended them away. I was trying to. Really hard. But then they just started bleeding out everywhere, every time I looked at you, and then I just . . . blurted out how I felt about you, and you said you felt it too, and – this sounds like such a cop-out, but I couldn't *not* kiss you. The way I feel about you is . . .'

Dylan broke off, pressing her fingers to her temples for several long moments. 'I haven't felt like this about anyone in a long time,' she said. 'It's electric. When I kissed you, it felt like I'd stuck a fork into a power point. It's amazing, but I kind of hate it, because it's so big, so overwhelming—'

'So out of control?'

She nodded. 'I wasn't expecting this, Mandie,' she said, something desperate in her eyes. 'I wasn't expecting *you*.'

'I wasn't expecting you either,' I said. 'I wasn't expecting anyone, not for a long time. I could barely even see a world where there could be an anyone again.'

She exhaled again, a shaky laugh. 'God, this is terrible timing.'

I shifted slightly, turning my body towards hers. 'Dylan,' I said, 'if this is what you want – if you and me is what you want – then we can make it work.'

She reached out and took my hand, raised it to her lips, and kissed it.

For a few glorious moments, I felt like I was everything

she'd written on those affirmation cards. Everything that had ever been on my list. I felt like Queen Shit.

But then, 'It's more complicated than that,' she said quietly.

'Why?' I said, pulling my hand away. 'Do you really like man-Dylan so much? Are you really that into him? Is it really better than what we have? What we could be together?'

She shook her head.

'Then why not?' I demanded. 'If you feel the way you say you do about me, why not?'

She leaned her head back against the cabinet and closed her eyes. 'Because,' she said, 'I have to win this show.'

16

It took her a long time to tell me the full story. 'I signed an NDA, so you can't tell anybody about this,' she said. 'If you do, I'm fucked, Mandie. Promise me.'

'Of course I promise,' I said.

It had started the day we'd met, at auditions.

'You're a nurse?' Murray said.

'Yes,' Dylan replied.

'So you must be working on the frontlines with this new virus, right?'

'Yes,' she said. 'You're going to be lucky if you get a season this year. With the way things are going, we're all going to be locked down.'

'It takes a hell of a lot to derail Marry Me, Juliet,' Murray replied. 'So why are you here?'

'To give myself an excuse not to be on the frontlines, honestly,' she said. 'I'm starting to realise that nursing is not

272

the life I want for myself. The work is hard and the hours are long and the pay is shit. I'm a single mother. Every hour I spend at work is an hour I spend away from my kid. And if this virus is as bad as I think it's going to be . . .'

Her voice trailed off. 'It's selfish,' she said. 'I got into nursing to help people. That's still all I want to do. But I can't live a life where I never get to see my son. Where I'm in danger every day. Where I risk having him grow up without a mother.'

'Tell me more about your son,' Murray said.

'His name's Noah,' Dylan said. 'He's nearly seven. He's great. Smart. Funny. Huge personality. Heart of gold. I love him to bits.'

'Are you looking for a father figure for him?'

'He's got a dad. I might not like him all the time, but he's a good dad.'

'Interesting,' Murray said, scribbling something down on his clipboard.

'I think that's why he picked me,' Dylan said. 'I didn't say I was looking for love. I didn't say I was looking for a dad for Noah. All I wanted was an out.'

When we'd had drinks after auditions, and she'd got that text and had to leave, I'd assumed it was from her work or her babysitter or something. It wasn't. It was Murray, asking her if she could come back for a private chat.

'First of all, I need you to sign this,' he said.

'What is it?'

'It's a lot of legalese that says I can sue you if you ever talk about this conversation.'

'Whatever this is, I don't think I'm up for it.'

'It's nothing bad,' he said. 'I promise.'

After a few moments, Dylan scrawled her signature across the bottom of the paper. 'All right,' she said. 'I'm listening.'

'Are you a fan of the show?'

'I've watched every season,' she'd replied, 'so yeah, I guess you could say that.'

'Then you know we haven't had the best track record lately with our Romeos and Juliets,' Murray said. 'We've only managed two solid couples from the past four years of Marry Me, Juliet and Wherefore Art Thou Romeo?.'

'Basil and Megan and Luna and Roger. I know.'

'You might also know,' Murray said, 'about the growing movement online for us to cast more diverse participants.'

'They're right. You should.'

'I agree with you,' Murray said, 'but the network is hesitant.'

Dylan raised an eyebrow. 'Worried about losing their white audience?'

'Yes,' Murray said bluntly. 'But they've given us one shot to show that it could work. Just one. We've got to get it right.'

He put a headshot on the table in front of her. 'This is Dylan Jayasinghe Mellor.'

'I know this guy,' she replied. 'I know who he is, I mean. The guy who had the panic attack at the Olympics and still won a gold medal. He has that mental health charity.'

'He's our Romeo,' Murray said. 'How would you feel about being his final Juliet?'

'What?'

'We want this season to be the biggest, splashiest, most romantic fairy-tale season ever,' Murray said. 'We want to *tell the most beautiful love story we've ever told, and we want to do it with two likeable, charismatic people of colour. We want to get the best ratings you've ever seen in your life and to prove to the ancient racists at the network that we don't have to cast only white people to make this show work. So we're going to rig it.'*

'And that's what we did,' Dylan said miserably. 'We rigged it.'

'Let me get this straight,' I said. 'You and man-Dylan – that's nothing. That's not a thing?'

'I wouldn't go that far,' she said. 'I like him. We're friends, I guess. But this is not going to be one of those situations where people start off fake dating and it turns into real dating. This isn't *To All The Boys I've Loved Before: Marry Me, Juliet* edition.'

'I saw you on his boat.'

'What?'

'The day after the love machine date,' I said. 'We had the day off, because Heather had been eliminated and there wasn't going to be a Necklace Ceremony. I went for a walk, and I saw you and him together on his boat.'

'Oh,' Dylan said. 'That wasn't anything.'

'You looked pretty cosy.'

'I think we hugged?' Dylan said. 'Whatever you're thinking, it was the opposite. We were trying to get to know each other better without the cameras there, because we know we've got months and months of pretending to be in love coming up, but . . . realistically, it was even less steamy than that awkward kiss between you two I walked in on the other week.'

'It wasn't that bad, was it?'

'I'm sorry to tell you this, Mandie, but yes. It was a very awkward kiss.'

She closed her eyes and banged her head a couple of times against the bathroom cabinets. 'Don't listen to me,' she said. 'I'm sure it was fine. I was just jealous.'

'Jealous?'

'In case I've been too subtle,' she said, opening one eye, 'I'd much rather be the one kissing you.'

'If we're being honest,' I said, 'I'd much rather have been kissing you too.'

I wanted to make her smile, but instead she sighed. 'This is a huge fucking mess, Mandie,' she said. 'Not just for us. For man-Dylan too. I'm almost positive there's someone here he actually likes, but he's just as stuck as I am.'

'There's no way out of it?'

'No,' she said. 'We both signed our lives away. There's the NDA, to start with, so if we talk about any of it we can both be sued. But they're paying me too. A shit-ton of money. Enough that I won't have to go back to nursing for years. I won't have to risk catching the virus, which means I can have Noah home with me.'

Her voice cracked again, and a tear ran down her cheek. 'I miss him so much,' she said. 'I'd do anything for him. Anything. I thought coming here and pretending to fall in love with Dylan JM would be easy. I had all these ideas about how I'd use my new platform to be a public health influencer, so I could still help people even if I wasn't on the frontlines anymore. I had it all worked out. But I didn't count on – I didn't count on—'

'Me,' I said.

'I've been falling for you so hard, Mandie,' she whispered, turning to face me. 'I've been trying to pretend it away, but I can't. That was why I didn't tell you I was into women, even after you told me. If I put that out into the universe, you and I would suddenly become this possibility, and I couldn't let that happen.'

I turned my face to hers. We were almost nose to nose, leaning back against the cabinet.

She trailed her fingers down the side of my face, stroking my damp hair behind my ear. 'You're like this ray of sunshine,' she said. 'Proper sunshine, not city sunshine, where it's filtered through all that pollution and smog. Pure, clear, clean sunshine that warms you up, right down to the bone. Even that first day I met you, when you were so sad, I just wanted to be near you.'

'To sunbake?' I said, reaching up and hooking my fingers through hers.

'You joke, but honestly, kind of,' she said. 'I haven't had a friend like you in a long time, Mandie. A ride-or-die. And I managed to convince myself that was all it was until that fucking love machine date.'

I blinked. 'What?'

'When you built that catapult out of, like, three pipe cleaners and a blade of grass? And it worked perfectly? Babe, I've never been that turned on in my life.'

'Are you telling me,' I said, 'that love machines actually *work*?'

She laughed. 'Actually, I'm lying a little bit,' she said. 'Sure, the love machine really turned my crank, but it wasn't the first time. Seeing how much that fancy car turned *your* crank also turned mine quite a lot.'

'Considering you have a massive in with production,' I said, 'can you find out where that Lambo is? I hate to think of her languishing all alone. I'd take such good care of her.'

Her gaze was liquid. 'I'm sure you would,' she whispered.

Then her eyes drifted downward. 'Oh, hello.'

'Shit, sorry,' I said, pulling my towel back together. 'This is what happens when you don't give me time to get dressed, Dylan.'

'Stop.'

I stopped.

Her fingers traced the seam of the towel. 'Can I?'

I swallowed.

'You can say no,' she said. 'That's totally fine, Mandie. I absolutely understand why you would say no. I'm contractually bound to man-Dylan, and I know you're not all the way over Jac, and this whole situation is the hugest fucking mess in the world. If we want to stay friends, then doing this is probably the worst thing we could do.'

'Probably,' I said.

The steam from the shower was catching in her hair. Droplets were beading in it like little diamonds. Her skin was damp and dewy, glowing in the bathroom lights. There were two worry lines between her perfect eyebrows, carved deep.

I reached out and smoothed them away. Traced the line of one of those eyebrows with my finger, like I'd been wanting to do since the moment she looked into my eyes at the First Night Party and the whole world tilted on its axis.

'Do you know what my worst quality is?' I asked her. 'Worse than the fact that I cry all the time?'

'That you shit-talk yourself?' she said, one corner of her mouth curving up wryly.

'That's a pretty bad one,' I said, 'but this one is worse. This one gets me into all kinds of trouble.'

I leaned in. I didn't kiss her, but I let my lips hover, just above hers. I could feel her breath, hot and uneven, against my skin.

I licked her lower lip. She made a sound in the back of her throat, a hungry, desperate little sound. I bit her lip gently. She made it again.

'My worst quality,' I whispered into her mouth, 'is that I'm way too impulsive.'

'Yeah?' Her voice was an octave higher than normal, her eyes closed but her eyelashes fluttering.

I traced a line down her throat. I rubbed my thumb in the little hollow at the base of her neck, then pressed my lips there too. 'Yeah,' I said.

She made the sound again.

I pulled back. 'Open your eyes.'

She didn't. She was breathing fast and shallow, her breasts heaving above the neckline of her dress.

I shifted, throwing one of my legs over hers, straddling her on the floor. 'Dylan,' I said, cupping her face in my hands. 'Open your eyes.'

Her hands slid up my legs, gripping my hips. 'Mandie—'

'Open them. Look at me.'

She did. I let my thumbs stroke her temples, the same place she dug her fingers in whenever things got too out of control for her.

Then I pulled my towel off and threw it to the floor.

It was a little awkward. My towel might have been easy access, but she was still in her Last Chance Party gown. The zipper got stuck when I foolishly tried a high-risk manoeuvre and attempted to undo it with my teeth, and it was a real two-woman operation to get it off her.

Plus, the bathroom floor? Hard! The chances of nearly concussing yourself on a cabinet? High!

On top of that, Dylan was nervous. 'It's been a while since I've done this with a woman,' she whispered, her hands hot against my hips, her voice shaky, as I kissed my way across her collarbone in a cloud of steam. 'You're going to have to help me out, Mandie.'

'Don't worry,' I said.

I leaned up and kissed her – an earthquake of a kiss, an electrical storm – then I pushed her gently back, laying her down with her head on my discarded towel. 'I've got you, baby,' I said, kissing a line down her body. 'I'll take good care of you.'

17

'I should have guessed you'd be good with your hands,' Dylan said.

We were curled up in bed together. It was Marija's old bunk, this time. Given that the whole bedroom technically belonged to us now, we weren't picky about which bed we ended up in.

Kumiko was on her final four Friends and Family Date with Romeo-Dylan. Parisa was filming an ITM with Carrie. Murray and the rest of the crew weren't around, apart from the PA in the monitor room down the hall (we'd checked, he was wearing enormous headphones and didn't even notice us peering into the room). There weren't a lot of times we could be alone in the Juliet Villa, but we'd made the most of every single stolen minute.

I craned my head and kissed her, running my fingers across her jaw and down the elegant curve of her neck.

'If there's one thing I know I'm good at,' I said, 'it's making things go.'

She grinned, waggling those knife-edge eyebrows I was so obsessed with. 'Yeah, you are.'

'You know what I'm especially good at?'

'What's that?'

'Making things go *fast*.'

Then there wasn't any talking for a while. Although Dylan did have to jam a pillow into her mouth in case the PA down the hall took his headphones off.

It was perfect, being in bed with her. There was no other word to describe it. The situation definitely wasn't perfect, the sex wasn't always perfect (although don't get me wrong, it was *very* good), but being there, with her, in bed: that was perfect.

'I really don't want to go on this date tomorrow,' Dylan said softly, stroking my hair.

It was perfect, except when I remembered it couldn't last.

'I don't want you to go either,' I said.

She sighed. 'They're making me introduce Noah to him.'

'Wow.'

'I know it's only by Zoom, and a million of my cousins will be on the call too, so it's not like there won't be a buffer, but still.'

'Big step.'

'Big step,' she said, her fingers tangling in my hair and tugging a little too hard as she involuntarily tensed up. 'Too big.'

'Are you worried that Noah will get attached to him?'

I asked, gently pulling my hair out of her hand and propping myself up on my elbow so I could look at her.

'Not *that* worried,' she said. 'I've introduced Noah to people I've dated before, and it's been fine. Plus, it's only one Zoom call, there's a limited amount of damage it can do. Most of it will probably be Noah dealing with the fact that his name is Dylan too – "Wow, Mummy, he has the same name as you!"'

I laughed.

'It's not Noah I'm worried about,' she said. 'It's me. Introducing him to my kid is just one more step towards it being real.'

I pictured the three of them together. They would be exactly the picture Murray wanted so badly to paint – the fairy-tale family. They would be perfect, and it made my heart ache.

'But this is what's real,' she whispered. 'You and me, Mandie.'

I kissed her again, so I didn't have to reply.

'Are you worried about your Friends and Family Date?' she asked, when we finally broke apart.

'Honestly,' I said, 'I haven't thought about it that much.'

There are a number of very obvious issues with the classic Mandie 'Thinking about something before I do it? Never heard of it' approach to problem-solving. For example: problems don't work like trees falling in woods where no one can hear them. There comes a point where ignoring them just means the tree lands on your head.

'Hi Mandie!' Mum said, waving brightly to me on the Zoom screen.

'Hi Mum,' I said, trying to keep my voice steady and happy and bright. 'This is Dylan.'

'It's lovely to meet you, Mrs Mitchell,' Romeo-Dylan said, putting his arm around me. 'I've had the most wonderful time getting to know your daughter.'

He kissed my cheek. Mum beamed. Sitting next to my secret girlfriend's soon-to-be fake boyfriend, I felt like the worst lying piece of garbage on the face of the planet.

Mum and Romeo-Dylan got on like a house on fire, which just made me feel worse and worse. 'I was very worried about Mandie coming on this show,' Mum said. 'Her ex Jac really knocked her around emotionally.'

'I know,' Romeo-Dylan said. 'Amanda's told me.'

'I was worried that this was just another thing she was doing while she was sitting around waiting for Jac to come back,' Mum said. 'She can be whimsical, my Mandie.'

'Mum,' I said, 'we don't need to talk about this.'

'I never thought she'd make it this far,' Mum said, ignoring me.

'Mum!'

'You're exactly what I want for her, Dylan,' Mum said. 'Someone who likes her for her. Who doesn't try to change her. Who'll treat her well.'

I felt Romeo-Dylan's arm twitch around me. I wasn't the only one who was profoundly uncomfortable.

'Thank you,' Mum said, 'for helping my Mandie move on.'

On the Zoom screen, I could see that Romeo-Dylan's smile was just as forced as mine.

'Hey,' I said quietly to him, in the break between the Zoom half of the date and the cheeseboard half. Usually one of us would get pulled off immediately to do an ITM, but Murray was in an intense discussion with one of the soundies, so for once, we had an actual moment alone together. 'Um. My ex. Jac. I should probably tell you . . .'

'Tell me what?' Romeo-Dylan asked.

I put one hand over my lapel mic and one hand over his. 'It's short for Jacqueline,' I whispered. 'She's a woman. I'm bi.'

His eyes flickered sideways. Checking for cameras, I realised. 'You don't want to be out on the show?'

I shook my head. 'Not really, no. Murray knows, of course, but . . .'

'Don't worry,' he said, not making me finish the sentence. 'I'll keep it to myself.'

'Thank you.'

'Is there . . .' His eyes flickered to the cameras again and he lowered his voice even further. 'Is there a reason you decided to tell me?'

Underneath the hand I had over my mic, I could feel my heart start to pick up speed.

'I just thought you should know,' I said. 'It's not a big deal, but it is a big part of who I am. Relationships shouldn't start with secrets.'

I felt him flinch, ever so slightly. 'That's true,' he said quietly.

'Plus, if it was . . . you know, an issue for you or something . . .'

He smiled, a proper smile this time, one that made those creases appear in the corners of his eyes. 'Of course it isn't,' he said. 'Thank you for telling me. For trusting me.'

He hugged me. It was the perfect reaction. No one could have asked for more from Romeo-Dylan in that moment.

It would have made things so much easier if it wasn't the perfect reaction. That was probably part of the reason I'd told him, to be honest, even though it was much too petty a reason to admit. Everything would be simpler if he'd reacted in that gross pervy way that some men do, where they think they're going to be the centrepiece of a threesome. If he'd been super biphobic about it, and recoiled in disgust. If he'd done something, anything, that would make him seem like less of a perfect romantic hero, something that would make Murray say, 'Oh no, we can't possibly build the most perfect love story in the universe around this guy, we've got to change the narrative in a big way. Dylan G, we're tearing up that contract.'

It might even have been easier if he'd had the perfect reaction to my face, but been a little weirded out by it in private, and eliminated me at the next Necklace Ceremony.

But no. 'Amanda, I want to know if your heart is the other half of mine,' Romeo-Dylan said. 'Will you take this necklace and commit to finding out with me?'

I could have made it easier for myself by saying no, but I didn't.

'Who do you think it is?' I asked Dylan later that night.

'Hmmm?' Her fingers were tracing lines on my shoulder as we spooned.

'That man-Dylan really likes,' I said. 'You said you thought there was someone he actually liked. If it's not you, who is it?'

'Maybe it's you.'

'Dylan,' I said, as she stroked her thumb over the spot behind my ear that she'd very quickly worked out made me shiver, 'you *saw* us kiss.'

She chuckled. Her breath was warm against the back of my neck. 'I guess it has to be Kumiko, then,' she said. 'Parisa's gone now, so if it's not me and it's not you, then it has to be her.'

'They'd be cute together.'

'Don't make me think about that, Mandie,' Dylan said. 'If I start thinking about how I'm tearing him away from his one true love, it's going to make this harder than it already is.'

She leaned in and pressed her lips to the spot behind my ear. 'We've only got a few days left,' she said. 'I don't want to think. I just want to be in the moment, here, with you.'

Like I said, I don't have a whole lot of experience with being angry. It wasn't until the next morning, when I was in the shower, going over things in my head, that I realised that mixed in with the mess of wanting and longing and yearning and multiple orgasms, was still a solid dose of that exploding-heater anger. Not at Romeo-Dylan, or the situation, or even myself, but at Dylan, for not picking me.

287

. . . which was ridiculous. There were very good reasons why she couldn't pick me. She would get sued, for instance. No sensible person would ever pick a massive lawsuit over the most perfect fake boyfriend in the universe, a public platform from which she could change the world, and piles of cash so large you could swim around in them.

Especially not when there was a way we could make this work. 'I think we should stage a reconciliation scene,' Dylan said, as we did our skincare routines together in the bathroom.

'What do you mean?' I asked, adjusting the headband I was wearing to keep product out of my hair.

'They're telling a story about us feuding,' she said, dabbing moisturiser onto her face and then handing the bottle to me. I'd run out three days ago and now we were sharing. 'One of those classic "oh, they were such good friends, but then they got all competitive over the same boy and it ruined it" things. Let's take control of the narrative and do something different. Let's stage a scene where we're all "I've realised that your friendship is super important to me, so let's put our differences aside, and no matter who wins, we'll be friends *forever*!"'

'Won't that undermine your big love story with man-Dylan?' I gently rubbed the moisturiser into my skin.

'How would it undermine it?'

I shrugged, sliding the moisturiser back into her make-up bag. 'You know how it works. I know "not here to make friends" is a villain thing, but won't it look like you don't have your priorities in order if your focus isn't one hundred per cent on him? Isn't that why they normally separate the Juliets when it gets to final four?'

'No, this'll totally work, Mandie,' Dylan said, meeting my eyes in the mirror. 'For one, it'll fit with all the stuff man-Dylan was doing with Cece. He told me about it that day I went down to his boat. They set up this big storyline about how friendship is important too, and people can be friends without it being all sexy.'

I raised my eyebrows.

'Yes, I see the irony in that, babe,' she said, grinning at my reflection and then pressing a kiss against my headband. 'But it'll work. Plus, you know how people are always talking online about how it's so toxic that the women on the show are constantly tearing each other down, wouldn't it be great if there could be some sisterhood, blah blah blah.'

This show actively hates women, Jac whispered.

'So that would be a good news story for the show,' Dylan said. 'And good news for us, because it would set us up perfectly.'

She grabbed my hip and turned me to face her, leaning down to rest her forehead against mine. 'No one would question why we were seen together after the show,' she whispered. 'They'd just go, "Oh look, gals being pals." They'd have no idea. They'd never suspect.'

'So,' I said shakily, 'so you want to . . .'

'Be with you?' she said. 'Of course I do, Mandie.'

I should have been thrilled. I should have been ecstatic. I should have grinned hugely and kissed her and pounced on her and dragged her to bed and not let her out of it for *hours*.

'What about man-Dylan?' I asked.

'He won't mind,' Dylan said, rubbing her nose against mine, both slippery with the moisturiser we were sharing. 'I don't think, anyway. We're clear on the deal. We've got to stay together for three months after the finale airs. Which really just means being photographed together, honestly. And if you and I tell this "best friends" story right, no one will question it if you're in some of those photos.'

'You've got it all figured out, huh,' I said, stroking her hair behind her ear.

'You know I like to be in control,' she said.

'I don't know,' I said. 'I've noticed that you enjoy it quite a lot when I take the wheel.'

She grinned and kissed me. 'Then once my time with him is up,' she said, 'you and I can figure out our next move. Whether we want to keep being public friends, private girl-friends, come out all the way . . . we can make it work.'

I nodded, a lump in my throat.

'I know it's not ideal, Mandie,' Dylan said, 'but this is going to be fine. You and I are going to be fine. All we have to do is wait it out.'

It was easiest to go along with what she wanted, to follow the process she'd laid out for me, so we filmed the scene. 'You've become so important to me over the course of this journey, Mandie,' Dylan said to me as we sat on the Villa couches, camera crew all around, a boom mic dipping low above us. 'I don't want to lose that.'

'I don't want to lose you either,' I said.

'Can we just agree that no matter what happens with Dylan JM, you and I are good?'

'Of course,' I said, my mouth dry. 'You and I will always be good.'

'Plus, you never know,' she said. 'Maybe neither of us will end up with him. Maybe it'll be Kumiko.'

'Maybe,' I said, feeling a little sick.

'How was that?' Dylan asked Murray, when we'd finished.

'Good, good, fine,' he said, waving his hand. His hair was looking even scruffier than usual today, like someone had stuck their fingers in it and pulled it in as many different directions as possible.

'Can you promise me that it'll make the episode cut?'

'I can't promise anything.'

'Murray, please.'

'You do know I'm not the boss of everything, don't you, Dylan? I'm not the only person who decides what goes into episodes.'

'Will you try?'

He sighed. 'Fine, fine, I'll try.'

Dylan and I stood just outside the Villa and watched him leave, rocketing down the hill in his golf cart. 'Is he getting grumpier, do you think?' she asked, putting an arm around my shoulders.

'I think he's just tired,' I said. 'They're all stretched so thin. He's probably just not getting enough sleep.'

'Relatable.'

I smiled and put my arm around her waist, leaning my head on her shoulder.

'Hi guys,' Kumiko said, coming out to join us. 'So you kissed and made up, huh?'

'What?' Dylan said sharply.

Kumiko gestured at us. 'You're back to being friends.'

'Oh. Yes.'

'I was worried about you two,' she said. 'Being the only two in that bedroom when you're in the middle of a fight – that's rough.'

Kumiko put her arm around Dylan's waist too. After a moment's hesitation, Dylan put her other arm around her.

Just three gals, being pals.

'I'm glad you two sorted it out,' Kumiko said. 'I always hate it when friendships get torn apart over a man.'

'Yeah,' I agreed vaguely.

'I know we're all here for the Romeo, but the people we actually spend time with are each other,' she said. 'I hope we can all stay friends after this.'

'That's the plan,' Dylan said firmly.

The top three Dream Dates started the next day. 'All right, this is how these dates are going to work,' Murray said. 'It's a bit different from usual.'

'Because we can't actually go on a dream date when we're stuck on the one property?' Kumiko asked. 'Surely we've already exhausted every date opportunity this place has to offer.'

'Partially, yes,' Murray said. 'But it's also because of some clauses in Dylan JM's contract. He made it very clear that he's not sleeping with anyone, or even giving the appearance that he's sleeping with anyone, until he's picked his final Juliet, so the usual overnight deal is out. Instead, we're going to go with some classic intimacy over the giant sweeping sexy thing we usually do. Dinner and dancing.'

'Do we actually get to eat the food?' Dylan asked.

'You sound exactly like your boyfriend,' Murray said. 'If you get through filming fast enough, sure, you can eat the food. Also, it'll be brunch instead of dinner for you, Amanda. We're shooting Kumiko tonight, you during the day tomorrow, Dylan G in the evening, then the Necklace Ceremony right after. All back-to-back, so you can't compare notes.'

'Is there going to be some kind of surprise, then?' Kumiko asked.

'How about you start getting ready for your date so you can find out?'

Kumiko left for hair and make-up. The crew packed up their stuff. Dylan and I each filmed quick ITMs with Murray, and then we were by ourselves in the Villa.

'Do you know how many times when we were alone in here,' Dylan whispered against my lips, my legs around her waist as I perched on the bathroom counter, 'I thought about kissing you?'

She kissed her way down my neck. 'You'd just be standing there, brushing your teeth, or combing your hair, or taking off your make-up,' she said, her breath hot against my skin.

'Normal things. Everyday things. But you'd be driving me out of my fucking mind.'

I wasn't the only one who was good with my hands. When she touched me, it felt like the whole world was shaking.

I could do this. I could have this. *Marry Me, Juliet stars Dylan Gilchrist and Amanda Mitchell out to lunch*, the paparazzi captions would read. *Their friendship had some rocky moments during the show, but we're glad to see these two gals are back to being pals!*

They wouldn't know that it was like this when we locked ourselves in the bathroom. They wouldn't know that the second the doors were closed behind us we were tearing each other's clothes off. They wouldn't know that it was tectonic whenever we touched each other.

They were joined later by Gilchrist's boyfriend Dylan Jayasinghe Mellor, the captions would read. *It doesn't look like there's any hard feelings, even though Mitchell was one of the final contenders for Mellor's heart.*

'Are you with me, Mandie?' Dylan said, her breath coming heavy.

I wrapped my arms around her neck. 'I'm with you,' I said.

All I had to do was wait.

I didn't sleep well that night. When the first rays of sunshine peeked through the gap in the curtains, I was already awake.

'Where're you going?' Dylan mumbled.

'I've got to get ready for my date,' I whispered.

'Hhhhmmmmokay,' she said. 'See you at the Necklace Ceremony.'

I leaned down and pressed my lips to her temple. 'Goodbye, baby.'

She'd given me a hickey, I realised as I combed my hair out in the mirror. It wasn't in an especially obvious place – just above the curve of my left breast – but if I wore a low-enough cut top, you could see it.

There was a shirt I had that'd be perfect. It was the black one with the scoop neck that she hadn't let me wear on my Lambo date. I pulled it out of my suitcase and fingered the material.

But then I sighed, put it down, pulled a baby blue one with a higher neckline over my head instead, and went back into the bathroom to cover up the hickey as best as I could, just in case someone noticed.

They'd set up brunch on the deck of Romeo-Dylan's boat. He was waiting for me, wearing white shorts and a green shirt and a smile that didn't quite reach his eyes. When I went below deck halfway through our date to use the bathroom, I saw that his bed wasn't made, the sheets all rumpled and twisted like he'd been tossing and turning all night.

Apparently I wasn't the only person who was struggling. Probably not the only person who wished more than anything that the notion of Dylan + Dylan = A Love Story To Heal The Nation had never entered Murray's mind, either.

It didn't stop me wanting to push him into the lake. If only he weren't so fucking goddamn *perfect*.

'Are you okay?' he murmured to me as they struck our brunch set from the deck.

'Not really,' I whispered back. 'You?'

'Not really.'

'Shut up, both of you,' Murray barked. 'No talking unless we're filming.'

'I just want you to know,' Romeo-Dylan said.

'Dylan!'

'– that this wasn't my idea.'

I glanced up at him. 'What wasn't your idea?'

'Dylan!' Murray snapped. 'What did I say?'

'I asked them not to,' he said.

'Dylan!' Murray roared. 'Over here! Now!'

We went into ITMs before the next part of the date. Murray was with Romeo-Dylan, so Carrie was doing mine. 'What was Dylan JM talking about?' I asked.

'Just because I'm not as grumpy as Murray doesn't mean I'm going to tell you shit, Amanda,' Carrie said. 'Now. You know the drill. Answer in full sentences. How do you feel, knowing that today could be the last time you ever spend with Dylan?'

Once my ITM was done, I was led back to the boat. The deck had been redressed, festooned with flowers and greenery, a bottle of champagne sitting in a silver ice bucket, but instead of leaving me there to wait, they led me below deck.

Romeo-Dylan was already there. He stood up immediately, unfolding his long legs from under his absurdly tiny table. 'Amanda—'

'No,' Murray said shortly. 'Go back. Do the entrance again, Amanda. Dylan, stop acting like you're about to tell her that her dog got hit by a car.'

'What's that?' I asked, gesturing to the large screen they'd hung on one wall. 'Didn't we already do the Friends and Family Date?'

'Maybe,' Murray bit out, 'if you do your entrance again, you can find out.'

I did the entrance again. And again, and again, and again, until Murray was satisfied.

'Dylan, Amanda,' Z intoned, 'welcome to a very special part of your Dream Date.'

He was perched on the end of Romeo-Dylan's (now beautifully made) bed. I'd never seen Z sit before. It looked wrong, like he'd never quite learned how to do it.

'Things are different this year on *Marry Me, Juliet*,' Z said. 'Instead of being able to take in some of the most romantic sights and sounds in the world, we've been here, at this property, locked away from the world. This means that you haven't been able to get a sense of what each other is like in reality, when things are ordinary, instead of extraordinary. Of whether or not you could really make this work.'

Romeo-Dylan's hand found mine under the table. He squeezed my fingers, tight.

'Stop,' Murray said. 'Go back. If you're going to hold hands, do it above the table where the camera can catch it.'

'I'm so sorry,' Romeo-Dylan whispered to me as we obeyed. Murray growled at him.

'So behind the scenes, we've been thinking,' Z went on, 'how can we best help you get to know each other? How can we bring your everyday worlds here, to the world of *Marry Me, Juliet*?'

Romeo-Dylan squeezed my fingers tighter.

'Who can help you really understand what each other is like in a real, everyday relationship?' Z said.

Tighter again.

'There was only one answer,' Z said. 'We had to call up your exes.'

My heart stopped beating.

The Zoom screen flickered to life. I was frozen solid, like someone had cast a spell on me to turn my blood to ice. If a doctor came in to check my vital signs, they would probably have declared me legally dead.

The only movement I could manage was with my eyes. I looked at Murray, pleading. He looked back, impassive.

'What are you like in an everyday relationship, Amanda?' Z said. 'Let's have a chat to your ex to find out. Dylan, meet—'

'Mark,' I whispered.

Mark. Sweet Mark. Lovely Mark. Mark who had never done a thing wrong in his life, except take me to a wedding that Jac was at.

'Hi Mandie,' he said, smiling. His eyes creased like Romeo-Dylan's did in the corners. 'How are you? It's nice to see you.'

Romeo-Dylan exhaled in a rush next to me. Relief, I realised, in the one corner of my brain that was still functioning.

'Mark,' I managed to croak. 'It's been a long time.'

'Too long,' he said. 'I've missed you.'

'I've missed you too.'

It was the truth. Being with Mark had been so easy. No challenges, no pressure. No passion, sure, but God, easy could be so nice.

How had Romeo-Dylan said I made him feel? Steady? I'd brushed it off as a backhanded compliment at the time, but I shouldn't have been so hasty. Steady had some real positive qualities.

'I can see you've found yourself a handsome fellow,' Mark said. 'Introduce me to this guy, Mandie.'

'Oh. Of course. Mark, meet Dylan Jayasinghe Mellor, the Romeo. Dylan, meet Mark, my ex-boyfriend.'

'Nice to meet you, Dylan,' Mark said. 'I hope you're treating Mandie well. She's a special one.'

'She sure is,' Romeo-Dylan replied, finding his TV smile and his TV voice and slipping back into effortlessly charming mode.

It was easy for them to talk. Mark recognised Romeo-Dylan from the Olympics, and they fell into some conversation about sports to which I only needed to contribute an 'Oh?' and a 'Wow!' and an 'Oh my God, I didn't know that about you!' every so often. Working for so many years in shops full of men had given me a lot of practice autopiloting through sports talk.

It was a perfectly nice conversation. There were no gaps, no awkward pauses, no silences. We were just three per-fectly nice people, engaging in some perfectly nice, perfectly shallow small talk, in which we said nothing at all.

There was movement in my peripheral vision. Murray. He was holding up his phone. *ASK HOW THEY BROKE UP.*

Romeo-Dylan saw it too, and he squeezed my fingers briefly. 'So how did you two break up?'

I tensed, but Mark just smiled. 'It was kind of like sailing, I suppose,' he said. 'We were bobbing along together, and then a storm came in and blew her away from me.'

'Did you –' Romeo-Dylan paused, swallowed, licked his lips, '– did you fight for her? Did you fight for each other?'

'I could have fought harder,' Mark said. 'But if we'd been holding tight to each other, it wouldn't have been so easy for her to slip out of my grasp.'

I wanted to be angry with Murray. I wanted to be the kind of person that would storm up to him and jab their finger into his chest and demand an explanation.

I wasn't, of course. I managed to hold it together until after the cameras had stopped rolling and Murray had sent the crew away to prep for the next part of the date shoot, but then I buried my face in my hands, unable to stop the tears coursing down my face. 'How could you do that to me?'

'Hey, hey, hey, it's all right,' Romeo-Dylan said, drawing me to him. 'Don't cry.'

'I didn't do anything to you,' Murray said. 'I made you a promise, Amanda, and I kept it.'

'You scared me half to death!'

'I needed some kind of reaction from you,' he said. 'We're at the pointy end of the season. We need to up the stakes.'

'You could have at least let *me* know you weren't going to out her on national television,' Romeo-Dylan said, arm tight around my shoulders. 'I could have told her it'd be all right!'

'Were you listening to anything I just said? Do you think I would have got anything out of her if she'd known that all she'd be faced with was that wet blanket of a man?'

I couldn't stop seeing it. The Zoom screen flickering to life. Jac sitting there, leaning back in her chair, arms folded. *Mandie.*

Hi Jac, I would have whispered.

This is a new low, she'd say, *even for you.*

Romeo-Dylan would have interjected. *Hey, hey, hey,* he'd say. *Amanda's a lovely person. She's done nothing wrong.*

I see you've found someone else to get your validation from, Jac would say. *Someone new to wait around for. Adorable.*

I'd start crying. She'd roll her eyes. *And I see you still don't have any self-respect,* she'd say. *Or a spine.*

Romeo-Dylan and Murray were still arguing. 'If you're not worried about her, what about me?' Romeo-Dylan was saying. 'I had to sit through that whole brunch thinking you were going to violate her privacy in the worst possible way – knowing that, and not being able to tell her. Do you enjoy making me feel like the biggest arsehole on the face of the earth?'

'How you feel,' Murray said, 'is not my concern, Dylan.'

'Do you care about anything?' Romeo-Dylan demanded.

'I care about making good TV,' Murray snarled. 'Now shut up. It's time for ITMs again.'

'No. Not with you.'

'Fine. You go with Carrie. Amanda, you come with me.'

'You don't have to,' Romeo-Dylan said to me.

'Yes, she does,' Murray said.

'No, you don't,' Romeo-Dylan said.

His eyes were kind. His fingers were gentle around mine. 'Amanda, you don't have to do anything you don't want to, all right?'

I was going to miss him, I realised. I really did like him a lot. Steady was nothing to sneeze at.

'It's all right,' I said. 'I'm all right.'

'Are you sure?'

I nodded.

He pressed a kiss to my temple. 'I'm so sorry,' he whispered.

It was the most genuine kiss he'd ever given me.

'All right,' Murray said, once we were all set up for our ITM. 'Same deal as always. Full sentences. Look at me, not at the camera.'

'Wait.'

'We're on a schedule, Amanda.'

'This will only take a second,' I said. 'I just have one question.'

He leaned back in his chair. 'Spit it out, then.'

'Did you contact Jac? My ex-girlfriend?'

He raised his eyebrows.

'Did you reach out to her?' I asked. 'Did you ask her to come on the show? Did she say no?'

'Yes,' Murray said.

I closed my eyes. Blood was pounding in my head.

'However,' he said, 'if she had said yes, I wouldn't have let you go into that scene without some warning.'

'Oh, sure.'

He grunted. I opened my eyes again. 'You can believe what you want,' he said. 'If you need to believe I'm a monster, go ahead. No skin off my nose. Now can we get on with it?'

'Wait.'

'What?!'

'One more question.'

'Will you give me whatever I want in this ITM if I answer it?'

'Whatever you want,' I said. 'Just tell me what she said.'

'Amanda, I've had maybe two hours of sleep a night for the past five weeks. Do you think I have that kind of information in my head?'

'Jac's memorable,' I said. 'What did she say?'

He exhaled noisily. 'Something along the lines of no, she would not be participating in a show that hates women, that she was ashamed to know someone who was, and how did I get her contact information anyway. Does that make you feel better?'

'Yes.'

He raised his eyebrows again.

'Shall we get on with it?' I said. 'I promised you whatever you wanted. So tell me what you want.'

I've never been the kind of person who could tell you when and why I made my decisions. How did I become a mechanic?

I don't know, I always liked cars, I found an apprenticeship, I just kind of fell into it. How exactly did I end up with Mark, or any of the other people I'd been with? I don't know, it just happened. How did I decide to go on *Marry Me, Juliet*? I don't know, it seemed like a good idea at the time.

It had been that way with Jac too. She'd come up to me at that wedding, and then it was done. There was no real moment when I consciously decided to be with her instead of Mark. I just was.

There was even an element of that with Dylan. One minute, my towel had come loose while she was spilling her guts to me in the bathroom, and the next, I was her secret girlfriend, waiting around for her while she went through the motions of her contractual relationship with Romeo-Dylan.

It was ironic that I made the first clear decision of my entire life while I was waiting around for Romeo-Dylan – waiting around, just like I always did.

I was standing on the deck of the boat, next to the ice bucket, surrounded by flowers and the full trappings of *Marry Me, Juliet*. He was finishing up his ITM with Carrie. I looked out across the lake, and I decided.

It wasn't one of those magical moments where the sun comes down from the clouds and illuminates the perfect way forward. It wasn't like the epiphanies I'd had at various points in the last few weeks, where things had suddenly become clear to me.

Well, no. That's a lie. There were a few things I already knew that crystallised for me, like:

1) A lot of the things Jac said about me were wrong.
2) Some of the things Jac said about me were right, even if she phrased them in the meanest possible way.
3) I was in love with Dylan.

Knowing those things didn't help, though. If anything, they made it harder.

I was in a maze, but it wasn't the kind where I could just put my hand against the wall and follow it down a bunch of dead ends before it finally led me out. I didn't know what was down the different avenues in front of me.

But I still had to choose which way to go.

I had to make a real choice, not a fantasy choice. Choose what was right for me, even if it was hard. Would I remain Mandie 1.0, who fell into things, who let her impulses take her everywhere, who let processes take over instead of thinking for herself? Or would I become Mandie 2.0, who could restrain her impulses, who did her best to make good choices?

The sun was just beginning to set as we filmed the final portion of the date, turning the lake from gold into pink into red. Romeo-Dylan and I both had a glass of champagne and some perfectly nice, perfectly nothing-level small talk before he took my hand and asked me to dance.

There was no music. They weren't allowed to have music, because it would interfere with the sound quality, so they'd edit it in during post-production. For now, there was just me and Romeo-Dylan, swaying gently, surrounded by camera-men and soundies, to the sound of absolutely nothing.

His fingers were wound tight around mine, our clasped hands nestled against his chest. I let my head lean against his shoulder for a moment. I wanted to hate him, but I didn't. I wasn't very good at being a petty bitch.

'Dylan,' I said, pulling back so I could look up at him, 'I've had a lovely time with you over these past few weeks. You're such a nice man.'

I expected him to smile his TV smile down at me, thank me, perhaps, but his face stayed serious. 'I wish that were true,' he said. 'Being in this situation has made me feel like the opposite.'

'I want to make things easier for you.'

'You can't,' he said. 'I wish you could, but you can't.'

'I can.'

I drew away from him, so I was only holding his hands instead of being pressed up against him. 'We both know it's not me,' I said.

He didn't say anything. He wasn't even looking at me anymore. His eyes were cast down to the deck.

'I don't want to hang around in the background, being some side character in your love story,' I said. 'I – I have too much self-respect for that.'

His fingers tightened around mine. 'I'm sorry,' he said hoarsely. 'I'm so sorry, Amanda.'

'It's not your fault,' I said. 'It's the situation. But there is something you can do for me.'

He met my eyes. 'Anything.'

'Let me go,' I said. 'Don't make me wait for the Necklace Ceremony. I've done enough waiting. It's time for me to go.'

18

I wanted to feel calm. I wanted to feel centred and steady and sure, secure in the knowledge that even though I'd made a horribly tough decision, it had been the right one. I wanted to feel proud that for once I'd stood up for myself, stood my ground, put my foot down and said, 'No more.'

I didn't. I regretted making the right choice every minute, every second, every jolt of the golf cart as a PA rocketed me back up to the Villa to get my stuff. *What have you done?* I screamed at myself. *Why did you have to pick now to grow a spine?*

'Make it quick,' the PA said. 'Dylan G's in hair and make-up for her date, but we need to get you out of here before Kumiko comes back from her interview. They can't find out you're gone until tonight.'

I wondered if they'd bother staging a Necklace Ceremony. *Where's Amanda?* Kumiko would whisper to Dylan.

I don't know, she'd whisper back.

The worry in her face would be genuine. The tears that she cried when Z came out and said something like, *Juliets, as you can see, there are only two of you here. Amanda and Dylan JM had a long discussion earlier, and Amanda has made the decision to leave the Juliet Villa* – those would be genuine too.

I was hurting her. Badly. I was under no illusions about that.

I was in love with her, and she was at least a little in love with me. You didn't say things like *hey, let's have a secret relationship in private while I'm having a fake relationship in public, BTW I could get sued and lose everything if anyone found out* to someone you didn't care about. A lot.

But just because I loved her and she probably loved me didn't mean this was good for me. I'd spent enough time waiting around, stuck with one foot in a fantasy world, because I wasn't brave enough to take a step forward in the real one.

If I did what she wanted, and had some dishonest secret half-relationship with her while she pretended to be with Romeo-Dylan, I might as well shred my list of positive features and set those affirmation flashcards on fire. I might as well believe every cruel thing Jac had ever said about me. I would be stupid. I would be spineless. I would be a pretty face with no substance, a doormat that got walked all over, a child with no self-respect.

I shoved my clothes into my suitcase willy-nilly, trying to ignore the way they'd become intermingled with Dylan's on the floor. The tears were falling freely down my face, but

I let them. *This hurts, Mandie,* I told myself, *but it's the right thing to do.*

I packed the affirmation flashcards last of all. I thought about leaving them behind as a kind of goodbye, but – no. They were important. She was important. Even if us being together was bad for me, she'd given me one of the tools I'd used to put myself back together. I would always, *always* love her for that.

Of all people, I couldn't believe it was Mark – Mark! sweet, lovely Mark! – who had brought me to this realisation. *If we'd been holding tight to each other, it wouldn't have been so easy for her to slip out of my grasp.*

It *had* been so easy, to slip out of his grasp, to let him slip out of mine. But I'd been holding tight to Jac, and when she'd wrenched herself away, it had nearly destroyed me.

I knew myself. I was good at waiting. It would be so easy to wait for Dylan. To cling to one of her hands with both of mine while her other one was in Romeo-Dylan's. To hold tight to the idea of what we could be, and to not let go.

But even though I loved her, and she loved me, and we both wanted the situation to be different, I deserved someone who would hold tight to me. With both hands.

So I had to let go first.

'Are you ready?' the crew guy asked.

I took one last look around the bedroom that had once been ours.

'Yes,' I said. 'I'm ready.'

I had to wait in a caravan for several hours before they took me down to the Convent. 'We don't have the crew to film you arriving there,' the PA explained to me, 'they're all filming Dylan G's date,' then he vanished before I could ask any more questions.

I wasn't sure whose caravan he'd brought me to, but it was clearly well lived in. The covers on the narrow bed were tangled. A backpack sat next to it, lumpy with clothes. Three novels were scattered near the head of the bed. Romance novels, I saw when I picked them up. They must be using them for ideas.

A long red ribbon marked the place in one of them. I opened it up. Romance was the last thing I wanted to be reading about right now, but it was either that or stare at the wall, regretting making the right choice.

I'm not a fast reader, but I'd made it through about a third of the book by the time Murray came to get me. 'Come on, Amanda,' he said gruffly.

I set the book down and turned off the little lamp next to the bed. 'I didn't know the crew slept in caravans.'

'Where else do you think we sleep?'

He climbed into the golf cart and gestured for me to get in the other side. I hesitated.

'For fuck's sake, what is it now?'

'Does Dylan know?'

'That you're gone? Yes.'

'What did she say?'

He didn't reply.

'Murray, please tell me,' I said. 'What did she say?'

He sighed. 'It's better that you don't know what she said. Trust me.'

'Trust you?' I exclaimed. 'After today?'

'Amanda,' he said, his voice surprisingly gentle, 'if your ex-girlfriend had said yes, I would never have let you go into that scene unprepared. I told you I wouldn't out you, and I meant it.'

'Oh, yeah, sure, you were going to put my ex-girlfriend on national TV and you *weren't* going to out me.'

'I would have talked to you about it first. If you really didn't want to come out, I wouldn't have made you.'

'Why should I believe you?'

'Believe what you want,' he said, his voice shifting back to its usual gruffness. 'Get in the golf cart. Some of us want to sleep tonight.'

There was more I wanted to say. *It's not even the fact you were going to out me,* I wanted to snarl, *it's that you would have made me talk to her.*

But even if there was a way to express that – to make him understand the bone-freezing terror I'd felt at the thought of having to see Jac – there was no point. He wouldn't care.

After the relative emptiness of the Juliet Villa, the Convent felt like a noisy pub. I pasted on a big smile as I said hi to everyone, hugged them all, accepted the drinks they thrust into my hands. 'Oh my God, tell us everything,' Jess D said. 'What was the Dream Date like? What's the situation? Give us the whole story.'

Everything was bright and loud. The rooms were much smaller than the ones at the Villa, and it felt like the walls were closing in on me.

'Oh, Amanda, don't cry!' Parisa said, wrapping her arms around me. 'He's not worth it.'

'I'm okay,' I said, wiping the tears (again? would I *ever* stop crying?) off my face. 'It's for the best, honestly.'

'That's the spirit,' Naya said.

It was so nice of them. They were so nice. But God, all I wanted was to be by myself.

'Where are you going?' Marija said. 'You haven't even come close to giving us all the goss yet.'

'I'll be back in a minute,' I said. 'I'm just going to the bathroom.'

I stumbled blindly into the hallway, desperate for a moment of quiet. '. . . thought for sure she'd be in the final two,' I heard Jess D say.

'Me too,' Parisa said. 'He liked her a ton. Plus, that'd give them that perfect boy-choosing-between-two-besties story. Production'd cream their jeans over that.'

Were they right? Would I have got a necklace at the ceremony, if I hadn't made Romeo-Dylan send me away? Would I be curled up in a too-small bunk with Dylan right now, her fingers playing gently with my hair?

Oh God. What had I done?

I started opening doors blindly. Maybe there was a way out. Maybe I could leg it back up to the Juliet Villa. It was dark, sure, but I knew how to solve the maze. I could do it in the dark.

And then what would happen?

I'd get caught, that's what would happen. Murray would

probably chain me up in the basement. I didn't know if the Convent had a basement, but he'd make do.

Or I wouldn't get caught. I'd sneak back out before anyone was awake, back down through the maze. Then up again the next night, and again, and again, and—

And then, 'Dylan Gilchrist, your heart is the other half of mine,' Romeo-Dylan would say, and 'Dylan Jayasinghe Mellor, your heart is the other half of mine too,' she'd say, and even though neither of them would mean it, it would still be *real*.

'Whyyyyyyy,' I heard someone moan.

My fingers stilled on the doorknob. I squinted into the dark room.

It was a laundry. One of the other women was sitting on top of the washing machine, curled into a ball, head buried in her knees.

She looked exactly like I felt.

'You too, huh?' I said, the words spilling out of me before I was even really conscious of saying them.

She looked over at me. It was Cece, the woman I'd Mummy Mandie'd so hard on the first night. 'Oh,' she said. 'Hi.'

'Hi,' I said. 'Nice to see you again, Cece.'

'You too.'

I felt awkward as hell, standing there in the doorway. 'Sorry for barging in on you. I thought this was the bathroom.'

'No. That's upstairs. First door on the left.'

I wanted to leave, but I didn't. Once you'd decided to become someone's metaphorical mum, maybe you couldn't stop.

Or maybe sometimes the lure of other people's problems was a temptation you couldn't resist, especially when there was no way you could fix your own.

'You look like I feel,' I said.

'Like shit?' Her words had hard edges.

'I was going to say miserable, but "like shit" works,' I said, forcing a smile I hoped looked kind. 'Want some company?'

Cece hesitated. Then, 'Sure.'

I closed the door. The room fell into darkness, lit only by the moonlight streaming in through the window. It wasn't the same as being alone, but it was quiet, almost peaceful. Definitely better than being out there, having to listen to everyone talk about the inevitability of Dylan and Dylan.

I sat beside Cece on the washing machine. 'Do you sleep in here?' I asked, pointing to the mess of bedding on the ground.

'Oh. Um. Yes. Kind of.'

'Kind of?'

'Technically, I sleep in one of the bedrooms upstairs. But Lily kicked me out. She really doesn't like me.'

'Ah. Lily,' I said. 'I understand all about Lily.'

Which was a lie, obviously. I doubted anyone understood all about Lily.

'I bet you're looking forward to living with her again,' Cece said, a dry note in her voice. 'She's such a calming and chill presence to have around.'

'Is it weird if I say I kind of am?'

It was almost pitch-dark in the laundry, but I didn't need to be able to see; I could *feel* the look Cece gave me.

'The last little while has been so bananas up at the Villa,' I said. 'It'll be nice to be back on solid ground. At least with Lily you know what to expect.'

Solid ground. That's where I was now. That's what I'd chosen. No more earthquakes, no more fireworks, no more quicksand. Just nice steady ground, on which I could plant my feet, and take steps forward.

I let my heels drum the rhythm of my heartbeat against the washing machine. This was the right thing. I was in the right place. I'd made the right choice.

Even if it felt like I'd reached into my chest and pulled out some fundamental part of me that I wouldn't be able to function without.

Cece muttered something. 'Hmm?' I said.

'Nothing.'

'It'll be nice to get a chance to hang out with you, though,' I said, reaching desperately for Mummy Mandie. 'We never really got a chance after that first night.'

'Yeah. It'll be nice.'

'Even if it's only for a few days. It'll be – shit, shit, I'm sorry.'

There was a lump in my throat the size of a station wagon. Tears were suddenly streaming down my face like a waterfall. 'I'm sorry,' I repeated, trying to laugh it off, like hysterical crying fits were something that just *happened* to people, oops, how inconvenient, nothing to see here. 'This has just been . . .'

What had Dylan said, when she found out I was gone? Had she been angry with Romeo-Dylan for sending me away? With Murray, for letting him?

Or had she understood what I'd done? Understood that I had to let go?

I wanted to be with her so, so badly. I wanted her to be here, with me. To burst through the laundry door right now.

How could you?! I wanted her to scream right in my face. *How could you just leave me?*

'Oh God,' I managed, before the tears defeated me.

I buried my face in my hands, but I couldn't stop myself. I was shaking so badly that I would have fallen right off the washing machine if Cece hadn't put her arm around me. 'I'm sorry,' I sobbed. 'I'm sorry, I'm sorry, I'm sorry.'

'Hey, it's all right, Amanda. You're all right.'

'I'm not all right!'

The lump in my throat was so big it felt like I was going to throw up, my sobs turning into retches. 'It's killing me,' I choked out. 'It's killing me. Not being with Dylan – it's killing me.'

I could have had it. I could have had *her*. If I'd just waited! *Why* hadn't I waited? Why had I let her go?

Why was making good choices so fucking *hard*?

'Oh God,' I wept. 'Dylan.'

19

The next days were some of the worst of my life.

The crying stopped, eventually. Turns out you *can* run out of tears. But the feeling that a crucial part of me had been torn out didn't go away.

Sometimes it felt like the battery. I'd lie in my Convent bunk underneath Heather, and the thought of doing anything or moving even the slightest amount seemed impossible.

Other times it felt like it was the brakes. I'd be washing up in the kitchen or mopping the floor or even just sitting outside on the verandah, and even though I was doing something small and quiet, it felt like I was careening out of control. I was going to crash into that last day, the day when Dylan and Dylan told each other that their hearts were two halves of the same whole and walked out of here hand in hand, and even though I could see it up ahead, there was no way I could steer around it.

But realistically, it was the engine that was gone. No matter which way you looked at it, I just didn't function anymore.

You could build new engines. Better engines. I knew that. I'd done it. I would do it again.

But it wasn't easy, and it wasn't cheap, and it took a long, long time.

Our last day in the Convent should have been grey and stormy, but it wasn't. The sun was bright and warm, turning the lake a glittering silver. There were a few clouds, but they were white and fluffy, the kind a little kid would draw. As morning turned into afternoon, the light took on a golden tinge, like champagne. The network was going to get the perfect backdrop for the fairy-tale romance Murray had promised them.

He'd been here earlier, talking to Cece, who, it turned out, was set to be the lead on the next season of *Wherefore Art Thou Romeo?* – something that was going to be very interesting, considering what a disaster she was on camera. When he was finished with Cece, he sent Lily to get me. 'No,' I said shortly.

She'd raised an eyebrow. 'No?'

'No, I don't want to talk to him.'

'You don't know what he's going to say.'

'I don't care.'

Lily paused. 'Murray is not a nice man,' she said, 'but he's not a bad guy.'

When I looked over to where she'd been standing, she was gone.

The first limo arrived to take us away in mid-afternoon.

I was hoping I'd be in it, but the limos were allocated by producer, just like they had been that first night. Carrie's contestants went first. The second limo took Suzette's, leaving only Cece, Heather, Lily and I in the Convent.

Time stretched on. The perfect day was going to give way to a perfect night, the sky clear and full of stars.

That was probably why Murray was so late. He was holding back. He probably had the Dylans stashed away somewhere, waiting for nightfall, for the perfect backdrop to shoot them declaring their love for each other.

They'd put her in something white. No, silver. Sparkly. She looked great in sparkles. She'd look like the moon had come to life and descended to Earth.

The creases would appear in the corners of Romeo-Dylan's eyes as he took her hands. *Dyl, your heart is the other half of mine,* he'd say.

The stars would be a spray of pearlescent glitter behind them as they kissed, the perfect backdrop for the picture-perfect couple.

I got up and went inside. It was either that or throw myself in the lake.

Time ticked on. Murray still didn't come.

'How long do you think it's going to take?' I asked eventually.

Cece and Heather were in the room as well, but we all knew I was asking Lily. 'Who knows?' she replied. 'Depends how long the break-up with Kumiko takes, for one. Dylan's such a wet blanket that he'll probably spend forever comforting her.'

I wondered if it had been Kumiko who Romeo-Dylan really liked. I hoped not, for his sake. It would be horrible for him to have to take her hands in his, say, 'your heart is not the other half of mine,' and let go. It would be horrible to say that to anyone, but especially if it was a lie.

'And girl-Dylan's such a ball-buster that they'll have to spend a million years trying to make that big declaration scene look natural.'

'No, she's not.'

Lily raised her eyebrows at me.

'She's lovely,' I finished weakly.

'Oh, come off it, you think everyone is lovely, Miss Peaches and Cream,' Lily scoffed. 'She'll probably make him do a PowerPoint presentation on all the reasons why he loves her, and then she'll give him a score out of ten for each one.'

'That's not how it's going to go.'

It was probably happening right now. My Dylan would be walking towards Romeo-Dylan in her moon goddess dress. His mouth would fall open, because how could it not?

Everything would be black and white and glittery. The night would be quiet, until he opened his mouth to speak.

'Oh Dylan G, I love you. I want to be with you,' said Lily in a low voice.

Then she shifted to a high voice. 'Oh Dylan JM, I'm afraid I'm going to need to see that in writing before I can respond, and that'll take seven to ten business days.'

Back to the low voice. 'Oh Dylan G, I understand. I'll get this heart necklace right in the mail.'

The high one. 'Oh Dylan JM, please include a stamped self-addressed envelope in case I decide to return it.'

The low. 'Oh Dylan G, absolutely, it would be my honour, but would you mind if I kissed—'

'Stop!'

I didn't realise that Cece had also spoken until Lily looked from me to her and back again. She shook her head. 'You two are both such stupid saps, honestly.'

My bottom lip started to tremble. Lily rolled her eyes.

It would have been so easy for her to rip into me. If she wanted blood, I was easy pickings. I clearly wasn't enough of a challenge, though, because she just glanced at the ceiling for a moment, smiled to herself, said, 'Hey, racist,' and started a fight with Heather instead.

It was a long fight. If it had been a movie, they would have shown the hands on a clock going around and around. Pages blowing off the calendar. The seasons changing.

Outside, darkness fell completely. Murray still didn't come.

Was this some kind of punishment? Was he deliberately drawing this out, just because I'd refused to talk to him? Was he trying to show me who was boss?

Or had Lily been right? Were the Dylans wooden and unnatural with each other? Was he still trying to craft the perfect ending to his fairy-tale?

I just wanted to go home. I wanted to lie down in my childhood bedroom and cry. I wanted to hug my mum. I wanted her to stroke my hair and say, 'Oh, Mandie, again?' and then bring me a cup of tea and tell me that I'd done the right thing, that it was too soon after Jac, that being some-one's secret girlfriend was a horrible idea, that she was proud I'd decided not to wait around, that I was standing up for myself at last.

I started pacing. It felt like the Convent walls were closing in on me again.

How had I ever thought I was good at waiting? If I had to wait any longer, I was going to claw my skin off.

A horrible idea occurred to me. 'You don't think Stage Four restrictions have been extended, have they? I'm going to go out of my mind if I have to stay here any longer.'

'Relax,' Lily said. 'If there was a chance of that, they wouldn't have shipped everyone else off before.'

'That's true, that's true, that's true,' I muttered.

Deep breaths, Mandie. You just have to survive this for a little bit longer.

But I couldn't stop. 'What if they have to bring everyone back? Their limos might get turned around somewhere.'

'Then they'd move us back up to the Juliet Villa,' Lily said, sounding bored as she examined her manicure. 'They wouldn't keep us cooped up in this two-bedroom shack when there's a mansion at the top of the hill. We'd go up there and the Dylans would move in here.'

The thought made me nauseous. I excused myself and went upstairs to the bathroom.

I splashed cold water on my face and looked at myself in the mirror. There were no make-up artists for us down in the Convent, and I hadn't bothered to do my skincare routine or make myself up this morning. My face was gaunt. I had purple bags under my eyes to rival Murray's. I looked like death warmed up.

I closed my eyes and let myself imagine, just for a moment, that I was back in the bathroom at the Juliet Villa. *Someone didn't sleep well*, Dylan would laugh. *Give me your concealer, babe. Let me help.*

There wasn't enough concealer in the world to fix this.

I sighed and went back downstairs, curling up in an armchair and wrapping my arms around my knees.

Just a few more hours. I just had to survive the next few hours, and then I could go home to Mum and that cup of tea and the work of rebuilding myself from the ground up.

The French doors clattered as Cece stumbled in from the verandah. She looked like I had in the mirror, and the Mummy Mandie instincts that were hardwired in me pulled me to my feet. 'Hey, are you all right, Cece? You look like you've seen a ghost.'

'I'm fine,' she said, although she looked anything but. 'Murray's nearly here.'

Those words hit me like a bull bar to the chest.

Murray's nearly here.

'So it's done, then,' I said numbly. 'It's over.'

Dylan Gilchrist, your heart is the other half of mine, Romeo-Dylan must have said. *I love you.*

I love you too, she must have replied. Words she had never said to me.

'Yeah,' Cece said. 'It's over.'

My knees just about gave out. I sat down heavily in an armchair, covering my eyes with my hands, trying to force those traitorous hot tears back.

Just a little longer. I just had to not think about their perfect fairy-tale ending for a little longer. To not think about her moon goddess dress, the creases in the corners of his kind eyes, the jewel-studded backdrop of the night sky behind them as they kissed.

'I am fucking out of here,' Heather announced. 'I can't wait to see you three bitches never again – oh.'

'Dylan?' Cece whispered.

I can't tell you how fast I turned around. I don't think I even did, really. I heard her name, and then in the blink of an eye, I was looking at her.

Except it wasn't her.

'Cece,' Romeo-Dylan said hoarsely.

Murray had turned up, I dimly registered. Some cameramen, too, and some soundies. They were desperately trying to get footage. Heather was complaining. Lily was loving it.

'I couldn't do it, Cece,' he said. 'I love you too much.'

I burst into tears.

If the past few days had stretched out agonisingly long, the next few moments were agonisingly full. Romeo-Dylan declaring his love to Cece, again and again and again. Cece fainting. Murray shouting.

And shouting. And shouting. It was mostly Murray shouting, if I was being honest.

'How long has this been going on?'

Romeo-Dylan and Cece couldn't answer to his satisfaction, so he shouted some more. And more. And more.

Unbelievably, I was jealous.

How long has this been going on? Murray would shout at us.

In a physical sense? Not that long, my Dylan would reply. *In a real sense? Since the day we met.*

She'd look across at me, squeeze my hand, clasped tight in hers. *Sound about right, Mandie?*

Yep, I'd reply.

You signed a contract! he'd yell at her.

I know, she said. *But then I met Mandie.*

I glanced over to the door. That contract was null and void now, surely. The Dylan that was here, the one whose fingers were clasped so tightly around Cece's that both their knuckles had gone white, sure as hell didn't look like he was about to enter a fake relationship with my Dylan.

He'd come for her.

But she hadn't come for me.

'Did you know about this?' Murray demanded, turning on Lily.

Her lips curled upwards in that half-smirk of hers. She didn't say anything, but she didn't need to.

'You knew these two were undermining the whole show and you didn't say a word to me?'

'I'm not your servant, Murray,' Lily said. 'You know that very well.'

'They didn't undermine the show.'

I barely realised I'd spoken until Murray had turned on his heel, directing his fury at me. 'What?'

Under normal circumstances, I might have quivered, but my anger muscles had got a workout over the last few weeks. 'They didn't undermine the show,' I said through gritted teeth. 'It's supposed to be about falling in love, isn't it? They fell in love.'

I reached my hand out to Cece. 'I'm happy for you,' I said. 'Truly, Cece. You too, Dylan.'

Cece brushed her fingers against mine. 'Thank you,' she said.

'Yes,' Romeo-Dylan said. 'Thank you, Amanda.'

The emotion in their eyes, on their faces, in their voices, was genuine. They were so sincere.

I wasn't. I hoped they couldn't tell.

Why you? I wanted to scream at both of them. *Why you and not me?*

Murray was yelling at Romeo-Dylan about money now. 'You've broken your contract! You're going to be paying back a shit-ton of money!'

Like that mattered. Romeo-Dylan was rich.

My Dylan wasn't. She would have had nothing to gain from reneging on the deal. Everything to lose.

She couldn't do what Romeo-Dylan did. She couldn't just cut and run. That option just wasn't on the table for her.

She could have followed him down to the Convent, though. She could have been right on his heels at the French doors. *I love you, Cece,* he would have said. *I love you, Mandie,* she would have said. Murray would be yelling at four people now instead of two, and everything would be all right.

But she hadn't.

Because of me. Because I'd let go.

Because I'd made the fucking *right choice*.

Out of nowhere, I wanted to laugh. I'd actually become the person I'd been trying to be all this time. Mandie 2.0, who didn't just let her impulses run away with her, who made good choices even when they were difficult. I'd put myself first. I'd shown myself some respect.

And this was what I got for it.

If I'd just done what I normally did and *waited*. If I'd said goodbye to her first, explained why I had to go, then done what Belinda did and broken up with Romeo-Dylan at the Necklace Ceremony. If I'd been brave enough to speak to her instead of just running away, instead of throwing what we had away without a word, then – maybe – maybe –

'I've got to get back to the Villa,' Murray said. 'Kumiko's already left, so I'm now short a lead for *Wherefore Art Thou Romeo?* and I'm going to be royally fucked if Dylan G doesn't want the gig.'

Of course. She was the perfect candidate. I could see the posters now. She'd be smiling, ever so slightly, one perfect eyebrow arched, a necklace dangling from her finger-tips. The tagline would say something like *she's not letting one bad break-up get her down*. There'd be a crowd of men behind her – hell, probably women too, Dylan wouldn't be too chicken to come out on TV – all vying to be with her. *I've picked one for you*, Murray would say, *sign here*, and she'd do it, and he'd hand her a cheque, and it would be the first season of the Romeo and Juliet franchise in history that I didn't watch because it would hurt too much.

'Then you're royally fucked.'

It took me a second to realise what was happening. Who was speaking.

'I don't want it,' Dylan said.

I'd been wrong. They hadn't put her in white or silver. She didn't look like a moon goddess. Instead, she was in a baby blue halter-neck dress, the fabric slightly iridescent, her hair pulled severely back from her face.

It was a dress I might have worn, but it didn't suit her. Wardrobe hadn't done right by her. Neither had make-up. She looked . . . tired.

She was still the most beautiful woman I had ever seen.

I wasn't conscious of standing up, but somehow, I was on my feet. 'Dylan,' I said.

Then I stopped. What could I say? What was there to say?

'You're here,' I finished lamely.

She didn't smile. The lines of her face were drawn, set, serious.

'Mandie,' she said. 'Can I steal you for a second?'

'No,' Murray said. 'Absolutely not. We had a contract, Dylan. You have obligations. I don't have time for you—'

'Murray, shut the fuck up,' Lily said.

He wheeled on her. 'Don't,' he said. 'Don't start with me, Lily. Don't you dare. I can't even look at you.'

'First of all, what do you think you're doing right now?' she said. 'Secondly, are you really that far up your own arse?'

The sound he made in his throat was like a volcano about to erupt.

Dylan grabbed my wrist. 'Come on,' she whispered.

She pulled me outside. I couldn't miss the fact that she let go of my hand at the first possible opportunity.

I paused on the verandah. 'Dylan—'

'Not yet,' she said. 'Not where they can interrupt us.'

She jumped down the stairs. I stayed where I was.

She looked up when she realised I wasn't following. 'Mandie, please.'

'I'm sorry.'

'What?' she said. 'Why on earth would you be sorry?'

'For running away,' I whispered. 'I didn't even tell you why. You deserved more than that.'

'Mandie, no!'

She vaulted back up the stairs, taking them two at a time. 'Come here,' she said, and wrapped her arms around me.

I wanted to clutch at her like a koala clinging to a tree. I wanted to hold on to her forever.

I gave myself a few seconds, and then I made myself pull away.

'I'm sorry,' I said again.

'You're sorry?' she said. '*You're* sorry? Fuck, Mandie.'

She sank down on the stairs. 'I offer you the worst deal in the history of time, and you're apologising *to me?*'

'I'm sorry.'

'Don't apologise!'

I didn't know what to say to that.

She sighed, and tried to run a hand through her hair, but was stymied by all the hairspray and bobby pins. 'Fuck,' she swore. 'Fuck, fuck, fuck.'

'Do you want some help?'

She looked up at me.

'With your hair, I mean,' I said.

'Fuck my hair. I just – sit with me, Mandie?'

She patted the step next to her. After a few moments, I sat.

The night sky was just as I'd imagined it, a crisp, clear black, the Milky Way spilled across it like droplets of sparkling wine. The air was cold. I hugged my knees to my chest.

Dylan didn't seem to notice. She was staring at the ground, her fingers twisting together in her lap.

'Whatever you need to say to me,' I said, 'can you just say it, please?'

'I'm sorry,' she said. 'I'm just trying to find the right words.'

She swallowed. 'The first thing I want to say is that I'm sorry,' she said. 'I asked way too much of you. Hell, I didn't even ask. I just *assumed*. I just took control. I mapped out this perfect plan of how things were going to be in my head, and I slotted you right into it and assumed you'd be cool with it without even asking you. Like, *oh, we're going to secretly date while I publicly date this other guy, that's the way it's going to be.* Who *does* that?'

She dug her fingers into those perfect eyebrows. 'You did the right thing, leaving the way you did,' she said. 'I deserved it.'

'No, you didn't,' I said. 'You deserved an explanation.'

'It's not like it needs spelling out,' Dylan said. 'I wouldn't agree to be someone's dirty little secret. Why would I expect that of you? *How* could I expect that of you? Fuck, Mandie, I love you, and I've treated you like absolute shit.'

I didn't say anything.

'Oh,' she said. 'I love you. In case that wasn't already obvious.'

She took my hand in hers and pressed my knuckles to her lips. 'I love everything about you, Mandie,' she said. 'I love how kind you are. How big your heart is. I love how you're so goddamn nice. But sometimes you're not nice, and I love that too. You've got this snarky, dry sense of humour that comes out. It makes your eyes sparkle, and you get this mischievous little smile, and it's the most adorable thing.'

She kissed my hand again. 'You're beautiful, obviously,' she said. 'Anyone can see that. But it's not when you're all dressed up in some Necklace Ceremony ballgown that you're the most beautiful. It's when you're excited about something. There's so much passion in you, Mandie. I don't just mean in bed, although Christ, some of the things you know how to do blow my fucking mind. But when you get all excited about something, invested in something, and that passion spills out, it's the sexiest thing I've ever seen. And then there's—'

'Stop,' I said. 'Please.'

'I know it's tough for you to hear nice things about yourself,' she said, 'but these are all true.'

'That's not it.'

I took my hand out of hers, pretty sure I was making the worst decision of my life. 'I can't be something you just fall into, Dylan,' I said. 'I know Man-Dylan broke your contract so he could be with Cece, so he's not in the way anymore, but I can't be with you just because it's suddenly convenient now. That's why I left. That's—'

'Babe, we both broke the contract.'

I stopped.

'It wasn't just him,' Dylan said. 'It was both of us.'

'. . . What?' I said.

'We got all the way up to the final declaration,' she said. 'We were holding hands, we looked each other in the eye, we both took a deep breath, and then we were both like, "nope, not doing this" at exactly the same time.'

I stared.

'You can ask him if you want,' she said. 'I mean, I wouldn't ask him now, he seems a bit busy having a screaming match with Murray, but tomorrow—'

I kissed her.

She pulled away after a few moments. '. . . Should I have led with that?' she asked, sounding a bit dazed.

'Should you have led with "Hey, Mandie, I just risked everything because I love you"?' I said. 'Yes! Yes, you should have!'

I kissed her again, hard, then I took both of her hands and kissed them too. 'I love you too, Dylan,' I said. 'So much.'

'Oh thank God,' she said, the relief spilling out of her like a waterfall. 'When you left, I – fuck, Mandie, when you were gone, and I really sat down and thought about what I'd done to you, and that I might have lost you, it just about ruined me.'

She laced her fingers through mine and held on tight. 'I'm going to work hard every day to deserve you,' she said. 'I'm never going to take you for granted again. I'm never going to just decide how things are going to be without discussing it with you. I'm going to be a much better girlfriend from here on out. I promise.'

'Don't shit-talk yourself,' I said. 'Am I going to have to make you some affirmation flashcards?'

She laughed and kissed me, smiling against my lips.

'There's one thing I don't understand, though,' I said after a while.

'Hmmm?'

'Why were you late?' I asked. 'Romeo-Dylan was down here for ages declaring his love for Cece before you turned up. If you both decided you were out at the same time, where were you?'

'Oh!' she said. 'That was what I wanted to show you. Come with me.'

I followed her down the stairs and around the back of the Convent. 'Because I've been so unfair to you, I was trying to find the best way to apologise,' Dylan explained. 'I was late because I was putting together my big romantic gesture.'

I clapped my hands to my mouth.

'You like it?'

'You found her!'

I ran my hands reverently over the hood of the Lamborghini, parked behind the Convent. 'You didn't take her off-road, did you?' I asked anxiously. 'Her suspension really isn't built for that.'

'That,' Dylan said emphatically. 'That look right there. The way your eyes light up when you get excited. That's the one I love.'

'How can you see it?' I asked. 'It's the middle of the night.'

'And there's that dry little sense of humour.'

'It wasn't a joke, it was a legitimate question. And so was the first one. Tell me you didn't take her off-road.'

'Does that little road around the lake count?'

'You poor baby,' I crooned to the beautiful Lambo. 'As soon as it's light, I'm going to take a good look at you, all right? I'll make you feel better.'

'Can I watch?'

'If you want,' I said. 'I don't know if it'll be very interesting for you, though.'

'Trust me,' she said, grinning wickedly, 'I'll get a lot out of it. Especially if you manage to get some grease riiiiiight –' she ran her thumb along one of my cheekbones, 'here.'

I turned and bit her thumb. Her breath caught in her throat.

'I'm normally very tidy when I work,' I said, kissing my way slowly up her wrist, 'but I think I can make an exception for you.'

'Good to know,' she said, her voice a little higher than normal. 'Compromise is important in a relationship.'

I kissed the crease of her elbow. 'There are some things I'm not willing to compromise on, though.'

Her free hand feathered across my hair. 'Of course,' she said softly. 'There are things I'd never ask you to compromise on, too.'

'Good,' I said, kissing my way to her shoulder and then up her neck, pressing my lips to her jaw and then tugging her earlobe gently between my teeth. 'Because this car is ours now, and I'm not compromising on that.'

She laughed and turned her head to kiss me. 'No compromise needed,' she said. 'I'm fully intending to hold this car hostage in case they try to sue me for breaking the contract.'

'You think they will?' I asked. 'Sue you?'

'They might,' she said. 'I'm hoping they'll be too focused on man-Dylan breaking the contract to pay much attention to me, but . . . yeah, it's possible.'

'If they do, you know I'll be there, right?' I said, brushing my nose against hers. 'I'll help however I can. We could sell our story to a women's magazine for a shit-ton of money. Sell the film rights. Sell – I don't know, something. Kidneys, maybe? We'll figure it out.'

'Mandie,' she said wryly, 'you are not selling a kidney for me.'

'Dylan,' I said, 'you are not the boss of me. I will sell a kidney for you if I want to.'

She laughed against my lips. 'God, I love you.'

I kissed her again, then took her hand. 'Come on.'

I opened the door of the Lambo. Dylan got in the passenger side. 'Where are we going?' she asked.

'Nowhere just yet,' I said. 'I need to check her out before we take her anywhere. Plus, she's worth so much that Murray would *definitely* sue if we kidnapped her.'

'Out of interest,' Dylan said, 'how much is this car worth?'

I told her.

Her perfect eyebrows shot practically into her hairline. 'I just drove a car worth that much money?' she said faintly.

'Relax, baby,' I said. 'I told you. I'll look after her in the morning. Nothing to worry about.'

I turned the engine on and listened to her purr, leaning my back against the headrest with my eyes closed. 'God, I love that sound.'

'It's okay?' Dylan asked. 'I didn't break the most expensive car in the universe?'

I opened my eyes and turned the engine off. 'She sounds fine,' I said. 'Better than fine, actually, but . . . I won't bore you with the details.'

'Mandie,' she said, turning towards me, 'you can talk to me about cars as long as you want.'

'Good,' I said. 'Because if we're going to make this work, you're going to need a pretty high tolerance for car talk.'

She smiled. 'I promise.'

I leaned over and kissed her lightly on the lips. 'We might not be able to take her anywhere, but there are two reasons I wanted you to get in the car with me.'

'Oh yeah?'

'Well, no,' I said. 'That was a lie, sorry. There are three. I genuinely did want to listen to the engine. I worry, you know. And I *really* love the sound.'

'I know you do,' she said, kissing me lightly back. 'I was there the day you made man-Dylan turn it on so you could press your ear against it, remember? I saw the expression on your face.'

'That actually leads me pretty neatly to the second reason,' I said, kissing the tip of her nose and then leaning my forehead against hers. 'You know how I feel about this car, right?'

'Of course I do.'

'Dylan Gilchrist,' I said, 'I love you more than I love this car.'

She started laughing, her nose knocking against mine almost painfully as her body shook. 'You are so adorable,' she said. 'God, I love you so much.'

'I'm glad,' I said, 'because I'm hoping you'll help me out with the third reason I wanted you to get in the car with me.'

'I'm sure we can come to some kind of arrangement,' she said, still laughing.

'Have I ever told you –' I let my lips brush gently against hers, 'about the calendars all the dudes at my work have? Hot women draped over cars?'

'Babe,' she said, her thumb feathering over the spot behind my ear, 'if you want me to lie on the hood, all you have to do is ask.'

'No,' I said. 'That's not what I want. I have too much respect for the paint job.'

I kissed her again. 'It turns out my fantasy is a little different,' I said. 'They fantasise about hot women *on* cars. I fantasise about hot women *in* cars.'

'Is that so?' she said, smiling against my mouth. 'You're in luck, Mandie Mitchell, because I think I can help you out with that.'

'Really?' I said, reaching behind her neck and untying the halter of her dress.

'Really,' she said, her fingers slipping under my shirt. 'I'd be delighted to. You look so hot in the driver's seat.'

Epilogue

The network didn't sue Dylan in the end, thank God. Partly because Romeo-Dylan was as good as his word and paid back his full appearance fee. Partly because we were very cooperative when it came to all the reshoots Murray insisted on so he could re-edit the story for the season. (We, apparently, were much easier to deal with than Cece, who'd never quite got over all her camera issues. We refrained from telling Murray that he'd probably dodged a bullet in not having her as the lead on *Wherefore Art Thou Romeo?*.)

They even paid my Dylan the full fee she'd been promised when she signed the Dylan + Dylan = True Love contract, as well as a (smaller, but not small) bonus to me. 'If you sign this, then your love story is officially part of this season,' Murray said gruffly, handing me a pen. 'You sure you want to be out on TV?'

I didn't hesitate. 'Yes,' I said, and signed.

I might not have been quite so hasty if I'd read the small print. I couldn't tell you the legalese, but it basically said *in return for this sum of money, Amanda Mitchell will go to any and every damn event we tell her to.*

Which was how Dylan and I ended up here, hosting the official *Marry Me, Juliet* finale watch party event along with Lily and Kumiko at a massive city bar.

The bar wasn't even close to full. We might have been out of Stage Four restrictions, but there were still pretty strict rules about how many people you could have in a space at one time. They'd picked such a huge place because they were only allowed something like twenty-five per cent capacity.

It *felt* full, though. People followed me wherever I went, and despite security guards constantly reminding them, they weren't even trying to social distance. 'Please tell me you and Dylan G end up together,' someone begged me. 'Please.'

'You'll just have to wait and see,' I said, smiling and signing the shirt they'd thrust at me. 'You know I'm not allowed to give any spoilers.'

'If you two don't end up together, I'm giving up all faith in love. I mean it.'

I only realised as I handed the shirt back to them that it had mine and Dylan's faces on it. *BICONIC*, it read, in huge capital letters.

The four of us had to do a countdown to the start of the finale like it was New Year's Eve. We were standing on a little stage in front of banners for Ties Out For The Boys (Romeo-Dylan's charity) and SweetHearts (the women's heart health foundation my Dylan had become the spokeswoman for).

'For fuck's sake, you two can't stand together, it'll give away the ending,' Murray ordered Dylan and I gruffly. 'Kumiko, Lily, you're in the middle.'

'So you're speaking to me now?' Lily said.

Murray growled.

'Of course it's just to tell me what to do,' she muttered.

Things got a little less chaotic after the countdown. There was still a buzz of chatter, but people quietened down to watch the episode, and the throngs crushing in around us got less throngy.

'You've become so important to me over the course of this journey, Mandie,' the Dylan on the screen said to TV me. 'I don't want to lose that.'

The most tragic romantic music cue in the world started to play. 'I don't want to lose you either,' TV me replied.

The whole crowd said *awwwwwwwwwwwww*. I very studiously did not look at Dylan in case I gave something away. Even now, so close to the end, I didn't want to make Murray any angrier than he already was.

The scene switched to something with Romeo-Dylan and Cece, and the crowd's attention shifted away from me. I took the opportunity to escape to the bar. 'Champagne, please.'

The bartender nodded, turning away to the fridge.

'Hi.'

I blinked. 'Hi.'

Jac leaned a casual elbow against the bar, turning slightly to face me. 'It's been a while.'

'It has,' I said. 'Eight months, maybe? Nine?'

I accepted my glass of champagne from the bartender.

'What are you doing here?' I asked. 'I know how you feel about the show.'

'I wanted to come and show my support.'

'Support for what?'

'This story you're telling. The representation. It's brave. I didn't think you had it in you.'

'I don't really care what you think, Jac,' I said, and walked away.

There was a little VIP/backstage area that we were allowed to go to if we needed a bit of privacy. ('You're on the clock,' Murray had growled, 'legally I need to give you breaks.') I carried my champagne in there and took a couple of deep breaths.

Dylan followed me in a few moments later. 'Hey, babe,' she said, leaning over to kiss me on the cheek. 'You all right?'

'Yeah, I'm fine,' I said, and meant it.

'No, you're not.'

'Baby, I really am.'

'No, you're not,' she repeated. 'I just got my lipstick all over your cheek. Shit. Murray's going to kill me.'

'It's okay,' I said, putting down my glass and opening my handbag. 'I think I have some concealer in here somewhere.'

Dylan followed me into the bathroom and reapplied her lipstick as I got rid of the mark she'd left on my face. 'This feels like déjà vu,' she said, blotting her lips on some paper towel. 'Any minute now Lily's going to hammer on the door and start yelling, and—'

The door opened so suddenly and sharply it smashed right into the wall, and in walked Lily. 'Oh, for fuck's sake,'

Jodi McAlister

she snarled, seeing us both. 'You think sneaking away to hook up in the bathroom is keeping the ending a secret? Get back out there.'

And she left again, the door slamming shut behind her.

Dylan and I stared at each other in the mirror, agape.

'. . . Am I magic?' Dylan said. 'Did I summon her, somehow?'

'If you did,' I said, 'can you please make sure you never mention her once we move in together? I feel like she'll scare Noah. And also me.'

'Yes. Absolutely. Deal.'

I put my concealer back in my bag. 'She's right, though,' I said. 'We should get back out there.'

'I wish we could stay a bit longer,' Dylan said, playing with the thin strap of my black dress. 'You look so pretty tonight, babe. I wish I'd worn more sensible lipstick.'

'One, that lipstick is gorgeous, no regrets,' I said, tangling my fingers with hers. 'Two, you also look stunning tonight. And three, once we get through the next forty-five minutes or so and everyone knows the ending, you won't have to worry about how badly that lipstick smudges.'

'Oh, trust me,' she said, squeezing my hand, 'by the time we leave this bar tonight, we're both going to look like the Joker.'

I smiled up at her. 'I can't wait to tell people how much I love you.'

She smiled back. 'Me neither.'

Acknowledgements

Sequels are always harder to write than the books that precede them. I knew this when I went into writing *Can I Steal You For A Second?* – this isn't my first time at the sequel rodeo – but I blithely ignored it. I had such a clear vision of Amanda and Dylan G. I knew exactly what I wanted their romance to look like. Plus, as the book takes place concurrently with *Here For The Right Reasons,* a lot of the events were set out for me. Surely it couldn't be *that* hard.

Obviously I was wrong. Writing any book is always more difficult than you think it's going to be – and that's without taking into account that this book was written against the backdrop of 2021 in Melbourne, see-sawing in and out of lockdown, never quite sure when the ship would steady again.

One thing that was steady, though, was the support I got from the people around me. Without that, Mandie and Dylan's love story would still be nothing but a really nice idea.

First and foremost are the two people who have been the biggest champions of both this book and this series more broadly: my literary agent Alex Adsett, and my publisher Cassandra di Bello. I'm not sure if either of them know how much their constant support and belief has buoyed me through writing this series. They saw the place marked 'above and beyond', went there, said 'why stop here?' and kept going. I am unbelievably blessed and lucky to have them both in my corner.

Speaking of feeling blessed and lucky: I couldn't have asked for more from the team I've been working with at Simon & Schuster. There are a lot of books and a lot of authors in the world, but with the care and attention they have paid to me, I have never once felt lost in the shuffle. My publicity team Gabby, Kirsty and Emily have gone so far out of their way for me that I can't think of a geographical metaphor to adequately describe it. I've been so well looked after by everyone even tangentially involved with *Can I Steal You For A Second?*, and I would like to thank them all (especially Katherine and Lizzie, who have been endlessly patient with me, and my sensitivity reader, whose insights were very helpful).

I've also been extremely well looked after by the people around me in my personal life. Writing can be a lonely affair – and if you end up in a bit of a time crunch, you can effectively disappear for weeks on end. Thank you to all my dear friends, who pulled me out of the cave/my own head when I needed it, and who offered me a wonderful variety of pep talks: Steph, Mel, Sonya, Mabel, Rashmi, Anna, Meg,

Claire, Katie, Maria – you are all singularly and collectively the best.

There are two people that I have to especially single out. It's not a joke to say this series would not exist without my friends Kate Cuthbert and Adele Walsh (you can refer to the acknowledgments of *Here For The Right Reasons* if you want the full story!). They have supported me professionally (thank you, Kate, for your editorial genius!). They have supported me personally. They have let me drag them to no fewer than four different wine regions and have let me monologue about grape varietals for far longer than any reasonable person would want to listen to. They have taught me about action movies, a genre in which my knowledge is sorely lacking. I love you both, and this book is for you.

Finally, I want to thank everyone who has picked up this book. If you followed me here from *Here For The Right Reasons* or my recaps of *The Bachelor* or my scholarship or any of the seven thousand different things I write – thank you so much for reading and engaging with my work. And if you're brand new – thank you for taking a chance on Mandie, Dylan, and all the shenanigans going on in *Marry Me, Juliet*.

And I hope you're ready for some more shenanigans, because there's no way we're leaving the Villa before finding out what the hell is going on with Murray and Lily Fireball . . .

About the Author

Jodi is an author and academic from Kiama, a seaside holiday town on the south coast of New South Wales. Her PhD was awarded by Macquarie University in 2015, and she is currently a senior lecturer in Writing and Literature at Deakin University in Melbourne. Her academic work focuses on the history of love, sex, women and girls, popular culture and fiction. It means that reading romance novels and watching *The Bachelor* is technically work for her.

You can find Jodi on Twitter at @JodiMcA, where she tweets regularly about her research, her writing, cool things she finds interesting, her hero worship of Kate Bush, and her slightly-too-intense passion for *The Bold and the Beautiful*. She is the author of young adult novels *Valentine*, *Ironheart* and *Misrule* in the Valentine series, as well as her first adult novel, *Here for the Right Reasons*.